SORCERESS RISING

LISA BLACKWOOD

SORCERESS RISING

A GARGOYLE & SORCERESS TALE / BOOK 2

LISA BLACKWOOD

BOOKS BY LISA BLACKWOOD

Gargoyle & Sorceress

Dawn of the Sorceress

Sorceress Awakening

Sorceress Rising

Sorceress Hunting

Sorceress at War

Sorceress Enraged

Legacy of the Sorceress

Sorcery & Firedrakes

Scion of the Sorceress

Sorceress Eternal

In Deception's Shadow Series (Epic Fantasy Romance)

Betrayal's Price

Herd Mistress

Maiden's Wolf

Death's Queen

The Prince's Gryphon (forthcoming)

Ishtar's Legacy Series (Epic Fantasy Romance)

Ishtar's Blade

The Blade's Beginning (short story)

Blade's Honor

Blade's Destiny

The Blade's Shadow

First Queen of the Gryphons

The King of the Anunnaki (forthcoming)

The Anunnaki's Blade (forthcoming)

Huntress vs Huntsman (Epic Fantasy Romance)

Master of the Hunt

Night Huntress

Dragon Archer

Soul Mage (forthcoming)

Sorceress Rising

Ignorance nearly killed Lillian once.

That time, she'd known nothing of magic until Gregory, her Gargoyle Protector, awoke from his stone sleep and saved her from demons escaped from the Magic Realm. They defeated the demonic Riven at great personal cost, one which forced them both to hibernate for months while they mended.

Healed, Lillian wakes to a world greatly changed, one where her sleepy northern town has been overrun by military, scientists, and paparazzi. Apparently, her battle with the Riven didn't go completely unnoticed, and her actions put her Coven family at risk of exposure.

These new tensions unearth another concern. Lillian and Gregory may be one being in the Spirit Realm, soul mates in the most literal sense, but it doesn't guarantee a perfect accord here on Earth, especially when Gregory's clearly defined sense of good and evil urge him to eradicate anyone he deems as evil—which, to her dismay, includes a good chunk of humanity.

But their troubles are not limited to humans, not when another, older power rises from the ocean's depths. Tethys, a siren of the ancient world, has her own plans for Gregory. For the first time in their many lives, Lillian finds herself at odds with her other half.

And if she doesn't master her own magic, this battle will become her greatest defeat.

SORCERESS RISING

PROLOGUE

A tremor shook the silent, underwater world. Fish darted into the safety of large schools as other marine life took shelter in the deep crevices of the living reef. A moment later, the ocean floor bucked and shivered in the grip of an earthquake. Fierce shockwaves rolled out from the underwater epicenter, displacing vast quantities of water. As the pressure built, water rushed toward the distant landmass —a series of enormous waves building in height and power.

Deep in the heart of the coral reef, the siren shifted and turned in her sleep. Chunks of calcified reef broke away. The tiny bodies of coral from centuries past crumbled, sprinkling her with sediment.

The earthquake, and the destructive monster it had unleashed, registered on Tethys' consciousness. The great waves were within her power to control, yet they were a normal part of the balance between life and death. Great destruction would come this day, and new life would arise from the old. All was as it should be. She shifted again, content to return to sleep, for the Mortal Realm would continue as it had for all the ages of her long life.

She drifted closer to sleep, but the ocean currents, disturbed by the earthquake, filled her living tomb with fresh water and new scents. An unknown flavor coated her tongue and tingled along the scales of her lower body. Her gills burned with it.

Heavy. Oily. A smothering chemical taste.

Like—and yet not alike—what the vents on the ocean floor spat up.

The siren opened her eyes for the first time in well over a thousand years. Even while she slept, Tethys was aware of the passing of time, the earth's cycles of renewal and destruction, but this was not nature's work. It did not belong in her world. A foreign taint. Unnatural. This was nothing the earth would spawn—but there was one creature upon the land capable of such depravity.

With a spark of rage, her magic expanded outward. The coral reef trapping her body burst apart, and she thrashed free of her resting place. Fish and other reef-dwellers darted away or sought fissures to hide in. Free at last, she hovered in the water, surveying her surroundings. Near at hand, a sleek, agile predator sliced through the water, drawing closer with each flick of its tail. She sensed its cold frustration at having its hunt disrupted first by the earth's trembling and now by her rising.

Unable to give voice to a song of enchantment while underwater, the siren hummed instead. The deep sound carried far out into the surrounding ocean.

Currents swirled at her command, coiling and dragging the shark closer. It fought water made solid by her magic. She swam a circle around her prey, coming ever closer with each revolution. Even helpless in her power, the shark still struggled. Reaching out, she slid her fingers along his smooth, sleek skin.

The male's thoughts were clouded with panic and base instinct. Through all the chaos, memories flickered across her mind, slippery and hard to hold. After focusing her magic, only one image came clear to her. Tethys frowned. She would get nothing useful from this one. She must try something else, locate one of the other sea creatures capable of understanding her.

With a gentle pat, she released the shark. Her rage wasn't directed at him, after all. Her effort wasn't entirely without benefit. She'd gotten one clear image from the shark, that of a strange two-legged creature peering at it from within a great metal cage, and accompanying it was the familiar oily scent. Though much weaker than what tainted the ocean, it was alike enough to confirm her earlier assumption. Humans were behind this catastrophe.

She'd hoped the passage of time would grant the young species wisdom.

Apparently, it had not.

It was time for another lesson.

CHAPTER ONE

Gran bustled around the kitchen in a whirlwind of activity, shifting dirty bowls into the sink, snatching clean ones out of a cupboard, and then gliding over to the stove to pull a tray of muffins out with one hand while sliding a sheet of cookies in with the other. Before the oven door had fully closed, she was already halfway across the room, attending to what Lillian could only assume was the beginnings of French toast. Gran possessed a culinary efficiency Lillian—and most everyone else—lacked, but at this exact moment, it was Gran's ability to compartmentalize emotions she truly envied.

She currently would have benefited from a large dose of Gran's stoicism, too. It might help numb some of the environmental 'noise' rubbing her newly heightened senses raw. Even watching her grandmother work almost caused Lillian vertigo. Sounds came too clear and sharp. What were once subtle scents like the salty, warm scent of butter melting in a pot, the hot, metal smell of the oven, or maple syrup and brown sugar—she now found overpowering to the point of inducing nausea.

In a desperate attempt to tune out some of the other senses, Lillian fixated on the heavy earthenware mug between her palms with its rich, dark coffee. A small chip marred the rim, but she couldn't bring herself to toss out her favorite cup over so small a blemish.

Tiny drops of coffee slowly slid down the side of the mug where her trembling hands spilled it over the edge. Her vision swam, and her head took up a steady pounding.

She closed her eyes for a moment but snapped them back open as a sharp tearing sound assaulted her ears. Her focus zoned in on Gran where she stood at the sink, innocently enough, just pulling labels from jars destined for recycling. Lillian's ears twitched in time with each auditory detail.

Focus on the coffee, damn it. Just one thing at a time.

Strange how the scent of coffee, and the sight of rich cream clouding the dark liquid, had suddenly lost their usual comforting effect. Lillian gave her mug an idle swirl before raising it to her lips and inhaling a deep breath of the warm steam.

Nope, nothing.

She sipped at the coffee and grimaced. *Nope, not nothing...downright nasty.* Just three months before, she'd been a certifiable caffeine addict.

Who would have thought a three-month sleep inside a tree could cure addictions? Or heighten her senses to the point of pain?

And just what other changes, besides the ones I've already experienced, has my meddling hamadryad inflicted upon me while I lay senseless?

Truthfully, she knew without her hamadryad tree's aid, she would have died. And Gregory, noble, loving being that he was would have followed her into death.

Just thinking of the gargoyle, her soul mate in the most literal sense of the word, had her turning toward the door leading to the living room. Presently, the other half of her soul was showering in the upstairs master bathroom. It was the only one in the house big enough to accommodate a gargoyle's massive wingspan.

She'd finished her own shower a half hour ago, a long, arduous affair of scouring and scrubbing to rid herself of her tree's pitchy afterbirth—a somewhat disgusting side effect from hamadryad healing, apparently.

If only the other magical side effects were as easily washed away.

Magic had saved her life—probably even saved her soul. After Gregory had woken to her call, he'd examined her hamadryad and informed her the tree had also trapped the demon seed Lillian had been unwillingly incubating. Without it, she now felt lighter and cleaner—not so strange, she supposed, since the demon seed had been feeding on her spirit and magic.

She thanked her hamadryad tree for its many gifts, but it didn't lessen the slow, creeping fear from invading her mind. Honestly, the fear wasn't so much about how deeply magic had interwoven itself into her life, it was the fact what she *did* know about magic was so very slight.

Frowning, she acknowledged she could probably write everything she knew about magic on a sticky-note and still have room to spare. After emerging from her tree, she hadn't had much time to talk to Gregory before the rest of the family had descended upon them with hugs, laughter, and tears.

The snippets of what she'd been told only added to her uncertainty. Then Gran had chased everyone away—to give Lillian and Gregory a chance to clean up, she'd claimed. But Lillian would bet it was more a chance to collect their thoughts, for which she was grateful.

She was confident Gregory would be able to answer her questions. Now, if he'd finish up with his shower and get his big gargoyle backside down to the kitchen, she'd start asking those questions.

Warm amusement brushed against her mind, and she choked back a gasp of surprise at the intimate contact. Apparently, she had been more distracted than she knew.

"Easy, beloved." Gregory's calming influence washed over her mind and flowed out to every corner of her body. *"I am with you always. We will get through this new complication together."*

"What's happening to me? My skull feels like it's being inflated by an air compressor."

There was a long pause, which usually meant Gregory was hung up on a modern term. He rumbled to himself and then answered. *"I believe your gargoyle father's bloodline is asserting itself over your dryad mother's."*

"Am I about to sprout a pair of leathery wings?"

"Yes. If you don't get your cascading magic under control, you will shift."

The pounding in her head made it difficult to think. Lillian fought for focus to make sense of Gregory's words and the warning behind them. She'd shifted once before, back when the demon soul had full control of her. It was how she knew she possessed the ability. Thanks to the strength of her hamadryad, she was now free of the demon's dark menace.

Oh, but during that time, she'd been all instinct, base urges, and raw emotions. She'd blamed it on the demon soul, but what if that was what being a gargoyle was? Gregory hadn't alluded to such, but she hadn't asked him either. Cold uncertainty dispelled some of the heady magic rising within her. Her skin still felt too tight and her body overly hot, feverish to the point she wouldn't be surprised to see steam curling up from her body.

She clutched the edge of the table and told herself she wouldn't shift. There was no more demon soul to coerce or control her. "I'm in control. Of myself, my magic, and my fate," she mumbled under her breath.

It helped a little. Then the scent of forest, male, and what she'd come to think of as the distinct scent of warm stone surrounded her, seeping into her lungs, the pores of her skin, and maybe even her soul. A moment later, the warm weight of large hands settled on her shoulders. Eyes still closed, she turned her head and inhaled a deep breath of Gregory's scent. It calmed her, as it always did, and the pounding in her head subsided enough so she could think.

The hands squeezed gently as Gregory's voice washed over her. Calming, soothing, peaceful. "I'm here. My strength is yours. Think of your tree growing tall, casting her soft lacy shade throughout your glade. Your escape from the world. A place to rest and heal. A dryad's haven. Remember what it is to be a dryad."

Even if he had spoken in a language she did not understand, she would still have taken comfort in his voice. The tension in her shoulders and belly eased.

In truth, she knew no more about being a dryad than she did about being a gargoyle. But forests and glades, the scent of loam, the sharp sweetness of sap, and the ability to feel the land—all those things were a natural part of her existence. When she opened her eyes, her vision came into focus. Lights and sounds returned to their normal levels. She released a ragged sigh and tilted her head up toward Gregory.

Muscular and towering to a lofty eight and a half feet, he dwarfed her smaller frame like a tremendous hulking shadow. His wings, even folded against his back, arched high above his shoulders, framing his horns where they brushed the ceiling in two long, elegant spirals. His fearsome exterior housed a gentle heart, as well as the other half of her soul. When he'd first explained they shared one soul between them, that they were the mortal Avatars of the Divine Ones, she'd been doubtful. But no longer.

Her heart still pumped with fear, but whatever was happening to her, she knew they would face it together, for they were one being in two bodies, far stronger together than alone.

"Hmm." Gregory leaned forward and sniffed along her shoulder. "Entirely too close. The tight, narrow confines of the kitchen is no place to learn to shapeshift." His nostrils flared as he inhaled a second, deeper breath. With a snort, he shook himself, his thick black mane flying in all directions. The shiver continued down his body, morphing into a full-body stretch as it worked its way to the tip of his tail.

"Yes, don't break the china," Gran injected with a chuckle. "You know how much I hate shopping."

Gran's lighthearted banter dispelled some of the nervous tension, and Lillian was able to slow her breathing into something resembling a reasonable pace. Sweat still trickled down her back and along her temples, but otherwise, she was unharmed. However, something in Gregory's comment about the narrow confines of the kitchen made her think he downplayed the danger. She doubted he was worried about the kitchen; more likely he was concerned about the other people in the house.

As if Gregory knew her thoughts—which he probably did—he leaned closer until his muzzle brushed her hair and whispered, "Later, we'll go into the forest, and I'll assess your abilities and teach you control."

Lillian only hoped it was half as easy as he made it sound.

With a rattle of dishes, Gran brought over a steaming plate of French toast and warmed maple syrup. Next came a plateful of steaming muffins slathered thickly with butter and an assortment of jams and jellies to pick from.

"Let me help." Lillian stood and skirted the table. Guilt pricked at her conscience, if a tad belatedly. She'd sat staring at her cooling coffee, oblivious to everything going on around her when she could've as easily spent the time helping Gran with breakfast.

"No need, dear," Gran said with a snort. "The day I can't whip together a quick breakfast will be my first day in the afterlife."

Regardless, Lillian helped set the table, laying out settings for three, even though Gregory disdained cutlery, preferring to use his three-inch claws. Surprisingly, he was a dainty eater for an eight-foot behemoth with wings, claws, and horns.

The mindless routine of minutia helped Lillian conquer the last vestiges of the strange wildness surging through her blood. Calmer, she returned to her seat next to Gregory. She'd barely sat down on the tall stool before the warm weight of Gregory's tail snaked its way around her waist. The spade-shaped tip landed heavily in her lap. With a chuckle at his predictability, she obliged him with a firm pat before turning her attention to her food.

"So," Lillian said around a mouthful of French toast. "Let's talk about what we've all been avoiding since Gregory and I first awoke."

She didn't bother looking up from her food. Out of the corner of her eye, she saw Gregory's right ear swing in her direction, but he didn't move otherwise, remaining hunched over his meal, eating with the single-mindedness of a hungry male.

Waving a butter knife in Gregory's direction, Gran eyed the gargoyle with a smile large enough it crinkled the skin at the corners of her eyes. "First off—no more wandering around buck-ass naked in gargoyle form."

Gregory glanced first at Gran and then down at his attire, which consisted of his usual beaded loincloth and the wrist and armbands that Lillian had been quick to learn were anything but vain ornamentation. His ears swung forward in question then flattened along his horns in confusion, or more likely, annoyance. Gregory could be a little touchy about his appearance. And she was unsure of Gran's line of thought herself. If they were to compare prudish personality traits, Lillian was sure she'd come out ahead as far more prudish than her grandmother.

A full-bellied laugh escaped Gran. "If you two could see your expressions. I haven't lost my mind or suddenly turned into a dried-out prune. If our little town was as sleepy as it used to be, I'm sure Gregory could walk through the forest in broad daylight and no one would be the wiser, but things have changed."

Lillian arched an eyebrow. She'd known by the underlying tension something was bothering her grandmother, something more worrying than the possibility of the Lady of Battles invading sometime in a vague and distant future.

"In the last three months," Gran said, her voice souring. "Gods, I can't believe it has only been three months—what must be half the membership of the RCMP, the OPP, CSIS, and a whole multitude of military acronyms, have trampled through every fen, stream, bog, glen, marsh, and game trail, all in the name of collecting evidence. With, I might add, a total disregard for the delicate balance in some of those places." Gran snapped her teeth together. "And don't get me started on the more recent addition of the media hounds—they're worse than death hounds!"

The memory of a death hound, its steel-grey teeth exposed to rend and tear, flashed through Lillian's mind's eye. Somehow, she doubted simple reporters could compare to those deadly destructive, unnatural creatures, but she remained silent, leveling Gran with a probing look instead.

Gregory bolted to his full height and bumped the table hard enough to rattle dishes. "What form of creature is this Media Hound? I sensed no immediate danger to Lillian when I first woke."

She laid a restraining hand on Gregory's arm. "They..." Lillian frowned, trying to explain in a way that wouldn't end with innocent humans being hunted by her gargoyle. "They're...harmless truth gatherers."

"Harmless truth gatherers? *Really?*" Gran rolled her eyes. "Gregory, don't believe one word of the rubbish that just exited my granddaughter's lips. The media is far from harmless. The local human population saw something in the sky the night the Riven nearly sacrificed Lillian—a bright, swirling power dancing in the sky. It was snapped, filmed, Tweeted, Facebooked and YouTubed to every corner of the Internet before we even had a hope of containing the damage."

Gran stopped to pour herself some tea. Once she'd stirred in the perfect amount of milk, she glanced back up. "If that was the worst of it, we could have mesmerized scientists and officials into believing the event was nothing more sinister than the northern lights fluctuating in response to a solar flare, or some such web of lies. That would have been within the Coven's power. But no," Gran said with an uncharacteristic snarl and waved her teaspoon for emphasis. "Human authorities reached the site first, they found bodies. The bodies of cottagers and campers the Riven had fed upon and discarded."

Lillian shivered as a boy's image surfaced from the morass of her chaotic memories—a beautiful boy, his expression cherub-like and sweet. Her stomach soured. She might never know if the Riven's host body was a child he'd possessed or merely shapeshifted to appear as one. He and his fellows were the cause of so many deaths, she doubted if the demon would have spared a child.

"We tried to slow the humans." Gran took a sip of her tea and then continued. "The remaining dryads, with the help of Greenborrow, Whitethorn, and the dire wolves, laid false trails, but the humans were persistent. They found some of the Rivens' remains. Even in death, those misbegotten monstrosities manage to threaten our people. And science—

ever the nemesis of magic—may yet be our undoing. Two weeks ago, some of those images leaked onto the Internet.

"Now, every alien and monster hunter this side of the equator has been roaming through our forests. Even our spa is full of government types...yes, we had to reopen the spa early for fear our cover story of 'renovations' would be investigated. No small business would willingly be closed during the cash cow this episode has become."

Gran sighed and ran a hand through her long hair, which strangely wasn't in her customary braid. It appeared a touch windblown as if she hadn't had time to attend to it yet. Maybe she hadn't. Lillian wondered what else had happened while she and Gregory slept three months away. There had to be more. It wasn't like Gran to be fazed by government types snooping around. In all their combined history, the Clan and the Coven must have run into a similar event in the past.

Gregory's thoughts brushed hers, and Lillian knew he had come to the same conclusion. He stepped closer and prodded her in the shoulder with his muzzle when she didn't immediately ask Gran what she was hiding.

"Something else has happened to rattle you, hasn't it?" Lillian kept her voice gentle, for whatever could disturb her grandmother had to be something genuinely fierce in nature.

Gran dragged in a deep breath and let it out slowly. "While you both were sleeping and healing, the Lady of Battles sent two of her servants to investigate why Lillian had not contacted her as promised."

Outwardly, only the slight twitch of his blade-tipped tail told of Gregory's agitation. But tied so tightly to him, both physically and spiritually, Lillian sensed the cold fear slicing through him, the tension in his wings, the lengthening of his dagger-like claws.

She could feel his battle readiness so clearly, it could have been her own body undergoing the changes.

"Who did our enemy send?" Gregory's deep voice startled Lillian back to the present, and she distanced herself from his thoughts and emotions to better focus on the problem at hand. Later, she would dwell upon the new, deeper connection with the gargoyle.

"The Lady of Battles sent Lillian's parents." Gran fidgeted with her teacup before finally looking Gregory in the eye. "Lillian's mother we could have handled. A mere dryad, even strengthened by dark magic, shouldn't have been too much of a challenge for the defenses the Clan and the Coven erected to keep you and Lillian safe. But the dark lady didn't just send a dryad, she sent her pet gargoyle, too."

"So, Lillian's father was here?" Gregory mused. Lillian sensed he was mulling something over in his thoughts, something he wasn't willing to express just yet. "Were you or any of the others able to track him? Tell me in detail what he did while here. Every little thing that you were aware of, no matter how small."

"Unfortunately, we had no better luck at following or tracking him than we would with you," Gran answered, displeasure in her voice. "But we were present in the glade when he examined you at length. I couldn't detect if he wove some spell upon you or not. We feared he had. Then he moved on to Lillian's hamadryad and spent even longer with her. Lillian's mother did the same. They couldn't have missed the fact the hamadryad was healing her and killing the demon seed the Lady of Battles had implanted within her. They must have realized when Lillian emerged from her tree, healed and whole, she would no longer be the Battle Goddess's tool. Strangely, they both seemed pleased with what they found."

"There must be more," Lillian pondered.

"Lillian's mother uttered one sentence: 'We mean no harm and will return at the turning of the leaves for our daughter and her mate.' Then they left as quickly as they came. There was no fighting or bloodshed. They simply vanished as Gregory is able to do." Gran shook her head in remembered disbelief. "Knowing whom they serve, I didn't believe the 'no harm' for a second, and I fully expected them to return with an army at their heels. Days came and went, but no army appeared. Though I still doubt the wholesomeness of their words. Their version of 'harm' is likely very different than mine."

"And mine," Gregory rumbled in answer. "Though if they had indeed meant us harm, I should have roused, whether I was healed or not. That I did not and was not even aware of the visit, worries me."

Lillian glanced between her gargoyle and her grandmother. "We're both healed and awake. It's mid-August, probably a good six weeks before the leaves start to change. However, I wouldn't put much trust in their words either—we might see my parents long before the first shades of autumn."

"I fear that, too." Gran frowned down at her plate.

A strange, conflicting mix of excitement and apprehension swamped Lillian—though she wasn't sure which one she wanted to win.

From the few scraps Gregory had revealed to her about the time before she'd come into Gran's keeping as an eight-year-old child, Lillian sensed both her parents had loved her. But more troubling was the fact she also thought her mother worshipped the Lady of Battles without question. She didn't trust the mother and daughter relationship to outrank sovereign and servant.

"I will not sit idle and await Lillian's parents' return." Gregory stretched to his full height, his horns once again brushing the ceiling, tail flicking in a slow, measured pace. No doubt a reflection of his present mental state. "We prepare for war."

CHAPTER TWO

Gregory spun on his heels and headed for the kitchen's back door, already expanding his power out before him, seeking both enemies and friends. As he saw it, his enemies had a three-months head start, a possible fatal advantage he planned to neutralize as soon as possible, starting today.

He ducked and turned to ease his shoulders through the back door, forcing his wings tight to his back until he was through. The scraping of chairs and hurried footsteps followed him across the kitchen and outside.

"Gregory, wait," Lillian hissed, barely above a whisper. "Did you hear what Gran said about the authorities crawling all over the place? They might even have an eye in the sky trained on us!"

Gregory continued without slowing. He didn't know what an 'eye in the sky' was, though to judge by the mental images he gleaned from Lillian's mind, he guessed it was probably some strange piece of metal and motors the humans used to spy upon their enemies. Presently, he had greater worries to attend to and wasn't concerned about the humans. If they became a nuisance, he'd show them what an Avatar of the Divine Ones could bring down upon their mortal heads.

"Gregory!" Lillian's hiss had grown in strength. Her thoughts showed she worried humans would find him and somehow capture him. Inwardly, he smiled over her protectiveness. For whatever reason, in this life, his lady was always trying to protect him. It was cute.

Behind him, Lillian started to jog, attempting to match his longer strides.

"Stop!" Her voice came out strained. "Someone's going to see you. You're just remaining visible to vex me, aren't you?"

Gregory chuckled. Even angry, Lillian was adorable. Hmm, she sounded out of shape. Three months in the heart of a tree, cocooned in hamadryad magic had healed Lillian's wounds, but he'd have to work on getting her fit again, especially if her gargoyle bloodline was going to assert itself within the coming days. She'd need to be strong, both emotionally and physically.

He turned sharply at a fork in the garden path, taking the left branch. Within a few strides, he dropped to all fours and broke into a ground-eating lope. He continued down the manicured gravel path, beyond the great cedar maze, and farther still, to where a long, narrow meadow was hemmed in on three sides by forest.

This area had changed since he'd last seen it. A fence now enclosed the meadow, and the grass had been clipped by grazing. On the far side of the newly made paddocks, two shapes —one dark obsidian and the other dappled grey—grazed in the peaceful manner of horses. Though if these two were horses, he was a deer. Gregory snorted with humor, and the two equines trotted over to his side.

Neither showed the slightest hesitation at the fence and sailed over it, not bothering to hide their competitive natures. Upon landing, the dappled grey kicked out at his obsidian companion. *Make that combative natures*, Gregory acknowledged. At least not everything had changed while he'd slept in stone—the unicorn and the pooka still barely tolerated each other.

Gregory frowned at the two thoughtfully. It wasn't like them to live in a pasture, and certainly not in line of sight of each other. "Is there a particular reason you're living on this small parcel of land?" He paused then added, "Together? Pretending to be mortal horses?" The last he found to be the more perplexing question.

The unicorn tossed his forelock out of his eyes as he trotted closer. He halted a stride away and arched his neck until he could butt Gregory in the chest. While the unicorn nuzzled him for a scratch, he felt a slight tug on his magic—which was the real reason for the affectionate greeting. With a sigh and another chuckle, Gregory complied with both requests, both physical and magical, giving a good rub along the unicorn's neck and withers, while allowing a small trickle of his magic to flow into the unicorn.

The pooka snorted and rolled an eye in his direction. Gregory took it as an invitation to groom the smaller black equine, and nearly lost fingers to the surly creature. With a grunt, he slapped his tail along the pooka's flank and was rewarded by an indignant squeal.

"Serves you right, you disloyal beast. We're still going to

have a long talk about why you delivered Lillian into the hands of my enemies last spring."

The pooka pranced out of reach, while the unicorn, in counterpoint, circled closer, each revolution bringing him nearer until he squared up and faced Gregory.

"At the time, Lillian was even more fearsome than you," the unicorn offered with an equine squeal of delight. *"Perhaps the little black pony feared her."*

The pooka curled his lip, flashing very unhorse-like fangs. *"It was not fear. She saw to my obedience. I could not match her power."*

"Liar," Gregory huffed half-heartedly. "You were a willing victim. You wanted what she offered."

"Yes. I wanted to return to the Magic Realm." The pooka shook his mane and arched his tail, dancing around Gregory at a swift trot. *"This mortal world will be the death of us all. Her bargain was one I couldn't turn down. I would do the same if asked a second time. So, I lied to you, but I wouldn't be much of a pooka if I told the truth all the time."* The pooka edged close enough to reach out and nip at the edge of Gregory's one wing. *"While we speak of personal weaknesses, as I recall, you were Lillian's most devoted victim. I can read weaknesses in all beings, their darkest fears, needs, and desires. In you, I saw a readiness to surrender all you were to save her, even if it meant serving the dark."*

The pooka leaped into the air, bouncing away faster than Gregory's tail could land a blow. With a whinny of triumph, the black pony trotted back into range, taunting clear in his body language. *"Deny it if you wish, Gargoyle. But we both know the truth, how close you came to betraying all you stand for, all you have ever served. How an Avatar nearly betrayed his God."*

"You just spoke another truth, Pooka. We are both in danger of betraying our natures."

The pooka jerked his head high. *"You acknowledge your guilt? You surprise me."*

"Good." Gregory laughed openly. "The day I fail to surprise you will be the day a pooka has defeated me." Of all the fae, the pooka was perhaps the most honest about his nature. But as interesting as this was, he was wasting valuable time. "Now tell me why you are both playing at being horses?"

Gregory turned his attention back to the unicorn, wanting an answer that didn't require having to see through ten veils of deception just to get one simple bit of truth.

"Gran's orders. She doesn't want any of us to be seen in our true forms by the humans. She said horses wandering in the forests and fields would be more easily explained. And Gran is almost as fearsome as you, Master Gargoyle."

"We will all need to become fiercer in the coming days," Gregory said, conviction he did not want strong in his voice. "War is coming. We must prepare."

"Warfare?" The pooka's ears perked up. *"I have not rolled in the blood of my enemies in an age."*

The unicorn shuddered and made a series of distressed snorts. He edged away from the black pony until he was safely behind the shelter of Gregory's slightly mantled wings, only then did he scrounge up enough bravery to arch his neck to peer at the pooka. *"And you call yourself an herbivore?"*

A pale glow gleamed deep in the pooka's eyes, just a hint of yellow as if he thought about shedding his pony disguise.

Gregory was just drawing breath to defuse the situation when the sound of feet on gravel reached his ears. He swiveled one ear in the direction of the sound, judging distance. Lillian was coming fast, kicking up gravel as she ran. "Don't start fighting." He glowered at the pooka for good measure. "I have something of importance I wish to ask before Lillian arrives. Gran told me of Lillian's parents. Were either of you near when they came?"

The unicorn bobbed his head in assent, and then to Gregory's surprise, the pooka followed a moment later. He'd expected the pooka would have been nearby. Of all the fae, he most wanted to return to the Magic Realm, and Lillian was his best chance to accomplish his goal. But Gregory was surprised by how readily he was getting answers from the ornery beast. While he was getting answers, he might as well see what else he could glean from his new allies. "Later, when Lillian is distracted by Gran or others, I want you two to seek me out and divulge all you know of her birth parents and their possible intentions." For the pooka's benefit, he added, "I will be in your debt."

The yellow shimmer in the pooka's gaze intensified, and he stepped closer to Gregory. His warm breath puffed along Gregory's skin as soft whiskers brushed over his arm and up along his shoulder to stop at the junction of neck and collar bone. Mobile equine lips nipped softly at an artery before pulling away. *"We have a deal, Gregory. I imagine your blood is rich."*

CHAPTER THREE

By the time Lillian came pelting down the trail, Gregory was already leaning nonchalantly against the fence, and both equines were safely back on the other side of the rails, grazing like they'd been doing so all along. She skidded to a halt beside him, sweating and out of breath. He merely tilted his head in her direction in acknowledgment and waited patiently while she leaned over, held her side, and wheezed like she'd never run in her life.

When he stepped forward and placed an arm around her shoulders and urged her to lean against the fence next to him, she complied without hesitation and rested her hip against a post. "What's wrong with me? I'm as weak as a kitten."

"You still haven't completely recovered. Your hamadryad healed you, but now you must rebuild your strength and endurance. You shouldn't have run so far."

She jerked her head up and glared at him. "And whose fault is that? I wouldn't have had to run if you hadn't taken off. I still can't believe you just ran off," she growled in a remarkably good imitation of him. "Didn't you hear what Gran said about all the authorities lurking behind every bush? Or did you forget the meaning of 'stop' while you slept for three months? Because I'd be happy to give you a little reminder."

"I heard what Vivian said about these new human authorities. I simply am not concerned with them. Humans have no power to threaten, hold, or enslave me."

"But they can shoot your half-naked ass."

Gregory swallowed a growl, not wanting to fight with Lillian about so trivial a concern as humans, not when the Lady of Battles might already be moving an invading army into position at this very moment.

Lillian's seemingly peevish demeanor was nothing more than a disguise, one he'd seen many times since he'd first come to this world. He knew her outward crustiness had more to do with worry than annoyance at having to run after him. Besides, he already had a useful method for handling Lillian's fear.

Inching closer, he dipped his muzzle and licked her from chin to hairline. She responded with the usual squawk as she flailed at his muzzle with the flat of her hand. Her contact wasn't much more than a pat, so he took advantage of her hesitancy to do him harm by bumping her hands away with his muzzle and then landing another sloppy kiss across her face, and then a third along her neck.

He nuzzled aside the neckline of her top, and her giggles choked off on a gasp. Her fingers dug into his scalp as she grabbed fistfuls of his mane and nearly jerked it out by the roots.

"What do you think you're doing?"

"Attitude adjustment." Gregory chuckled at her affronted look. "You needed a distraction. You were allowing your fear to affect your judgment."

"Nice attempt at modern phrases." One delicate eyebrow shot up at his words. "Sadly, it falls flat when your reasoning is positively medieval."

Gregory's ears perked as hope flashed through his being. "Then I'll stop trying to adapt to this modern world. We'll both be happier."

"You say and do the oddest things." She shook her head at him. "Let's leave this entire episode as a species barrier incident, shall we?"

"As you wish, my Sorceress." With the danger of Lillian learning his true intent at seeking out the two equines bypassed, he shook the residual tension out of his wings.

Tilting her head back, her eyes flicked over his features in a way he knew was trouble. She crossed her arms over her breasts and said, "Don't 'My Sorceress' me as a deflection. You're hiding something. What did you say to the unicorn and the pooka you didn't want me to overhear?"

He winced inwardly at her astute observation. "I wish for them to find and bring Whitethorn and Greenborrow to me." Which was the truth, Gregory reasoned with himself. He'd planned to ask them to do that very thing after he'd talked of Lillian's parents. "We must discuss battle strategy. You're more than welcome to join the meeting, but I know both you and Gran would likely appreciate the time to catch up with each other."

His ears pricked up and his wings relaxed marginally—his words sounded plausible. She shouldn't take exception to them. As if on cue, the unicorn and the pooka lifted their heads from grazing and pointed their ears in Gregory's direction. With a snort and a bob of his head, the unicorn was the first to jump the fence a third time and take off down the trail, the pooka a dark shadow a short distance behind.

Gentle fingers curled around his muzzle and tilted it until she was able to look directly into his eyes—hers were full of sorrow. "Have I taught my Gargoyle Protector to lie? Is that the gift I have given him?" Sadness echoed in her voice even as the words were carried away on the afternoon breeze.

"Lillian."

She slid one finger against his lips. "Don't. Not if it's another lie. In the not so distant past, we both concealed truths with the intention of protecting the other. As I recall, it didn't work out so well for us." Lillian stepped up to him, surprising him with a fierce embrace, her arms squeezing him with all the strength she possessed. "I will never knowingly lie to you again. Please have the decency to honor me with the same promise."

Nothing and no one possessed the power to unman him as devastatingly as his Sorceress. He bowed his muzzle over Lillian's head, nuzzling her hair as his arms and wings encircled her smaller form. "Forgive me. Even if I learn nothing in this life, I will learn this lesson well. You have my word. I will not lie to you again." He dragged in a deep breath, savoring her calming scent.

Lillian held her silence as she petted his back in long soothing strokes.

To his shame, his wings trembled at her gentle touch, but something in his spirit eased, and the truth flowed from him freely. "I asked the unicorn and the pooka to tell me what they had learned about your birth parents. Both equines have a unique ability to read the heart of a person—to see one's hidden personality traits, their loves, hates, their deepest desires—what lengths they will stoop to complete a mission. Dark things no child should have to learn about a parent, beloved or not."

Lillian gave a bitter-sounding laugh. "Gregory, there is nothing the pooka and the unicorn can tell me that will be worse than what I already imagine. At most, whatever they say will only confirm what I suspect." She patted his shoulder in a companionable way before continuing, "Later—together —we'll listen to what the unicorn and pooka have to say about my parents."

"Your words hold wisdom." He gave her hand an affectionate lick.

She sighed predictably at the dampness covering the back of her hand, but the muscles of her jaw relaxed enough for a hint of a smile to show through.

"My words actually hold wisdom? Well, there's a first. Let's go find Greenborrow and Whitethorn." Her lips turned down in determination. "Battle plans await."

With a sharp nod of assent, Gregory dropped to all fours and bumped his nose under her hand. Her fingers skimmed over the curve of his muzzle and around the base of one horn before settling in his mane as she took up a long-legged stride, a perfect match for his ground-eating walk.

With the subtle contact, peace flowed between them and Gregory's world was back as it should be.

CHAPTER FOUR

*L*illian halted at the edge of the forest's shadowy perimeter. Gregory mirrored her motion, and she dropped her fingers away from his mane. The breeze blew cool across her heated face, the contrast raising gooseflesh along her arms.

The gravel path continued for another dozen feet before it turned, winding its twisting way through the trees and out of sight. They walked for perhaps another twenty minutes. All the while the forest grew thicker, the shadows darker, the rich scent of loam heavier in the air. As the forest embraced her, Lillian relaxed further.

Gregory stopped, lifted his head, and sniffed the air.

"Now what?"

In answer, Gregory stepped out around her, veered off the path, and disappeared behind an evergreen's dense foliage.

"Why Gregory, thank you for answering my question." With a snort, Lillian followed her gargoyle off the path and into the forest. They continued to walk, dodging tree trunks, craggy roots, thorny thickets, and boggy low spots. Lillian was used to the forest's tricky geography and kept pace with Gregory relatively painlessly, though she was envious of the way he moved so gracefully.

The shadows of the forest thinned ahead, and they emerged into a meadow. At the end of the clearing, the unicorn circled a large pine. He trotted with his neck arched and his tail a bright, white banner behind him. Every inch of his body language said he was pleased with himself.

When Lillian squinted at the shadows below the pine's sweeping branches, she could just make out another shadowy form. Unlike the unicorn, who showed no more concern for human authorities than Gregory did, the one under the tree was wise enough to want to hide.

Upon closer proximity, Lillian recognized the other fae's slender form and long silvery hair, the shimmering shade not one she'd ever seen on a human. She raised a hand in greeting to the sidhe leader. Whitethorn cast a glance around the meadow before he edged out from underneath the tree's canopy.

Only then did Lillian notice he had his bow at the ready, an arrow nocked. He lowered the point to the ground and jerked his head toward darker shadows to his left. There the forest thickened again, choking out the meadow grasses with the shrubby growth of understory trees.

Gregory skirted the meadow, and as Lillian paced him, she felt when he called on the cold magic of the Spirit Realm. The air around them became chilled like someone had opened a freezer door. A fine mist rose from the warm ground, and shadows beneath the surrounding trees deepened, blurring and softening the bright light of day into something more like twilight. Ahead, Gregory's bulk had vanished completely, and Lillian was willing to bet she was now invisible to mortal eyes.

But it didn't mean they were immune or hidden from a more technological variety of eye.

"Wait! Gregory, you might not be as concealed as you think."

She grabbed in the general vicinity of where his shoulder should've been and encountered a wing instead. Tugging forcefully, she attempted to turn him. "Humans have technology, science you have never seen, which can track things like body heat and movement from high overhead or a great distance away."

He became visible as he flicked his wing free of her grasp. "You doubt my ability to protect us from humans?" Then turning to her, he stepped closer until his muzzle was only inches away.

Lillian held her ground. "I'm not questioning your prowess as a protector, but there are things in this world you know nothing about that might be able to see through your cloaking magic."

"Then you need not worry." Warm breath puffed across her cheeks. When he smiled, she got a worm's eye view of his very white fangs. His deep voice rumbled in her ears when he spoke. "I sense no humans near us. There is a group within an hour's walk, but even if they stumble upon us, I promise to deal with them 'gently.' As for being seen from above, I have made it impossible."

Standing toe to toe, with his bulk dwarfing her, his massive wings curling to partially enfold her in their velvet expanse, it would have been easy to back down to his passive-aggressive stance. Instead, she tilted her head so she could meet his gaze and asked, "Care to elaborate on the last statement?"

He drew a deep breath which expanded his chest and leaned closer until they were nose to nose. "Not now."

Grumpy, she thought. *Now, who needs an attitude adjustment?*

"If you're not going to budge, why are we wasting time with this staring contest?" Lillian tossed back, and then placed a kiss on the tip of his nose. He jumped back, startled, and she hooted. "You moved, points for me."

Gregory huffed, folded his wings tight, and stormed off toward Whitethorn.

"Spoilsport," she called out to his retreating back. While she might not possess great powers like she'd supposedly once commanded, still she had a purpose—keeping her beloved gargoyle humble. And possibly guiding him through all the pitfalls he might encounter in the modern world.

"The pooka said you wished to speak with me, Lord Gargoyle." The sidhe leader's words were accompanied by a half-bow, the move more graceful than anything executed on a ballroom floor. Without the shimmering silver locks, pointed ears, and dark-grey brocade tunic, he'd look entirely at home on one of those polished floors as well.

Gregory's rumbling voice drew her back to the conversation. "Gran informed me that during the time Lillian and I rested and healed we received some unusual guests. We must conceive of a solution to our present problems."

"A wise idea. But not here where we are so exposed." Whitethorn drew back deeper into the shadows, gesturing for Lillian and Gregory to follow. "If Vivian told you of our visitors, she must have also warned you of the increased numbers of humans roaming our lands. It isn't safe to remain in the open."

Gregory's tail twitched at the word 'humans,' but he mellowed enough to follow Whitethorn without argument, for which Lillian was grateful. Perhaps she had an ally in the sidhe leader.

Deeper into the woods they finally stopped, and she perched on a fallen tree trunk. Gregory and Whitethorn both turned to look out beyond their circle, toward a small game trail to the right of where Lillian sat. She glanced in the same direction but saw nothing. It was on the tip of her tongue to ask what they found so interesting when she heard the soft clomp of hooves. Seconds later, the unicorn galloped down the path in their direction, Greenborrow clinging to his back. As soon as the unicorn halted, Greenborrow tumbled off.

A few choice words in an unknown language colored the small clearing. In more dishevel than usual, Greenborrow straightened his baggy clothes and squared his shoulders, growing taller as she watched. He stomped his feet a couple of times as if it would knock the wrinkles out of his long tunic, and then he closed his eyes and curled his bare toes into the forest loam. After a deep sigh, he opened his eyes and took them all in with a merry look. "That's better. Solid ground under my feet. No leshii was ever intended to ride horseback."

At the leshii's words, the unicorn neighed loud enough to echo through the forest.

"What's gotten into you?" Greenborrow leveled a glare at the equine. "Oh...horseback, unicorn, pooka...one's as unnatural to ride as another."

"Then walk next time!" With a twirl of his head, the unicorn spun and galloped back into the forest.

"That went well," Lillian mumbled under her breath.

"I thought so." Greenborrow bestowed her with a grin and a jaunty little bow. "Always nice to see you." Then turning to Gregory and Whitethorn, he became more serious. "Well, Lord Gargoyle, what thoughts do you hide behind those black mirror eyes?"

"Dark thoughts," Gregory said. He shook out his wings and sat down with his tail curled around his haunches. The other two fae joined him, and he gestured for Lillian to sit by his side.

She hadn't fully settled herself when a muscular weight landed in her lap. Gregory proceeded to coil his tail around her waist twice until the spade-shaped tip was again directly in front, conveniently under her hands. Inwardly, she smiled at the predictability of her touchy-feely guardian while she settled her fingers on the boney ridges and began to massage between the plate-like armor at the very tip.

Whitethorn arched an eyebrow before he continued the conversation from earlier. "If we don't take precautions, we may find ourselves fighting a battle on three fronts—the humans, the Riven, and the Lady of Battles. Even you, Avatar, must find those daunting odds."

"The Lady of Battles is my greatest concern. While she can't come here herself, she may send her warriors soon. My normal defensive weavings will not remain effective for any length of time in this Realm so I must try another method. I will gift any fae who wishes to join me with magic-forged weapons and personal defensive spells keyed to an object. It will protect the magic from the ravages of this Realm."

"Permanent talismans," Greenborrow whistled. "You, my boy, are planning on expending a great deal of magic. More fae will come, curious as they would be of any gargoyle in the Mortal Realm. Many newcomers have already arrived and felt your power even as you healed. Some of the oldest guessed who and what you are—the Avatars. In this magic-starved land, you, my darlings, are an unequaled banquet."

Gregory nodded. "And I welcome them to come to feast on magic cast-off as I forge weapons and spells."

"Is that a bribe?" Whitethorn asked, sounding almost incredulous.

"Yes, if it will sway more to my side."

"And if we are victorious?"

"My offer is still the same; there is no limit upon it. When I return home with Lillian, any Clan or Coven member wishing to come with me, may."

Greenborrow slapped his knees and chuckled. "And that, my fine gargoyle, is the best bribe of all."

Whitethorn's nod was dour. "Indeed."

"Why are we just sitting here? Are we waiting for the Lady of Battles to show up for tea?" Greenborrow stood up and bowed to Lillian. "Though your lovely grandmother might just be civil enough to bake for even her worst enemy."

"A word of caution," the sidhe leader stood in one graceful motion, "not all fae who come to you will be trustworthy."

"I don't expect them to be," Gregory said and glanced in the direction of a darker shadow, which coalesced into the pooka. "My personal standards are not as elevated as they once were."

Gregory unwound his tail from Lillian's waist. She missed the weight and the warmth, but also the gentle flow of magic between them; however, she didn't let it distract her from an earlier worry. "But what are we supposed to do with the humans while we wage war with the Battle Goddess's minions and the remaining Riven. Most humans aren't evil...for goodness sake, I thought I was human. The collateral damage of a war here in this realm will be immense. You can't expect me to stand aside and allow harm to come to the humans."

Gregory huffed.

Lillian frowned and then tried another tactic. "We're Avatars. Surely we must protect the humans of this world?"

"Perhaps, but it's not our primary purpose," Gregory said, looking thoughtful once more. "As Avatars, our first and foremost role is to act as physical vessels for the Divine Ones to pour their power and essence into so they can bring about change to the universe and sometimes beget offspring in a way that doesn't jeopardize all their creation. An age can come and pass before they choose to call on us for that task, but we have a long and varied list of other duties to perform when our primary function is not required."

"Yeah, I remember the 'coming together equals a glorious death'— as in ours— 'to give new life' speech. Someone needs to tell the Divine Ones that seems a steep price to pay for a little fun in the sack."

Gregory's one ear flicked forward and then back, but otherwise, he didn't move a muscle, trying to stare her down instead, she suspected. Or perhaps she'd struck him speechless.

Finally, he blinked and then started to laugh. "When this life is over, and we once again walk in the Spirit Realm as one being, we must remember to mention what you said to our creators. Perhaps they will grant us some freedoms in the next life they have never given before, and we have never thought to ask."

Lillian crossed her arms. "You're making fun of me again, aren't you?"

"Just a little."

"Thanks, love you too."

"Our thoughts, desires, and motivations are so different when we shed our mortal bodies and become one being in the Spirit Realm. I sometimes forget you cannot remember how it is. We have never been unhappy—frustrated, yes," he chuckled, "but never unhappy with our lot."

"I know. I'm sorry." Lillian sighed and fought to bury her more cynical side, the part of her that wanted to challenge and question and pick apart every little detail to understand what made them tick.

A throat cleared behind them, and Lillian remembered they had an audience—a rapt one, by Greenborrow's fascinated expression. Whitethorn, who had been the one to clear his throat, nodded his head in the universal signal to continue.

Lillian flushed slightly, then asked, "But you might be convinced to aid the humans?"

Gregory bobbed his head. "If they do not get in my way." He paused, and Lillian watched him struggle for the right words. "I cannot risk all of creation just to save a few innocent mortals."

Lillian could be just as stubborn. "But you will try to protect the humans if at all possible, yes?"

Gregory's ear flicked to half-mast position in what Lillian was coming to recognize as the gargoyle version of a flinch. "Yes. All innocents deserve our protection."

"Thank you." Lillian reached out and grasped his hands, wanting to show him she knew he wasn't finding this life or this world easy to acclimatize to. "I know all this would be so much easier if I had your Sorceress's memories."

Gregory stood and stretched, keeping her fingers trapped within his. "You will one day remember all that has been lost."

"I guess I'll just wait for that day," Lillian sighed out dejectedly.

"It will only be for a short while, as we judge time, before you regain your soul and your memories and all else you once were." Gregory sighed and butted his head against her chest hard enough to make her sway.

"Stop it. You've got work to do."

He sighed a second time, giving her a long-suffering look. "Yes."

Whitethorn bowed to them both. "I will ask all available sidhe metalsmiths to come to your aid, and Greenborrow will do the same among the rest of the Clan." He tilted his head in the leshii's direction. Greenborrow nodded his head in acknowledgment.

"In the meantime, until the metalsmiths have arrived, I will construct some defensive spells to warn us should the Riven attempt to invade our lands. While the spells will cover a vast area, they will be temporary, lasting mere days in this Realm. However, they will help until the next Wild Hunt can run."

"We are honored to have your protection." Whitethorn folded his arms across his chest and bowed at the waist.

"Until later, then," Gregory said and started away from the small clearing where they'd talked. Lillian followed, curious about how he would place magic enchantments over a large area. She might lack her own magic at present, but that would not always be the case, and at the very least she could watch and learn.

Gregory walked a short distance and dropped to all fours. He circled back and sidled up next to her. His one wing dipped in an invitation, baring his broad shoulders and back. His tail snaked around her hips before she thought to try and backpedal out of immediate danger. But it was too late, and his muscular tail dragged her closer to his back.

"I'm not tired. I can walk! Really!"

Gregory coughed, or it might have been a laugh. Lillian failed to find the humor in the situation. He wanted her to ride gargoyle-back, as it were, and she wanted nothing more than to avoid that fate.

Last time she'd found the whole situation too bumpy, too fast, too scary, and far too intimate—equal parts awkward and thrilling at the same time. And this time, she feared she might not find it so bumpy or scary.

"This is probably a bad idea." Lillian ran possible scenarios through her mind. "If we get too near humans, you might have to bolt in a hurry. I'll fall off and break something for sure."

"Now who is lying? Besides, I would hear humans long before they were a danger to us. And I won't let you fall." Gregory forced her closer. It was get on his back or be flipped over it to land painfully on the ground on the other side.

Lillian decided to save what dignity she still possessed and tossed a leg over his back and settled in place. Gregory's wings folded tight to either side of her thighs, locking her in place. She knew from previous rides she was as secure as she would be if she buckled herself into a car. Probably more so. Gregory looked out for her welfare—a car was far more indifferent.

CHAPTER FIVE

The siren glanced up uneasily at the ocean's ceiling. A mirror-bright, cerulean blue reflected from the upper realm, a world of air and strange destinies; a world she'd soon have to explore.

She swam for hours, unable to find the source of the oily taint she inhaled with each flutter of her gills. It was everywhere, had worked its way into every reef, school of fish, and patch of kelp she encountered. While she did find life, it was not thriving as it should. The underwater world, her realm to protect, was changing, its magic diminishing, its species no longer as numerous as they once had been.

Even the great whales were not untouched. From them, she gathered more knowledge. As she'd suspected, humans were responsible. The whales' perception of the source of the taint—some cataclysm—was vague, the details scattered and full of holes. They could only relate what they had heard, but they spoke of a family of dolphins that had witnessed the event.

With greater determination, Tethys set out to find the dolphins.

For leagues, the siren swam, her anger banked, but still glowing like a land-bound's fire. Around her, the ocean's waters raged in sympathy. White-capped waves rolled away from her location with greater and greater frequency.

A soft clicking sounded in the distance. Twisting her body, she whipped around, homing in on the location. The water carried the sound from a long way, but it was still distinguishable as dolphin speech even over the deep drone of the raging seas.

They sang their approach across the vastness of the ocean. A small pod of six pale-grey shapes drew closer, their compact bodies elegant in the water. As the dolphins neared, the ocean calmed, and Tethys let the last of her rage go. She'd never been able to remain angry in the presence of the playful ones.

With a lighter heart, she went to meet them. The first dolphin broke rank and bolted ahead of the others. A young male, his curiosity clear by his body language and chattering clicks. He swam close enough to bump his nose against her tail before his bravery deserted him, and he darted back to the rest of his family pod.

The other members of the family, perhaps older and wiser, held back, studying her. The young male broke rank a second time and slid closer. He continued to chatter at her, questioning what she was. She answered in kind, the clicks and whistles a language she'd mastered long ago.

At length, she explained to the dolphin family who and what she was, and they gave her their names in return.

A deluge of playful greetings distracted her from other, darker questions. It wasn't until they had hunted together and were well fed that Tethys asked about the condition of the air and water. Her line of questioning was too complicated at first. The results were a mix of confusing clicks and meaningless whistles.

She tapped the fingers of one hand along her flank and tried another question.

"What makes the water taste bad?"

There were more clicking and swift, darting bodies as the group worked out a spokesperson.

The young male ignored his elders' debate and answered the siren. *"The Not-Island sank."*

"Not-Island?" she asked, hoping for something more conclusive.

The oldest matriarch of the pod bumped the young male aside, scolding him in the process. Once she was finished, she came alongside the siren. They swam with near-perfect unity for several body lengths, and then Tethys reached out a hand to rest on the dolphin's side.

At the contact, a confusing series of images marched through her head. A great metal monster perched out in the ocean, close to shore, its metal roots burrowing deep into the earth's crust.

Above the surface, bright flames burned on the metal Not-Island. Darkness floated upon the water and impossibly, burned there, too. Great poisonous clouds billowed up into the air.

Humans had jumped from the metal island, trying to escape their own folly. The dolphin pod circled farther out, wanting to help the humans, but too afraid of the monstrous island to come near enough.

More humans arrived in boats, rescuing their fellows. They battled the fierce blaze for a time, but it proved too much, and the heat pushed them back.

Both humans and dolphin pod watched as the structure weakened. Then with a great, tortured groan, the whole of it twisted sideways. Pieces of debris sheared off, dropping into the water below with great splashes and much hissing of steam. Another long stretch of time elapsed, then finally the massive Not-Island died, collapsing down into the ocean. Like a leviathan with its spine severed, chunks of metal piping twisted and crumpled upon themselves as it made its slow, painful way to the ocean floor.

The fires on the surface burned out, the sounds of tortured metal ceased, and the ocean grew silent once again.

To Tethys's horror, she realized it was only the beginning.

Oily black death bubbled out of the earth as if a vein had been severed, spreading an ever-enlarging stain upon the ocean realm.

For days upon days, humans had scurried about in boats. Their actions desperate and ineffectual against such an insidious enemy.

The dolphins had stayed in the region to learn if the disaster would be contained, but the waters grew steadily more tainted, fish sickened and died or fled the area. Seabirds and other life succumbed to the black menace.

With no other choice, the dolphins abandoned their

hunting grounds, following the schools of fish, and left the humans to battle their mistake.

The siren sensed it took the humans days to stop the leak, far longer than it should have. A year passed, the ocean defused the toxins, and the humans' clean up continued. Yet she could still taste the legacy of disaster.

Her tail flicked with agitation and her mind filled with thoughts of hate and revenge, but she forced herself to calm as she faced the dolphin matriarch.

The dolphins were fond of the land-bound humans for some reason she'd never been able to comprehend.

"Where can I find knowledgeable humans? Ones with water and land wisdom?"

"You seek searchers and studiers?" the matriarch chirped.

Tethys nodded at the female's question. *"Yes, I require those with knowledge so I might learn from them."*

"Friendly ones that like us. We show you."

The dolphin darted off, angling toward the far, distant shore. The siren and the rest of the pod followed.

As they traveled just under the blue mirror, the young male who had first approached her bumped her again. In a burst of youthful enthusiasm, the youngling broke the surface and arched through the air.

With barely a splash, he dove back in, and with three powerful tail flips, he was back at her side, nudging her to play. Subduing her anger at the humans, she opened her heart to the dolphins' joy of life. Arching her back and swishing her tail in rapid, strong strokes, she clipped the young male with her tail as she darted toward the surface.

Chirping wildly, the male gave chase. Seconds later, they

broke the surface together, curving through the air before they fell back into the cool embrace of Mother Ocean.

The rest of the pod joined in the fun of surf dancing, leaping and twisting into the air. When they tired of the game, they hunted schools of fish. All the while, the dolphin matriarch guided her family under Tethys's watchful eye.

CHAPTER SIX

From her position near a giant grandfather of a sycamore, Lillian watched Gregory pace out an invisible circle, an area roughly the size of his outstretched wings. Periodically, he glanced up from his study of the ground and eyed the surrounding trees with a simmering intensity. After two more circles of the area, he returned to Lillian's side.

"This location will do. Here the land's magic is stronger than anywhere else we're likely to find within three day's flight."

"Whoa! The use of 'we' and 'flight' together in the same sentence is strictly prohibited."

His head cocked to the side. "You have always loved flying with me. I will help you overcome your irrational fear."

To cover up the rush of terror his words inspired, she tossed her hands up in surrender and then turned and stomped back to the shelter of the sycamore. The gooseflesh standing at attention all along her arms testified to the fact she wasn't fond of riding gargoyle-back. Not to mention her hardy dislike of anything that combined speed and heights. The mere thought of flying while perched precariously upon Gregory's back was the culmination of some unholy nightmare, only one she hoped to postpone indefinitely. "Good thing this spot will work, because there's no way you can just go for a 'little three-day flight' without finding yourself on the nightly news or the permanent guest in some super-secret government institution."

With another of his huffs of disdain, Gregory turned his back on her and mantled his wings. Less than ten seconds later, she felt him call magic. Whirls and eddies of cool air swirled around her ankles, raising more gooseflesh along her legs to match what was already gracing her arms. She held her position with her denim-covered butt firmly parked against the tree's trunk. If Gregory was going to cavalierly dismiss her concerns, she'd show him she could be just as stubborn.

It didn't matter what he was doing.

She wasn't curious in the least.

Not one bit.

A deep, rumbling laugh filled the night. "You're a terrible liar, my Sorceress. However, you are more than welcome to watch, pretend extreme indifference, or take a nap if you wish, but just stay close." Gregory gave her one of his wicked, toothy gargoyle grins over his shoulder before he turned his attention back to his spell.

Lillian pursed her lips.

He was correct on all counts.

Damn.

But she wasn't about to take a nap on his command like some naughty child.

She pushed off from the tree and walked around Gregory until she could peer around his half-mantled wings.

He'd burned a magic symbol into the very air—she couldn't think what else to call the glowing, tightly knotted flecks of light hanging suspended at waist height. A second was forming next to the first. On the original's opposite side, a soft glow soon developed into a third pale-green symbol, this one shot through with silver spots of brighter intensity.

Gregory shifted from his hunched position to stand upright, his wings stretching until they were fully extended.

Anticipating his next move, Lillian sank down into a cross-legged position. Safely out of the way, she leaned back against the tree's trunk and watched him work.

As she half-expected, he pushed the glowing symbols with a gentle sweep of one broad wing. The misty lights flashed brighter as they floated away from each other with increasing speed.

Wanting an explanation, she craned her neck to look up at Gregory.

He stood with his head bowed, eyes closed, expression relaxed. His arms rested at his sides, and his tail lay curled around his ankles, the picture of peaceful contentment.

Why shouldn't her gargoyle be happy? He was working powerful magic from the Spirit Realm, doing what he was designed to do. She swallowed back her questions to simply allow him this moment.

Only his wings held any tension as they fanned the air slowly, stirring up a slight breeze as he called a greater flow of magic and shaped it into more of the fire-bright symbols.

After each was made, they hovered in a group a few feet away. When he had another half-dozen of them, he fanned his wings with more power and sent the new spells out into the surrounding forest in pursuit of the first round.

She was still watching their graceful flight when the excited baying of a hound reached her ears.

CHAPTER SEVEN

*L*illian lunged to her feet as more barking pierced the air, closer this time. Too close. She returned to Gregory's side and placed a hand on his upper right arm, being careful not to interfere with the spell he was still calling into being.

"Gregory, I think those are police or military dogs. We're about to get uniformed visitors." Lillian forced herself to take one step away, not liking how she was about to leave him at what could be a very vulnerable time but seeing no other choice. "Stay, take the time you need to finish the spell. I'll delay our company."

Magic brushed against her skin and in the touch, she felt Gregory, his thoughts sharp with alertness, but not undue concern. *"Be careful, my Sorceress. I sense no evil in the humans coming near, but they are well-schooled in the weapons of this world and smell of anticipation and a touch of fear. Never a good combination."*

"Guess I better be careful not to surprise them then."

After one last glance in Gregory's direction, she started back the way they had come. The dogs were closer now, the tone of their cries fiercer. In the distance, lights flickered through the dense undergrowth. Lillian began to run, wanting as much distance between the newcomers and her gargoyle as possible.

As her long-legged strides closed the distance, Lillian realized she reacted with her usual rashness and absolutely no plan. Out this deep in the forest, with darkness falling, she needed an ironclad explanation, and she imagined anything as mundane as a simple walk would be sure to catch the interest of whatever investigator would be accompanying the dogs. No one was stupid enough to wander the forest at night, at least not without good reason, a strong flashlight, and a backpack —or a campsite nearby.

"I have none of the above. And no wits to save me, either," Lillian muttered to herself in disgust.

"No great lady, you may not have yet gained wisdom in this life. But that is why you have allies." A dour voice invaded her thoughts. And accompanying it, the pooka trotted out of the darkness between two trees. *"You have two groups of humans converging on your location."*

"Which one of the Fates did I piss off to warrant so many?"

The pooka snorted as he came alongside her shoulder. A bright, yellow halter encircled the pony's head, the color a near match for his normally bright yellow, otherworldly eyes —though at least his eyes were a nice normal brown at the moment. A lead was already clicked to the halter. The pooka held the excess clamped firmly in his teeth. With a shake of his head, he tossed the lead at her. *"Take it. And try to look like you know how to lead a horse. When the humans arrive, you will say a predator spooked your horses, and you followed our trail into the forest."*

"Would a horse bolt into a dark forest where a who-knows-what-kind of predator could be waiting in the shadows for its next snack?"

The pooka chuckled. "No, but when they find us and assume their dogs have been trailing me and the one-horned fool over all this distance, they will be so disgusted with themselves and the dogs, they will call off the hunt."

Being within touching distance of the pooka was not always the best place to be, but once again she found herself grateful to the evil-tempered beast. Following his instructions, she took the lead he offered and looped it around her hand, and then glanced in the direction of the lights.

"What part of 'look like you know what you're doing' didn't you understand? Don't loop it around your hand—unless you want to get dragged to your death! And stand on my left."

Lillian juggled the lead rope, and then situated herself at the pooka's shoulder, still fighting to untangle the line.

"Left! My other left. Hurry!"

Lillian grumbled and switched sides. She didn't have long to wait. Two excited dogs, their handlers only a few feet behind them, burst from between the trees. Retina-searing light flashed directly in her face, blinding her for several, vital seconds. She raised a hand to shield her eyes from the bright light.

One of the dogs, a wiry-haired terrier and the smaller of the two, jerked away from its handler and streaked past both Lillian and the pooka with barely a glance. Nose to the ground, it leaped over an old, rotted stump and vanished down the path leading toward Gregory. The last Lillian saw was its short tail wagging hard enough to snap off.

Its handler cursed, flexed his fingers like he was checking to see if they were all accounted for, righted his jacket, and then glared at Lillian as he stomped past like it was all her fault.

"Gregory," Lillian reached for his thoughts, *"a small dog is coming up your trail, and his handler will be not long behind him. Watch yourself."*

A mental chuckle was his only reply. Lillian didn't have time to interpret his mood. The other dog was alternately sniffing, barking, and lunging at the pooka in a way that had Lillian worrying for its little doggie life.

For his part, the pooka was playing the role of spooked pony too well. He bolted in a half-circle, dragging Lillian along for the trip. He slammed his shoulder into a large, bearded man with a really big gun pointed at the ground. His fatigues registered on her senses a moment later. Next to the soldier, the surprised dog-handler fell backward with an astonished expression. Lillian spotted RCMP on the shoulder patch of his dark jacket. The pooka spun around, pinned his ears, lowered his head, and kicked out at the next closest human.

With a yell, the man dodged to the side. He stumbled into the man next to him before finally coming to a painful-looking stop by slamming into a conveniently located tree. While the newcomers fell like dominos, she felt the itch of the pooka's magic, confirming the source behind all the chaos.

Swearing, Lillian turned to the pooka in time to see him strike the police dog. The blow glanced off the dog's flank, leaving a mark in the fur and probably a nice bruise come morning. But it wasn't a killing strike. That told Lillian the pooka was playing nice. The dog rolled away with a yelp but circled around, coming at the pooka from a different direction. The pony swung his neck to face the still-barking dog. A wash of the fae's power slid along Lillian's skin, then on by her, to where the dog continued his mad barking.

Lillian knew the exact moment the pooka's magic impacted the dog. It jerked its head to the side, tucked its tail so far between its back legs it was a wonder she didn't see the tip between the front two, and loosed a mournful whimper before belly crawling back to its handler where he was picking himself up off the ground.

The pooka snorted, shook his mane out, and then trotted back over to Lillian's side, entirely too pleased with himself. Belatedly, Lillian's shocked mind realized several sets of eyes, both human and canine, were focused on her.

"I'm so sorry!" She rushed the words together as she pulled the pooka over to a tree where she proceeded to tie him up. He snorted with displeasure, but she didn't care and tightened the knot.

"You should have used a quick release knot," he whispered in her mind.

"Shut up! You've done enough damage. I'll be lucky not to get charged for assaulting a police officer with the stunt you just pulled." Lillian ignored the pooka's angry snort and faced the humans. Her face burned with heat, and her body was bathed in a nervous sweat. She would have preferred to meet one of the Riven—at least they would not make her fill out paperwork.

"Hi," Lillian ventured into the silence. "Sorry about the fuss. Your dogs frightened my pony. He's worked up over getting loose and losing his way in the forest. He can be a touch reactive on a good day. Is everyone okay?"

Grumbles and cursing echoed in the forest. A gruff cough was quickly followed by a clipped, "Miss, this is a quarantined area. You don't have authorization to be here."

Lillian glanced at the speaker. It was the big guy with the sunburn and black beard she'd noticed earlier, the one the pooka had slammed with a shoulder, and the man didn't look happy.

"Oh! Sorry." She faked a nervous, fearful squeak in her voice. "As I said, something spooked my horses, and they both bolted into the forest. I've been trailing them for the last four hours. I just found one—well actually, he found me. But the grey is still missing. I was about to go back and get my brother, some flashlights, snacks, and a few bottles of water before resuming the search."

"You'll have to come back with us, ma'am. I'll radio about the other missing horse." The soldier didn't break eye contact as he pulled a radio from one of many pockets and raised it closer to his face. "You can stand down. The dogs were tracking a horse. We found the owner and one of the animals." The soldier continued to give a description of Lillian's appearance, including her hair color, height, weight, and clothing.

His exceptional attention to details registered on Lillian's mind and worry flashed to life. He had no reason to relate her description with such detail. It occurred to her they might be looking for someone fitting her description. And if they were interested in someone matching her description, then they must know something more than Gran had suspected. And it didn't bode well for either Clan or Coven.

"You're Vivian's granddaughter, aren't you?"

"Yes, may I ask how you know that?"

He smiled, but it wasn't the type to put one at ease. "She has pictures of you and your brother on her mantle. When I was there, I noticed them. I never forget a face."

"Oh." Lillian laughed but didn't relax. "Gran always plasters our pictures on just about every surface she can find. It's embarrassing."

"Must be difficult to find the real estate for pictures with that extensive sword collection she has on her walls."

Lillian swallowed the next bit of fluff she'd been about to spout and frowned as she juggled several possible responses. "Some of those have been with the family for generations—Gran didn't start the collection. She is more a curator of sorts."

"I thought she said you and your fiancé were still up in Kirkland Lake for the rest of the summer."

Lillian's mind scrambled to keep up with the soldier's rapid change in topics. Trying to follow his logic was as dizzying as trying to track a chipmunk jacked up on an energy drink. His quick change of subjects must be some method to catch her in a lie, and if it was, she was already a suspect.

Damn and double-damn. It was just her luck. Of all the soldiers she could have run into in a forest, it looked like she'd tripped over a military interrogator or something similar. Her usual luck.

"Yes, we were there looking into some property. Gran wants to expand the family business, possibly opening a chain of resorts. Anyway, our plans changed when we heard about the rumors. We just had to come back and see what all the media frenzy was about. Now I wish I hadn't, you know, not with all the talk of monsters and aliens. Can you believe people?"

With another gruff chuckle, the bearded man glanced over Lillian's shoulder, out beyond the dark trees. "I never believe people."

"Ah." Lillian floundered for some response.

The soldier snapped his intense gaze back to her as quickly as he'd taken it off. "Have you seen monsters in the forest, Lillian?"

His question so caught her off guard, she had to snap her jaws closed, and could only stand there and look upon him with utter disbelief.

"Monsters?" She cleared her throat. "I've seen the news and heard all the rumors—terrorists, cults, monsters, and aliens. I have to say I'm on the side of those who believe it was some kind of twisted cult, or an elaborate hoax gone wrong."

"The way those bodies were torn apart and scattered around the forest was no hoax," the soldier said in a clipped tone.

Lillian's stomach dropped as a cold wave of fear slid across her skin, followed by a swift blanket of gooseflesh.

"We need to get out of here." The pooka's voice in her mind was calm, though he had started to jerk on his lead rope, likely as fearful of a trap as she was. *"These humans know more than the other fae believed. The soldier wouldn't otherwise mention any details about an ongoing investigation. He's fishing. We need to retreat and regroup before your gargoyle comes crashing through the forest to rescue you. I can't stress how unfortunate such an event would be."*

Lillian swallowed as she met the soldier's gaze. "You mean

it wasn't a cult murder-suicide like the media believes?" She cast a nervous glance over her shoulder purely for show. "Are you saying there is something or someone hunting in the forest and it killed those people?"

"The investigation is ongoing—we're still analyzing evidence."

"Is that code to say you're hunting for urban legends like the rumors suggest? Sir..." Lillian gave his fatigues a once-over, looking for a name or something with his rank, but realized she still would not have known what the bars and badges met anyway.

"Major Resnick, CFB Petawawa," he supplied. "And no, I'm not hunting for a yeti."

Lillian's chuckle sounded nervous to her own ears. "Glad to hear it. I wouldn't like to think I've been exploring the forest for all these years when there might have been something else studying me in return."

"However, while I have you here," he said, a glint of something in his eyes that hinted he was fishing for more than just random information. "Have you ever seen or heard something out of the ordinary in all your exploring? Anything at all? It might not have seemed like much at the time, but anything you remember might have importance. We've been interviewing many of the locals."

While he used the word 'interviewed,' Lillian imagined 'interrogated' would have been a more accurate one. She frowned and pretended to think for several moments. "My family runs a spa, and we've had some unusual patrons from time to time, but I can't think of having seen anything out of the ordinary."

If you don't count a gargoyle and numerous Clan and Coven members.

The pooka nickered.

"However," Lillian continued with more authority. "I saw some signs of bear, a mother and cub by the tracks—the bears might have been what spooked the horses in the first place. And I certainly don't want to lose the one I just found...so if you don't have any more questions..."

A rustling in the underbrush along the path saved Lillian from having to continue. The small, wiry-haired terrier burst out from behind cover and bolted between Lillian and Major Resnick and then proceeded to run full-out, all four legs churning at maximum speed. Two seconds later, the dog was well up the path and out of sight.

Everyone stared after the dog for a few seconds more, then turned to look the way it had come. Lillian turned too, fervently hoping not to see Gregory pursuing it.

He wasn't.

She released the breath she'd been holding. All her plausible lies would have been for nothing if there had been a gargoyle galloping up the trail in pursuit of the dog.

The terrier's handler jogged up the path, cursing as he came. He stumbled into their midst holding his side and sucking back deep breaths. "Something big spooked Socrates. Didn't get a good look, but it was a damned big son of a bitch."

"Bear," Lillian commented nervously, but for different reasons than the handler. Gregory must have finished with his spell.

"Gregory," Lillian sent, *"I assume you intentionally just scared a year off that man's life on purpose."*

A grumbling huff answered Lillian's mental comment. All the humans twitched, and their hands darted to their weapons in a way that made Lillian genuinely nervous.

"Don't come any closer. The humans are twitchy enough as it is. Let me handle this."

Gregory's thoughts touched hers, confirming what she feared. *"I do not care for the emotions I'm picking up from the humans. Extract yourself now, or I will deal with them myself."*

"Dammit. You might be the other half of my soul, but you can be such a pain in my ass! At present, I'm not in any immediate danger."

"Yes, you are. Their leader is thinking of taking you to a secure site where there are many more of his kind. I can see it clearly in his thoughts." Another huffing rumble issued from the darkness behind her.

"Stay out of this. I'm leaving. They don't have any reason to hold me at the moment. Don't give them one." Out loud she hissed, "Bear!" loud enough to draw everyone's attention away from the area where Gregory was making a tree shake. She bolted for the pooka and worked loose the knot that tied him to the thick branch.

The pooka arched his neck and sniffed at her fingers. *"In the future, I'll instruct you on how to create a proper safety knot. You wouldn't be having trouble if you'd done what I told you."*

"Stop fussing with the pooka and get out of there now," Gregory injected from an unknown location.

"Quiet! Both of you."

Lillian jerked on the knot until it came free and then she hauled the pooka around by his head, uncaring if she was rude. As she and the pooka made it past Major Resnick's position, she glared at him. "Tell your men to fall back. It's probably the same mother bear I saw earlier. Don't order your men to shoot the poor bear just because she's protecting her young."

She didn't wait to see what they would do. Instead, storming on down the path that led to civilization, and probably more uniformed military types, but she didn't have any choice. Not if she wanted to find a peaceful end to tonight's outing.

"Let her pass," Major Resnick called. "Everyone fall back, nice and slow. Get the other dog out of here, and then bring up the tranquilizer guns."

The forest around Lillian came alive as a second military team she hadn't even known was there eased out of their hiding spots. She didn't even try to hide her shock, it probably looked innocent enough. Beside her, the pooka started trotting, his motion more up and down than forward in his excitement. Lillian didn't think his agitation was an act. She had the impression of big guns, night-vision goggles, and more camouflaged fatigues.

As Resnick continued to call out orders, the military unit split in two. Four men spread out to take up the rear and guard the others' retreat, always keeping themselves between the main group and Lillian's 'bear.' Presently, her 'bear' was following a few paces behind the last human. While Gregory was actively cloaking himself in shadows and magic, he didn't bother to hide his presence or his simmering displeasure from her, and she had a difficult time keeping her eyes forward.

Gregory worried for her safety, and she, in turn, worried for the humans should he decide they were an immediate threat, or they were simply too close to her.

"They most certainly are too close, my Sorceress." Gregory's

annoyance came clear across their mind link. *"You said you would extract yourself from them."*

"I tried. They followed. They're not going to just let me walk off into the forest. They're like burrs or gum; I think I'm stuck with them."

"Find a way." Gregory's thoughts were almost a shout.

She covered her flinch by pretending to swat a mosquito, then she directed her thoughts back at him. *"Something else is wrong. I know if I were in immediate danger, we wouldn't be having this conversation, and the poor soldiers wouldn't know what hit them. They're not the enemy; they simply have a job to do. But you know that, or they would already be smoking-black smudges on the forest floor. What's really bothering you? Are they leading me to a prison cell?"*

"No." His short answer told her nothing useful.

"Then what?"

"Earlier, some of them watched you."

"Watched me? They were probably bored out of their minds after tromping around the forest day after day for the last three months."

"Their thoughts were not the thoughts of a 'bored' male." His clipped tone told her much more than his earlier one-word answer.

Oh boy.

The pooka loosed a distressed whinny. *"Merciful Mother, he'll annihilate them. My Lady, your gargoyle is enraged by their lack of respect. He's never had to deal with people who do not know to respect the Avatars."*

She didn't need the pooka's commentary to tell her how bad the situation could get. *"Gregory, it doesn't matter. It means nothing."* Lillian kept walking, she and the pooka doing their best to keep the soldiers to a fast pace. The sooner they could part company, the safer everyone would be.

"It is not nothing! Their leader still thinks about detaining you, taking you back for more questioning, holding you against your will. That they would hold such disrespect for the Mother's Avatar, Her mortal vessel!" Gregory roared.

Every gun jerked up as the soldiers reacted to the unknown danger.

"Bear, my ass," Resnick said, then started shouting orders. "Get the civilian and her pony out of here. Daniels, call for back-up. I think we found something."

Hoping to distract the snipers, Lillian loosed a terrified shriek, but the pooka one-upped her, and bolted forward, knocking into the soldier directly in his path. She kept a tight grip on the lead rope and allowed the pooka to drag her along.

"Your gargoyle seems to be in a bad mood today," the pooka said as he rolled an eye in her direction. *"But at least Gregory knows how to get the humans thinking about something else other than taking you in, I suppose."*

She might have found the pony's comment humorous if she wasn't worried about Gregory being riddled by bullets. *"Dammit, Gregory! Was that really necessary?"*

"Yes!"

CHAPTER EIGHT

Gregory glowered at the humans circling his lady, blocking him from going to her side. Even the pooka, a creature he'd usually dispatch long before it could even scent his Sorceress, was presently closer to Lillian than he could manage. His rage building, he sent his magic outward. It rustled in the leaves and caused branches to moan. The humans twitched badly, and he smiled.

His actions were petty—spiteful, even—and out of character, he knew. But he couldn't help himself. This world was nothing like he'd ever experienced. His relatively short time here was not enough for him to adapt to this Realm's...ignorance.

Evil he knew how to handle. The endless battle between good and evil was familiar to him. It gave him purpose in this strange new world and up until now had allowed him to ignore the things he secretly found distressing about this part of the Mortal Realm. There were far too many humans, far too out of balance with the natural world. Too much noise, too many bodies clustered together, too many souls in too close of quarters, too many chaotic thoughts and emotions bombarding him from all directions. The soul of the earth was bruised, he could feel her pain. And it was a great evil brought about by the humans of this Realm. Part of him wanted to restore the balance.

But he couldn't, for it would mean the deaths of millions of humans. His Sorceress of old would have understood, would have aided him with what needed doing if they were ever ordered to complete such an unpleasant task, but Lillian was like a creature newly made—innocent, gentle, naïve. She'd already made it clear she sided with the humans, and she expected him to—if not love them—at least tolerate them.

And she was correct—these humans, even the male who had gazed upon Lillian with lustful thoughts, were not evil. In their own way, they served the Light—protecting, bringing peace when they could. What little he knew about the humans of this world he'd gathered from touching Lillian's thoughts. He'd gleaned most of the destruction the humans caused was brought about due to ignorance, greed, and neglect more than willfully serving evil. It was a common failing with a young species.

The vast majority of humans still had potential.

He *should* view them with the tolerance he would grant any youngling.

But being rational was difficult when others were surrounding Lillian, keeping him from her side.

They'd only had a handful of days between when she'd first called him from his stone sleep, to when she'd had to merge with her hamadryad to heal. It wasn't enough time. Under normal circumstances when they were reborn, they grew up side by side, studying and training until they matured into their full strength.

Until this last time when the Lady of Battles interfered. He hadn't realized how vital childhood was to them—it gave them both a chance to adapt, to relearn how to function as two separate beings when they'd recently been one being in the Spirit Realm.

"Oh, Gregory." Lillian's thoughts merged fully with his. *"I'm so sorry. I didn't remember what our childhood was supposed to be like. I only knew I needed to be near my gargoyle statue, I couldn't remember anything else."*

Gregory jerked in surprise, his wings twitching so hard he snagged one in a low hanging spruce bough, causing the whole tree to shake. He darted off to the left as three of the soldiers aimed their guns where he'd just been.

"Gregory, are you all right?"

"Yes," he admitted a touch sheepishly. *"I was distracted and gave my position away."*

"Now that I know why you've been distracted," Lillian mused, *"I have a better idea how to help us adapt. I may not have much magic, but I have myself. I'll make time for us, even if I have to barricade us in the wine cellar."*

The accompanying image her words inspired gained a chuckle from him. While he'd never been fond of fermented drinks, their taste and smell too strong for a gargoyle's heightened senses, he didn't doubt Lillian could still entertain him even in such a dark and chilled place.

With her promise, he found he could tolerate the humans with some semblance of benevolence even if they were closer to Lillian than he'd wished. He even dropped back a few paces, so he wasn't tempted to antagonize the nearest male.

Which, he mused, was rather generous of him, since the man was the one who had entertained the offensive thoughts.

The humans' leader made subtle gestures with his hands, which Gregory interpreted as silent orders. As the soldiers spread out, hastening to obey in a coordinated fashion, he moved out of the way of any soldier who settled too close to his position. Once the soldiers became stationary, and the forest was quiet again, he acknowledged with a touch of respect they were very good at blending in with their environment. They had arranged themselves in a loose circle, with Lillian and the pooka once again in the center. Neither one looked happy to be there. But with the soldiers' weapons pointed out into the surrounding forest, it was the safest place for his dryad mistress.

He hunched down near the base of a great old spruce; its wide trunk offered enough cover to hide him even if he wasn't cloaked in his own magic. He thought he understood Resnick's reasoning. By ordering his men to dig in, they could set up a defensive perimeter, use Lillian and the pony as bait, and wait to see what came sniffing after them. It was the safest strategy until reinforcements made it to their location.

He didn't have long to wait to confirm his theory. Silent, black shadows eased through the trees to the south. They moved with a smooth, deadly grace Gregory admired. Not as elegant as a sidhe warrior, but as close as a human could come. The newcomers merged seamlessly with the soldiers already in position.

Resnick and another officer, a female by her scent, conversed with each other in hushed tones. Gregory held his position and waited for the two soldiers to come to a decision. Calling a trickle of magic, he sent it outward, scouting the newcomers, looking for even a hint of evil. It flitted from human to human, brushing against bare skin as it passed. More than one shifted uneasily at the touch of magic, but none seemed overly suspicious. To them, it should feel like nothing more than an unusually chilly breeze gusting through the forest.

Lillian arched an eyebrow in his direction.

"Do not worry," he reassured her. *"It was only a small spell to learn their intentions."* He dropped to all fours and padded out from behind the tree. *"I detect no evil on either of them."*

"Good. We're in enough trouble as it is. We don't need more." Lillian narrowed her eyes. *"Speaking of trouble—are you intentionally trying to find some?"*

"No," Gregory replied but didn't deviate from his route.

"Then why are you making a beeline for me?" Her frustration and worry bled across her thoughts. *"Use common sense for five minutes, or you're going to get your ass shot off."*

"They cannot see me." Moving silent and swift among the soldiers, he stalked Lillian as if she was his prey.

"What if they have some piece of technology which can see through your spells?"

"They would have already attempted to take me down."

Lillian muttered a curse under her breath, but he felt when she gave into his wishes. She couldn't stop him anyway.

Obeying another silent command, the soldiers rose to their feet. Some broke away from the group guarding Lillian, quickly replaced by the same number of newcomers. When they had sorted themselves out, he studied the newcomers' weapons—they were of a different type.

"Those are tranquilizer guns," Lillian said into his mind. *"They fire a dart filled with a substance which puts its target to sleep. Better*

than bullets, I suppose, but I don't know what effect they would have on a gargoyle. Let's not find out."

Gregory acknowledged her words with a nod, knowing she was the only one presently able to see him.

When the humans guarding Lillian moved out, he followed, leaving Resnick and the other soldiers to hunt for a ghost. They wouldn't even find tracks.

CHAPTER NINE

It felt like the longest walk of her life. In reality, she'd only been walking in the company of the tight-lipped soldiers for less than two hours, but the worry that Gregory would get captured or have to fight his way free made it feel much, much longer.

Gran was correct. Gregory needed to take human form—she knew he could do it. He had for short times before, when he felt like it. Right now, his best non-lethal defense was to play human. Now she'd just have to convince him, which would be no easy task. But that conversation would have to wait until later. They were nearing their destination. She could see floodlights through the trees. Her internal compass told her they would emerge from the forest at the north end of town, near the arena.

It made sense. The arena was the only space clear of trees and large enough for a field command.

They walked out of the forest and onto a paved road. She sensed when Gregory stopped at the edge of the forest, still in the shadow of the trees. On the other side of the road was the arena—though it looked vastly different than she remembered. The entire parking area had been fenced off. Within the new compound, trailers and other kinds of portable buildings took up most of the space. What was left was occupied by military vehicles. There was even a heavy-bodied helicopter off to one side.

Lillian was brought up short by the lead attached to the pooka. He'd planted all four hooves like he didn't plan to move one step farther. Squinting against the bright floodlights, she understood the pooka's reluctance. *"Will your glamour hold up to scrutiny under their lights?"*

"I would prefer not to test it." He tugged on the lead a second time, nearly pulling her off her feet. The pooka continued his 'spooked pony' routine, lunging to the side and trotting a nervous circle around Lillian. Soldiers scattered out of the pooka's path, cursing the black pony.

Only Corporal Mackenzie, a tall, muscular woman with a dark complexion and her hair done in corn rows, laughed at the pooka's antics. The female soldier with the no-nonsense attitude had been assigned to lead Lillian back to civilization. Now she faced the pony and, much to Lillian's surprise, cooed to him in a gentle voice, approaching him with a calm manner. She pulled a carrot from one back pocket and after glancing at Lillian for permission, offered it to the pooka.

Where the heck had the soldier pulled a carrot from, Lillian wondered?

The pooka pinned his ears and glared at the offering disdainfully.

"Oh, come on. I know you want it deep down in your little black heart," the soldier said with a laugh.

The pooka sniffed for a moment and then snaked his head toward her. Lillian thought he was going for fingers, but he surprised her by only snapping up the carrot.

"Well," Corporal Mackenzie chuckled, not put off by the show of bad manners, "I see your big, grey companion is the nicer of the duo."

Lillian realized she must be talking about the unicorn—who had taken on the glamour of a dappled grey gelding. "You found my grandmother's other escape artist?"

"Yes, he's a sweet boy. I wondered where he came from. Your grandmother—she's the owner of the spa?"

"Yes." Lillian wasn't in the most talkative mood. She was tired, dirty, bug-eaten, and hungry, but even so, she liked the woman. Anyone who liked a pooka must have a big, compassionate heart, or be a total badass, in the cool kind of way.

"I saw your grey gelding running loose at the edge of the forest near the intersection just west of here. A group of us herded him down this way where others had constructed a temporary pen to hold him. It's just around the bend, butted up against the forest. I acquired some carrots from the market to entice my new friend into the enclosure. Thought he might be more relaxed away from all the lights and noise of HQ."

"Thank you for the help. Really."

"No problem. I rode as a kid. Think mom was trying to seduce me away from the military even then." Corporal Mackenzie laughed. "My dad is military, and four of my five brothers are career military as well. It's in my blood. Mom didn't have a chance, not even with the aid of ponies."

The other soldiers parted company with Lillian and Corporal Mackenzie, heading toward the main gate. Lillian, with a bit more than a mote of surprise, realized she wasn't going to get detained for 'trespassing' on her own property like she'd half-expected.

"I'll help you get your boys through the barricades and checkpoints." Perhaps seeing Lillian's surprise, the woman laughed openly, then clarified. "I'm not aiding and abetting. Major Resnick's orders were to get you to civilization and then send you on your way."

"Thanks," Lillian said, not knowing what else to say, so stayed with the truth. "I could use the help with the horses. They belong to Gran. I just help out from time to time."

"No problem. Come on." She jerked her chin in the direction she wanted Lillian to go.

Lillian led the pooka down the mostly deserted road. Gregory kept pace in the forest running alongside. She was more than happy he hadn't decided to pad down the center of the road, certain her constant staring would give him away.

They retrieved the unicorn without incident and made it through all the barricades and checkpoints. When Lillian parted company with the other woman, she released a loud sigh, not quite believing they'd made it out of enemy territory. As she continued home, leading the two horses and Gregory trailing behind, she half-expected to hear shouts of alarm and sounds of pursuit. She still didn't relax until she walked up the long lane to the cottage. Never had its rough, stone walls looked so welcoming.

Then Lillian noticed Gran on the porch. Pacing.

"I've been worried sick. Why didn't you send word?"

Dammit, Lillian cursed in the safety of her own mind.

By her grandmother's tone, she hadn't avoided an interrogation after all.

CHAPTER TEN

Several body lengths above the siren's head, a small boat, its metal hull silhouetted against the sky, rocked gently upon the waves. A small anchor held it in place.

She eyed it. Debating whether she should drag the boat out into deeper water or risk capturing the humans this close to shore. The pod still circled, watching to see what she would do. They'd led her to this spot, a little alcove frequented by curious humans. From what she'd gathered from the dolphin's minds, these humans were researchers, and as such cared for the oceans and what went on in them.

If it was true, how could they stand by and do nothing to prevent an abomination like the metal Not-Island from coming into existence in the first place?

Perhaps these humans were little more than peasants, unable to dictate change to the ruling nobility. The dolphins couldn't give her insight into this—such a rigid structure wasn't the dolphin way, and they did not understand the ultimate rule of a king.

Frowning up at the boat hull, she saw shadows moving as the humans went about their mysterious purpose. With a flurry of activity, a large cage was dropped over the side. Other objects were dropped in next, things suspended on long lines.

The dolphins had positioned themselves a short distance away at the first sign of activity, but with a series of questioning chirps, the young male was back at her side. Reaching out, she brushed a hand along his side, and he calmed, floating contentedly at her side.

Something splashed against the surface. Blood scent coiled through the water as bright red clouds trailed along the ocean surface, carried away by the current. Fish blood. Fish bodies. The smell reminded the siren it had been a few hours since she'd last fed. Magic sustained her throughout her long sleep, but upon waking, she needed to feed often for the first few days. Though dead fish didn't tempt her, she preferred hers fresh.

The dolphin matriarch rejoined her and said, *"Fish slurry for sharks."*

"The humans want to bring a predator to them? Whatever for?" she asked in genuine confusion. *"To hunt the shark? With their nets and boats, the humans could easily hunt other, less dangerous prey."*

"Not to hunt. Study." The young dolphin's excited clicks intensified.

"You have seen this behavior before?"

"Yes. They study and protect. Track numbers and movement."

A very passive form of protection, the siren decided. Another splash at the surface regained her attention. A human had plunged into the open top of the cage. While she watched, a second human joined the first. They wore sleek, black, second skins, and each had a large cylinder strapped to their backs. She studied them while they were organizing supplies.

The strange objects strapped to their backs supplied them with air. Whatever was held in their mouths issued a small storm of bubbles every other heartbeat.

Hmm, the land-bound ones had found a way to live within her domain, at least for short expanses of time.

She narrowed her eyes.

A very short time.

CHAPTER ELEVEN

*L*illian rinsed off the last plate and placed it in the dishwasher. The mundane routine of after dinner chores helped dispel the residual nervous energy from earlier. Gran had drilled her for every little detail during her exchange with Major Resnick. Gregory hadn't escaped Gran's tongue lashing either. She'd merely finished with him sooner and then sent him up to have Jason show him the inner workings of human clothing. Looking mildly contrite, Gregory had slunk off in the general direction Gran had indicated. Lillian had only stood and watched, utterly gobsmacked. That had been half an hour ago. Now all she wanted was to do a face-plant in her bed.

"Would you like some chamomile tea? It's good for the nerves." Gran gestured at the big, battered old pot sitting in the middle of the table.

"Thanks, but I'd probably fall asleep and—"

A loud crash echoed from the floor above followed by a

window-shaking roar. "On second thought..." Lillian scooped up a cup, poured herself some, and took a sip.

"Told you so." Gran smiled into her cup. "Better hurry before Gregory kills your brother. I know he can be a brat, but I still love my grandson."

"I'll send Jason down for a cup once I find which wall Gregory just put him through."

Lillian made her way from the kitchen and into the living room as she sipped from her cup. Before she reached the stairs, there was another loud thump. Moments later, she heard Jason cursing, which was a good sign. At least he was conscious, she mused as she took the stairs two at a time. She turned right at the top of the stairs and headed down the hall leading to her room.

Her bedroom door opened suddenly, and Jason bolted out. He didn't make it three feet before a long, muscular arm shot out of the billowing darkness and latched onto her brother's shoulder.

"Hey! I know you're pissed, but I warned you about zippers!" Jason screamed as he was dragged back into the room. The door slammed in Lillian's face. She sipped from her tea. There was another loud thump, then what sounded like a minor scuffle. Something heavy landed against the door, and she heard her brother curse before it was cut off. He continued to make noise, but it was muffled.

Lillian reached for the handle, but the door sprang open of its own accord. She backed out of the way just in time as her brother was propelled out with a good deal of force. He stumbled into the opposite wall.

She arched a brow at the sight her brother made—only to realize he couldn't see with a pair of boxer shorts over his head. Taking her time, she circled her brother and then pulled the boxers off his head.

She placed her teacup down on a side table. "I assume it didn't go so well?"

He glared at her when she smiled. He couldn't do much else, not with the sock jammed in his mouth like a gag and his arms trapped under what looked to be at least three layers of polo shirts over the top of his own clothes.

She pulled the gag from his mouth. "You okay?"

"Your gargoyle has anger management issues."

Lillian grabbed the bottom of one shirt and pulled it up over his head while he disentangled himself from the others. When he was standing in front of her with the clothes he'd started with, she laughed.

Her brother glowered, apparently not finding the situation particularly funny.

Between bouts of laughter, she finally managed, "What happened?"

"Gregory isn't a fan of modern fashion. Zippers in particular. I warned him to be careful with the zipper on the jeans... guess he understands why now." Jason made a grab at his crotch as his face screwed up in mock pain.

"You didn't..."

"Laugh? You bet. In sympathy, of course. Though it was his fault for going commando." Jason shrugged. "Unfortunately, I then might also have mentioned something about sending you up to kiss it all better."

Another ominous growl rolled out of the darkness behind her bedroom door.

"Ah!" Jason darted around behind Lillian, putting her

firmly between him and the black mist boiling out of her bedroom. "Think I've overstayed my welcome. Bye, Sis."

Without so much as a glance behind, Jason bolted for the stairs. His mop of unruly brown hair stood straight up in a near-gravity defying way as he vaulted off the top stair. He dropped out of sight and landed with a heavy thump before stampeding down the rest of the flight.

Gran yelled something at Jason before the kitchen door slammed with its usual creak. Lillian waited a moment more and then turned back to her room, boxer shorts and shirts in hand.

"Gregory?"

Nothing.

Bumping a hip against the partially open door, she eased into the dark room and tried the light switch on the wall. She flicked it a couple of times—still nothing. Great.

Her gargoyle was beyond 'pissed' if his concealment spells had dampened the lights.

"Gregory, love. I know you can see in the dark, but I can't."

A rumbling huff echoed from three feet in front of her. Her searching fingers collided with warm, leathery skin, so soft it was suede-like. A wing membrane? Then it pulled out of her grasp as if he was turning away.

The sound of tearing cloth was loud in the silence. Equally noticeable was the pounding pressure of Gregory's magic against her skin. It hummed in her blood with each lungful of air.

"Hmm." Lillian wasn't too concerned. She liked the wild essence pressing against her skin. And it was Gregory with her, after all. However, it would still be nice to see what was going on. "Light, please?"

He huffed again, more growl this time, but his magic retreated, and the lights flickered back into existence.

"Thanks." She blinked against the suddenly bright room. When she could see again, her gaze sought out Gregory. He stood with his back to her, in gargoyle form—though by the shredded clothing clinging to him, he'd been in human form until recently.

She came up behind him and plucked a mangled patch of what was once a nice oatmeal-colored knit sweater from the clawed joint of his right wing. Another larger swath of tangled yarn was draped over his other wing joint. Unwinding it, she brushed the rest away without comment.

The remaining portions of the sweater were draped loosely across his broad shoulders and chest. A glance down confirmed a pair of blue jeans hadn't fared any better. The seams had burst over his powerful thighs and calf muscles. And his tail hadn't done the back of the jeans any good, either.

One large hand came up and gripped the material at his right shoulder. With an interesting ripple of muscles along his back, he tore off a good half of the offending sweater.

"I probably shouldn't have enjoyed watching that as much as I did."

Lillian touched the back of one of his arms, keeping the contact light as she stepped around in front of him. When she was squarely before him, she transferred her fingers to his chest, gliding them under the torn sweater. Continuing up and over his shoulder, she pushed the knitted material away from his body and down his arm.

Gregory didn't move, not so much as a twitch, but she could feel his intense gaze locked onto her. Perhaps it was the decision of a coward, she mused, but she kept her eyes level with his well-muscled chest, neither looking up nor allowing her eyes to drift down below his waist. She pulled another scrap of material from his opposite shoulder and watched as the bit of sweater remains hit the floor. She pushed it off to the side with her toe, the soft rustle of fabric unnaturally loud in the silence.

The weight of a long-fingered, talon-tipped hand coming to rest on her shoulder startled Lillian into looking back up until she was eye-level with his chest again. She only then realized she'd been staring at the floor because her confidence had fled.

His fingers began to knead her tense shoulder in a gentle, rhythmic manner.

Forcing her eyes higher, because she *would* overcome her personal cowardice and be the partner the other half of her soul needed, she finally met his intense gaze. Her throat tight with nerves, she swallowed past the lump. "No permanent damage?" she asked, her voice soft and unsteady, even to her own ears.

"Just to my pride." His warm breath washed across her one ear and on down her neck. "Nothing that won't heal."

So, he had done himself some harm. In a spur-of-the-moment, she-wasn't-really-thinking-about-what-she-was-doing move, she glanced down and started to reach for the split and sagging material of his jeans.

Gregory moved at the same time, and Lillian jerked back. Her face heated in a fiery blush, thinking he was going to push her hands away from a place they had no business being in the first place.

"Sorry." She rushed on. "I don't know what I was...it's not like I still have any healing powers...it was some knee-jerk instinct..."

"It comes naturally to us." Gregory's voice was deeper than normal, velvet and sinful. "We would commonly inspect and heal each other's smallest injuries. It was one way we could show our deep love for each other without breaking our oaths to the Divine Ones." Gregory enfolded her hands in his and drew them back to his body, curling them gently around the slight protrusion of his hip bones. "There is no shame in this."

He tucked his muzzle against his chest and closed his eyes but made no other move. Clearly, he was leaving the next move to her. Even motionless, he was still an imposing wall of muscle and sinew. His bulk of wings, horns that brushed the ceiling, and broad shoulders that dwarfed her smaller frame, all added to his overall air of menace.

Yet, as different as they might be in body, they were one soul.

And right now, her other half needed her. Touching him, she could feel what he felt, his bone-deep terror she would fear him and turn away, that she would not be, could not be, what he needed.

She took one step into him, pressing her cheek to his chest as she sealed the length of their bodies together.

"No shame," she whispered against his chest. "None ever between us."

Gregory released a deep, rumbling sigh as the tension melted out of his body. His arms encircled her shoulders, and his tail wrapped possessively around her lower legs. They stood there unmoving for several moments. Gregory seemed willing to just stay like that, but Lillian knew she had a little more to do in order to be what he needed.

She unwound her arms from around his waist and hooked her fingers in the top of his ruined jeans. It was easy enough to push the torn denim down his hips. Gregory shifted his weight for her, making it easier to shove the pant legs on down. When it was low enough, he kicked free of the shredded material and then went still once more.

Almost done, she thought. Giving herself silent orders seemed to be the only thing holding her confidence in place. If she was standing in front of anyone other than Gregory doing this...

"I would do them serious injury." Gregory's voice rumbled over her head.

"There is no one else I would do this for." Her voice had steadied, but when she reached out and pushed against one hip to urge him to turn toward the light flooding from the bathroom, she couldn't hide the nervous tremble in her fingers.

It wasn't the first time she'd seen Gregory completely bare. He had little concept of human modesty. The other two times had been when he'd been in the shower. Both those times she'd averted her gaze within seconds but had still been left with the knowledge Gregory was impressive in every aspect. He was utterly hairless but had the correct number of parts to be mostly human-shaped, which maybe wasn't so strange, since gargoyles and dryads did interbreed upon occasion. And dryads and humans were nearly indistinguishable in appearance.

She arched an eyebrow in thought. Still, if Gregory was an average example of his species, dryads were made of sterner stuff than she'd credited them with. Lillian might be of dryad blood, but she wasn't sure if she possessed the courage to tackle a gargoyle. Even at rest, he was larger than what a similarly proportioned man would have possessed.

Gregory's body language was still relaxed, but his thoughts hinted at an underlying sense of anticipation. She moved her hand from his hip and stroked her fingertips across his belly and was rewarded by the subtle flex of the muscles spanning his abdomen. He shifted his stance as he grew semi-hard at her touch. It was one of the sexiest things she'd seen.

Her breath rushed from her lungs. She had to remind herself this was supposed to be an inspection, not a seduction. Though, she imagined, she was the one getting seduced by Gregory's undeniable, virile nature.

Inspection.

"It's just an inspection."

Gregory laughed, his voice a dark caress along her overheated body. "Then, by all means, inspect me, my Sorceress."

His baiting had her blood rushing to answer his challenge, and she made herself take a lingering look. "Everything looks...in order. You have fully healed?"

"Yes." It was more growl than word.

"You're in no pain?"

"No, but..." He groaned and stepped closer. "I need you near."

His arms and wings settled around her, their warm weight a reassurance. A moment later, his tail coiled around her hips.

She hugged him with a fierce strength, knowing he needed this intimacy, needed to feel the other half of his soul near.

And it soothed a hunger in her body and soul to hold him so close.

"Would you like to shower with me?" she found herself asking.

"Yes, my beloved Sorceress." His muzzle dipped down to nose past the neck of her tank top. He pushed the fabric out of his way until he encountered the black lace of her bra. His lips caressed the valley between her breasts. "You're wearing too many layers."

"I am," Lillian agreed.

Gregory stood, hardly daring to breathe for fear the slightest movement would startle Lillian into bolting from his side. But her confidence held, and she took his right hand in her much smaller one and tugged him in the direction of the bathroom.

She was doing this for him. He knew it. He also knew she wasn't emotionally ready to take their relationship into these new, dangerous waters. In his current touch-starved state after sleeping in stone for twelve years, he doubted he was any better equipped to deal with this part of their relationship. He should stop this before it went further.

Oh, but her smaller hand felt good in his, as did the weight of her eyes every time she looked at him with a mix of innocence and desire. More than a few times in their past lives, they had played this dangerous game, caressing each other as lovers when the loneliness of being separated outside the Spirit Realm became too much to bear.

Always before when they took turns giving and receiving pleasure, it was with their duty and its restrictions held firmly in their minds. Without the strong, disciplined mind of the Mother's Sorceress overseeing him, he wasn't sure if he could trust himself not to go too far. And Lillian, as much as he was coming to love her all over again in this life, was not the Sorceress of old. She could not hold him back by the sheer strength of her mind alone.

Yet, all the same, he would not crush her fledgling courage, which led her to come this far, to strip him bare, to study and accept him and all his fierce differences. He'd craved her acceptance since he'd emerged from his first stone sleep. He would in no way endanger it by rushing Lillian into something she wasn't ready for, so he'd let her choose when and how events would unfold.

Lillian led him into the master bath, and after fiddling with the shower taps and adjusting the water temperature several times, she hesitated.

Sensing her confidence about to flee, he playfully tapped the spade-shaped tip of his tail against her nearest arm. She startled at the contact and looked over her shoulder with a wide-eyed gaze. With a gentle nudge of his muzzle under her chin, he sighed with contentment and whispered against her skin, "Little dryad, this need not be anything more than a shower."

The tension in her shoulders eased visibly, and a warm smile brightened her expression to something truly beautiful. "I know. That's why I trust you so much." She worked loose the strange fastenings of her human garb, disrobed quickly, and then took his hand and tugged until he stepped in the shower with her. "However," she said, with a mysterious little smile. "I do hate personal cowardice and would use this opportunity to work upon my own underdeveloped confidence."

"So very formal," he said as happiness swelled in his heart.

"Formal? Ha! It's all your fault. Your archaic way of speaking is infectious." She stepped into him, raised herself up onto her toes, and placed a kiss along the underside of his jaw, effectively taking any sting out of her words.

"Mmm," he rumbled softly, backing farther into the shower at her gentle insistence. He did so enjoy her method of apology. "I would be honored to offer up myself as a means to help you become more comfortable with our relationship."

In answer, she poured soap on what she called a shower sponge and applied it to his shoulders and chest. Mild disappointment flooded him. It was her hands—not an indifferent sponge—he wanted on his flesh.

Her free hand suddenly came up and caressed the curve of his hip, tentative at first and then with a bit more boldness. His eyes drifted closed as she ventured farther afield, her delicate touch gliding lower.

Belatedly, he realized his private wish had made his control slip, and she'd picked up the thread of his thoughts. But he didn't feel guilty about it, especially not when she dropped the sponge and brought her other hand into play, stroking soap suds across his chest.

A deep, rumbling purr escaped him. He wanted to return the caresses, but he held himself passive. It was more important for his other half to learn him and the limits of her courage.

There would be time for his own exploring in the days to come.

CHAPTER TWELVE

A soft, persistent knocking registered on Lillian's senses. She tried to ignore it and burrowed deeper under the covers—wanting to escape the noise and the bright light flooding in the windows that declared it was morning. Gregory seemed to have a similar idea and attempted to bury his muzzle underneath her hair. She was draped over his chest, a leg sprawled over his powerful thighs. They were both completely naked. One part of her mind said this was probably inappropriate, but another part liked it rather too much to move.

And after their shared shower last night, modesty was likely no longer an issue.

Though, as he'd promised, the shower was no more than a shared shower. Afterward, he'd toweled her dry and then bundled her into bed. He'd joined her once he was dry. And she'd soon discovered he liked to cuddle. Which was how she'd come to have her limbs entangled with a gargoyle's this morning, feeling warm, protected and cherished. It was a surprisingly pleasant way to wake up.

Better still, the knocking on the door had stopped.

Grinning, she stretched, enjoying the delightful feeling of his warm skin brushing against her body.

Mmm.

She most certainly didn't feel like moving. Gregory didn't seem inclined to either—well other than one part. His tail was flicking lazy caresses up and down her back. Lillian smiled and returned the favor, running her hands along his sides.

"What if I'd been a team of commandoes?"

Gran's voice jolted through Lillian's sleepy mind. She jerked fully awake, but Gregory replied first.

"I'd have spread their ashes across the three Realms." His chuckle shook Lillian's entire body. "You're lucky I'm fond of you. Besides, you feed me."

Her face burning, Lillian rolled off him and buried herself under the blankets. Gregory had no such concerns or modesty. She peeked out in time to see him throw off the blankets and stretch, before leaning toward the plates Gran held out to him.

"My goodness!" Gran gave an approving purr. "Now, I know why dryads have a preference for gargoyles."

"Gran!" Lillian bolted upright, but kept hold of the blankets, not wanting to flash the room.

"Don't be a prude, darling. I'm old, not dead. I still have hormones enough to appreciate a fine-looking specimen when one is presented to me." Gran then turned her attention back to Gregory and bestowed a smile on him. "I brought breakfast for you both."

Lillian tried another angle. "You could have just called through the door. What if we had...we'd been..."

"Having sex?" Gran started to chuckle again, belly laughs this time. "If you had, the whole house would have heard. Gregory has a tendency to roar. Besides, I didn't hear any headboard cracking last night. And the house is still standing —no stray flares of creative Avatar magic."

Lillian collapsed onto her pillow and tossed the sheets back over her head.

"No time to hide." Gran tugged on the blankets. "You need to eat and then get dressed. The Fae Council arrived in the night. We need to discuss what to do about the military problem. And Gregory, dear, you need to pretend to be human. No more dragging your feet about it."

He grunted around a mouthful of food but nodded his head.

"Good. When you are both presentable, come down to the kitchen. We have work to do." Gran patted Lillian's blanket-covered leg and placed a plate of food in her hand.

Lillian eyed the plate of bacon and eggs. Not exactly a romantic breakfast in bed, but she was hungry, and it would be a waste of perfectly good food if she didn't eat it. Picking up a fork, she started to work her way through breakfast.

Gregory stood before her and gave her his best annoyed gargoyle scowl. Strange how well the look transferred to his now fully human form. Another minor feat she wouldn't mind mastering was his ability to look equally noble and stern in nothing but a pair of silky, black boxer shorts. Perhaps it had something to do with him being comfortable in nothing but his own skin.

Lillian admitted it was a little disconcerting having a nearly naked human man in her bedroom. On the one hand, she knew it was Gregory, and yet on the other, she could see very little of her guardian in this tall, dark-skinned man with his brown eyes, dark hair, and severe expression. Somehow, this felt different than when Gregory wandered around half-naked in gargoyle form. Maybe it was because her eyes kept telling her she was standing across from a stranger she'd only laid eyes on a couple of times before.

She held out a pair of black jeans, then gave them a little wiggle when he didn't take the bait.

"Oh, come on—you're worse than a two-year-old. They're just jeans, not a viper about to bite you."

He frowned at her tone but stepped forward and snatched the jeans out of her hand.

"I thought the worst thing about the Mortal Realm was its lack of magic," he muttered as he jerked on the pants, though was cautious about doing up the zipper, "but I was wrong. There is one thing worse—its fashion. Humans wear so many layers, even their clothing has clothing. It snags, it rubs, it bites, it pinches..."

It seemed her gargoyle needed a little incentive.

Lillian stretched up and pressed a quick kiss to his lips. "If you wear the clothing today, I'll help you out of them tonight."

His lips parted, and his eyes widened ever so slightly. Secretly, she was pleased she could still surprise him. The kiss had the added benefit of stilling his tirade.

"I'll play at being human—but I only do it for you."

Gregory held out his hand for the T-shirt she still held. "Though, you are welcome to kiss me whenever you want, if you think it will make me more malleable to your diabolical plans."

A pearl of laughter escaped her. "You're such a terrible actor—though I like your sulk. It's cute." And she also liked this new playful side of Gregory. Seeing him happy warmed her heart, and she wanted to do whatever was required to keep him happy.

He pretended to sulk at her words—but his expression was so off, she laughed even harder. "Enough, you great ham. We have a Fae Council to pacify and a large military problem to resolve."

Gregory sobered and nodded.

Lillian held the door and motioned him forward, wanting to make sure he didn't try to ditch some of the clothing on his way down. When Gregory frowned at her, she knew she had hit on the correct plan.

With a huff, he stomped past, still pulling at his T-shirt and the waist of his jeans as if trying to make them more comfortable. Halfway down the stairs, he gave up and fisted his hands at his sides.

When they reached the bottom, Lillian could hear the voices drifting from the kitchen. By the sound of it, the council meeting was already underway. Gregory shoved the kitchen door hard enough to make it groan in complaint. If there had been anyone on the other side, they'd have been laid out by the blow.

"The door is not to blame for you having to wear cloth-ing," Lillian stated under her breath.

Gregory stopped, turned swiftly, and smiled what could

only be called a devilishly handsome grin. "Keep it up, and I'm going to revert to my true form, march over to the human military compound, and strut naked past Major Resnick. Twice. In case he misses it the first time."

"That's sure to stir the hornet's nest." A great, gruff hoot was followed by a hand slapping a thigh. "If you do, make sure to let me know in advance. I want to be there to witness it."

Gregory grinned and nodded to the stranger. Lillian froze, her mind trying to place where she'd seen the older man before. He was familiar, but she didn't know from where. Or why he was in Gran's kitchen. He was dressed in faded and patched jeans, an old flannel shirt, and his feet were encased in rubber boots. Upon first glance, Lillian might have taken him as a farmer.

But she could 'feel' the power hidden inside him.

"The council members are using glamour to hide," Gregory replied to her unasked question. "If you look with more than your physical eyes, you will recognize them."

Lillian scrutinized the man. "Greenborrow?"

He gave her a courtly bow. "In the flesh, great lady."

Gregory skirted the table and took one of the seats beside the leshii. While Lillian made her way around to sit in the other chair, she cast subtle glances at the other three people already seated.

Gran wasn't presently in the kitchen so she couldn't look for hints there. And while by Gregory's easy manner, it was clear he knew everyone in the room, Lillian was still annoyed enough with him she wasn't about to ask him for information.

Two of the occupants were women in their forties. A third was a tattooed and pierced young man with spikey black hair, a black leather jacket, and worn blue jeans. He looked to be in his early twenties—not much older than Lillian herself if she was to go by her eyes alone.

She focused on the man first, not because she was ogling his tattoos and piercings—though they were something to behold—but because she expected the sidhe lord, Whitethorn, to be at this meeting. She couldn't imagine him not being there. Unless he was running late. She narrowed her eyes again trying to see something of the sidhe in the young man sitting at the table.

His smile was neither overly friendly nor outwardly cold, which was very much the sidhe lord's personality. Ah, she was right. "Whitethorn?"

A regal nod greeted her question.

"Hmm, isn't the whole idea of the glamour to blend in?"

"Yes," Greenborrow cut in before the sidhe lord could reply. "But we make do with what humans we can take by surprise and won't be reported as missing to the authorities. Whitethorn lost the bet and won the 'honor' of taking on the little drug lord's seeming."

Lillian arched a brow in question.

"In the past, we've found the easiest identity to use is one already created." Greenborrow shrugged. "It has the added benefit of sending the authorities off on a wild goose chase if we make a misstep."

Knowing some of the fae as she did, a nasty thought occurred to Lillian. "Just curious, but what happens to the humans you impersonate?"

"We put them in a safe place where they sleep for a day or two, depending on how long we need to move around in the human world." Greenborrow gave a little shrug. "And, no, we don't kill them. Once they are no longer needed, we give them false memories and then allow them to wake."

"Glad to hear it."

"Dead bodies cause too many questions." Greenborrow sounded mildly disappointed.

Whitethorn turned what might have been a laugh of genuine amusement into a cough.

Her eyes rolled back toward Whitethorn. At least she now knew who the tattooed personage was.

One down, two to go.

Looking over at the women, she debated for a moment. One was friendly, her cheerful grin contagious. Likely one of the sprites. But which one, mother or daughter? If Whitethorn wasn't averse to taking a form that looked much, much younger than his years, Lillian wouldn't put it past the mother and daughter duo to play around with their ages, either.

"Goswin?" Lillian took a stab, figuring she had a fifty-fifty chance.

The sprite nodded.

As for the other woman, she gave nothing away in her expression. Lillian frowned, a touch unhappy at failing what felt like a test.

"The banshee," Gregory supplied, his attention still half on adjusting his clothing. He tugged at the neck of his T-shirt with a little too much force and Lillian heard the telltale popping of a seam giving way.

A huge grin lit up Gregory's face, and he fisted the front of his T-shirt.

"Don't you dare do an imitation of a drunken redneck at a tailgate party! T-shirts don't grow on trees, and you already destroyed one outfit last night. Which I think is plenty for now, don't you?"

Gregory froze, his brows furrowing in confusion.

Gran walked into the kitchen, saving Lillian from having to explain 'redneck' and 'tailgate' to her gargoyle.

"Good," Vivian said, "you're all here. And I see my granddaughter even got Gregory into some clothing."

Gregory grunted something dark under his breath but didn't verbalize further.

Gran sat down in the chair next to Lillian and nodded to Whitethorn.

The sidhe lord glanced around the table. "Most here know the problems we need to solve and solve quickly, but Lillian, you and Gregory have only just awakened and possibly haven't had time to fully understand all the ramifications."

Gregory sat up straighter in his chair, and Lillian found she mimicked him without conscious thought.

"We can hide from the humans to some extent," Whitethorn continued, "but there is one time each month when we run a greater risk of exposing ourselves to them."

Gregory leaped to the answer before Lillian even had the first stirrings of an idea. "The Wild Hunt."

"Yes," Whitethorn said. "We've been lucky until now. The power both you and Lillian raised in the last Wild Hunt sustained the boundary wards of our land and fed our people what magic we needed to survive, but it has now dwindled to a level where we must risk a Hunt or weaken to a dangerous point. And the humans are not our only enemies—the remaining Riven are still very much a threat."

Greenborrow reached across the table and patted Lillian's hand. "You broke the Riven's foothold in this world, but they are far from defeated. We've found traces of them far north of us. They've retreated to the northern wilds to lick their wounds and to avoid contact with the humans. But I believe they will only stay away until they've grown strong. Then I fear they will return, and they might not take as much care to avoid human notice as we have. If the Riven reveal our existence to the humans, it could prove more damaging to us than any battle the Riven themselves might wage."

Whitethorn gave an almost defeated sounding sigh. "The Wild Hunt must ride to shore up our defenses, for we will need them in the coming days and months."

"However, we can't risk the Hunt for the very reason it could expose us to the humans," Gran countered, an arched eyebrow aimed in Whitethorn's direction. "Round and round we argue and still no progress." She stuck her spoon in her tea and gave it a good stir as a way of punctuating her statement as she continued to glower at the fae.

By the exchange of dagger-like looks shooting between Gran and Whitethorn, Lillian could only assume the Wild Hunt was a sore point between the two. Silence held for a heartbeat more, and then the entire table erupted into a chaotic debate strident enough to make a politician proud.

Lillian didn't venture into the verbal warfare, instead studying Gregory for any reaction. He leaned back in his chair, crossed his arms, and tilted his head first at one arguing fae and then another. Not one soothing word or sage piece of advice did he utter into the debate. Instead, he studied the others with a glint in his eyes that clearly said he found the whole situation humorous.

When she raised an eyebrow in question, he merely nodded his head in a barely discernible motion. Then along a private link, he added, *"If you find a peaceful resolution to allow the Wild Hunt to ride while at the same time protecting the humans from themselves, I will make certain the Clan and Coven abide by your plan."*

He was leaving it up to her?

Well, it's settled then. She'd just have to come up with a solution to the 'human' problem and prove to Gregory his trust in her wasn't misplaced.

She pursed her lips. Between the military, the media, and an army of scientists, Lillian had just set herself a near-impossible task.

How did one hold the Wild Hunt without the risk of discovery? How indeed?

The problem with the hunt centered on the initial raising of power, and the subsequent magical blast wave it pushed out across the land, which washed away all but the most powerful of pre-existing spells. The usual concealment spells the fae used to hide, and perhaps even some of Gregory's shielding spells would be washed away by the new tide of power released across the land, exposing the fae to the humans.

Normally the risk wasn't too high, as the Wild Hunt was held at night in relatively unpopulated areas. But with military, police, media and a host of other people roaming the forests, that presented a problem.

The fae needed to hide in plain sight. In essence, they needed to be visible and yet not draw attention to themselves. Or maybe to simply not stand out as unusual.

A diversion!

They needed to pull off a bait and switch trick worthy of a great magician.

When the bare bones of an idea came to her, she grinned so hard it hurt her cheeks.

"The Wild Hunt needs to come out of the closet to hide in plain sight." Lillian smirked as those around the table fell silent one by one and turned toward her. When she was certain she had their full attention, she continued. "We need an ironclad cover story to offset the danger of discovery during the Hunt. Give the average human a plausible, mundane explanation for anything strange they might happen to see, and their reasoning mind will be more than willing to believe the lie instead of an impossible truth."

Greenborrow wheezed rather loudly. Lillian took it as a sound of encouragement.

"If you want to hide the Wild Hunt, then all you need to do is throw an elaborate masquerade ball. Give the humans illusions, parlor tricks, and true magic. They won't know truth from fiction, and the secret of your existence will remain safe. And if any of the fae are spotted, it will be easy to discredit any news stories that might arise. Most people don't believe in monsters or aliens or magic."

Lillian held her breath, waiting for the first denial. One minute stretched into a second, but no challenges came. She released the breath she'd been holding and glanced around at the other fae. Each, in turn, had a thoughtful expression, their gazes turned inward in calculation. It was Gran who finally broke the unnatural stillness by picking up her cup of tea and sipping from it.

"Well?" Gran directed the one word into the silence. "Personally, I think Lillian's idea has merit. What says everyone else?"

Whitethorn cleared his throat. "If this masquerade is to

work, it will need to be substantial to draw the numbers required, covering a large region, community-wide at least."

"There could be more than one venue," Goswin suggested. "A parade, or a theatrical performance, a renaissance fair. Music and dancing and drinking."

Greenborrow laughed. "Lots of drinking. Get them drunk, and any stories will be easy to discredit."

The banshee shifted in her chair and pulled absently at her clothing like Gregory had been doing earlier. "Will not those persons seeking the truth behind the more fanciful imaginings—such as Major Resnick—be suspicious of something like this? What possible reason could we have to host a...medieval fantasy renaissance fair?"

"Greed." Lillian laughed at the banshee's questioning look. "This whole situation has drawn in huge crowds of people, and those people have money in their pockets. Any business-minded local is going to be brainstorming ways to part people from their money. I bet we can get all the other local businesses on board with this as well, especially if we do the heavy lifting."

"I really can't find fault with your reasoning," Greenborrow commented. "Though your plan may draw suspicions directly upon your family and the Coven by association."

"From how Major Resnick was questioning me and by what Gregory picked from his mind, we know we are already in their crosshairs. The problem isn't so much whether we can completely fool the authorities, but whether we can hide the Hunt from the vast majority of humans. The Hunt must happen. How many days to the next full moon?"

"Twelve," Gran said, her brows furrowing in thought. "Twelve days to pull off the bluff of all bluffs. Leave this to me, I'll rally the Coven. We'll see to the human threat, and it will leave the Clan free to help Gregory to prepare for a war with the Battle Goddess's forces."

Lillian had almost managed to put that particular danger out of her thoughts, but it was just as real as the human military—and far more dangerous, as the demon seed presently trapped within her hamadryad proved. But as dire as the situation was, it was really just a waiting game. In time, her tree would finish killing the demon seed, and Lillian would be free to rejoin her hamadryad, reclaim her soul, and take up the mantle of her power to become an Avatar once again. Then they could face the Battle Goddess on a level playing ground.

Easy as one-two-three.

Sure. As if anything in her life was ever easy. But presently, there was nothing she could do about it, which left her to help with more mundane difficulties. She turned to Gran. "Since the masquerade was my brilliant idea, how can I help?"

"Flyers," Gran stated with a chuckle. "Your expertise on the computer would be lovely."

The impromptu council meeting broke up. Whitethorn, Greenborrow, and the banshee herded Gregory in the direction of the back door, while Gran and Goswin ushered Lillian off to the one corner of the living room that doubled as the home office.

CHAPTER THIRTEEN

All around her, the ocean realm called to Tethys, urging her back into the depths where she belonged. Unfortunately, that would have to wait for some days yet. She had a task to complete, which was why Tethys currently found herself stationed under a small boat as she waited for the sharks to come like they had the last time the human's had put out bait to draw the predators close. Once the humans were distracted, she would ease up closer to the boat, within striking distance.

Half hidden by the boat's shadow, she studied the two humans. An older male and a younger female occupied the cage. With their backs to her and their attention focused on their equipment and the milling sharks, they were oblivious to the danger that even their stout cage wouldn't protect them from.

Yet Tethys hesitated.

As far as humans went, these ones were better than many she'd met over the centuries—their hearts held kindness, their minds a sharp intelligence, an essence bright with potential. She would regret snuffing out that rare quality.

She reached through the bars of the cage and then hesitated a second time. Unnoticed by her prey, she fought a silent debate within her own heart. These ones thought of themselves as protectors of the ocean realm. And perhaps in a better world, that would be enough.

Yet, more was needed. Their lives would continue to serve the ocean realm. She whispered a prayer for them as she reached her hand inside the cage a second time. Her fingers closed around the male's ankles, and she commanded the water magic to swirl the breathing device from between his lips.

The male tried to free his feet and simultaneously make a grab at his breathing tube. When he realized it was out of his reach, he struggled harder as panic set in.

She allowed the male enough freedom to fight harder, his exertion would end his suffering faster. The female she buffeted with ever-changing water currents, slamming her from one side of the cage to the other.

After a short time, the male's struggles lessened. As the siren waited for his end, she took no pleasure in it but wasn't overly moved by his fear either. She did feel guilt, for her actions stressed the dolphins—peaceful, forgiving creatures that they were. Once this unpleasantness was over, she would make amends to them.

Her gaze traveled from the dolphin pod disappearing in the distance and slid back to the cage and her work. The human male was dead. But she noticed her momentary distraction had almost allowed the female to escape. She'd managed to fight the currents long enough to climb halfway out of the cage. As Tethys watched, her head broke the surface, and she heard the woman scream for help. Another human from aboard the boat leaned over the side and grabbed the woman's arm.

As her intended prey was pulled over the side and out of sight, the siren dropped away from the cage. She circled the boat at a leisurely pace, listening to the woman's hysterical cries.

In the world above, the two remaining humans had edged closer to the side of the boat. Their frightened visages peered back at her, tracking her movement through the water. She didn't hide from them, wanting their attention.

Another powerful tail flick and she surfaced to study the humans in turn. The male seemed to be the same age as the female. Both were young—adults, but not far into adulthood. Flicking her glance back down to the cage below, she wondered if the older male was a mentor to these younger ones.

Perhaps it would have served her better to keep the older one alive. He may have been more knowledgeable about this new world and everything going wrong with it.

No matter. It was too late for regrets. Her power was great, but even she could not heal death. The young male would have to do.

Rising a bit higher out of the water, the siren spat salty brine from her lungs and out her gills and dragged in a lungful of air. It tasted odd. Not oily like the water, but oddly heavy with strange odors.

She drew a second breath, then on a third, she began to sing. Within the first few notes, she'd snared the male, as was clear by his mesmerized, vacant look and the easing of tense muscles.

The human's companion wasn't as affected by her song, which was very rare. This female must have suffered damage to her hearing at some point in her life. With the slightest change in her song, Tethys ordered the male to sit. His female companion started shaking his shoulder, shoving him sideways with the strength of her grasp. But Tethys's influence was more powerful than simple gravity, and the male swung back into position without a flicker of emotion on his face. His companion backed away, her horror almost a tangible flavor on the back of the siren's tongue.

The human continued to backpedal until her legs touched the edge of the boat's one side.

With a nod of her head, Tethys acknowledged the human's survival instincts. But even with an entire width of the boat between them, the female still wasn't safe, and perhaps the human was intelligent enough to know it, for a sad, desperate look flooded her features.

Tethys hesitated and then gave the human an equally sad smile. She would take no joy in this one's death either. The human was a fighter, young though she was, and perhaps deserved a better fate than the one planned for her.

But the ocean deserved a better fate than what humans had left it. With a powerful flick of her tail, Tethys drove herself higher out of the water. Between the webbing of her tightly fisted fingers, a power built, water aided by magic solidified into a long trident with bright, crystalline points.

Half-twisting in a powerful thrust, the siren sent the trident flying. It speared the female in the upper chest, sending her flipping over the side of the boat to land with a great splash on the other side.

Tethys moved quickly, darting under the boat and up the other side to the body's location. The woman was already dead, a clean, quick death. Grasping the corpse, she heaved it up and out of the water and onto the boat where it would be safe from sharks, since she still needed the body.

Once done, she sank below the waves in search of the one whose distress was so suddenly overwhelming.

She sang Surefin's name as she swam.

CHAPTER FOURTEEN

*L*illian thumbed off the phone and tossed it to the opposite end of the couch with a practiced accuracy as she finished scrawling contact information on her notepad. "The fairgrounds are booked, and the call just before that one was the jousters confirming they can make the three-day midweek appointment. They can't manage the weekend, they're already booked for another fair. The hall just called back to say we can have it for Saturday after all, so the medieval banquet has a location."

"Told you not to worry." Gran didn't look up from where she sat at the desk, leaning over her keyboard typing.

"It really was a miracle getting the hall last minute. There had been a wedding booked, but the bride just contracted chicken pox." Lillian groaned in sympathy for the unknown woman. "Poor thing, guess she never had them as a child. But the timing."

"She'll recover."

Lillian stopped sorting papers and glanced up at Gran

with growing suspicion. After staring a hole in the back of Gran's bent head didn't elicit a response, Lillian tried polite tact. "Pardon?"

"Yes, dear?"

"Tell me you didn't somehow give the poor woman chicken pox."

"Me directly? No."

Lillian was just drawing breath when the phone rang again. She huffed, aimed a glare at the cordless and then a second at Gran for good measure, before snatching up the phone. Her 'hello' had a bit more force than intended.

Lillian thumbed the 'off' button hard enough to make the plastic and rubber creak and then heaved it at the end of the couch, where it bounced before coming to rest precariously close to the edge. She pinched the bridge of her nose and rubbed at her eyes in a futile attempt to soothe away the deep-seated, ever-present throb of a headache.

She never did get back to the conversation about the woman with the chicken pox.

In the four days since she'd come up with what she now thought of as the 'moment of insanity' plan, she'd thought about nothing but the masquerade, arranging, verifying, and playing phone tag for what seemed like weeks. If she ever wanted to start a career along the lines of a wedding planner, she imagined she now had enough experience to add a line to her resume.

She glanced around the living room, hoping for a distrac-tion from all the notes scattered across the coffee table, all of which still required a follow-up phone call. But she didn't see a single distraction.

In fact, she hadn't talked to anyone face-to-face in hours, and today's four-plus hours talking on the phone after a quick lunch didn't count as basic human contact. She hadn't seen much of Gregory the last few days, either. Needs had them keeping opposite hours.

Gregory and the other fae did most of their spell work at night, using the cover of darkness to help shroud their work. Lillian, Gran, and several other members of the Coven worked in the daylight hours fielding phone calls and whatever else needed doing in the daylight.

Come each dawn, Lillian would get up, pack a hearty breakfast, and seek out Gregory. When she found him, she ached at seeing firsthand the steep toll it cost him and the other fae to cast great works of magic in this magicless realm. She would curse fate silently for the set of circumstances that prevented her from helping Gregory in his monumental task.

Gregory and the other fae metalsmiths were usually putting finishing touches on the newest batch of spelled weapons when she arrived with breakfast. Yesterday morning, Gregory had been too exhausted to eat, his complexion a paler grey than his usual lustrous, ebony tones. A caress of fingertips along his shoulders proved the greyish tone was, in fact, his skin starting to turn to stone.

He'd seemed unconcerned and simply nuzzled her in greeting and then leaned some of his weight on her as they walked back to the center of her maze. Once there, he'd hoisted himself up onto his pedestal and turned to stone before her eyes.

While Gregory seemed unconcerned for himself, Lillian worried on his behalf.

This morning when she'd gone to take him breakfast, it was to find he'd finished early. A quick search found him already turned to stone on his pedestal. She'd sat on his stone knee and ate a tasteless breakfast.

Yet another day of phone calls and errands helped her focus on other things, but it did not banish the worry and fear. And suppressing those emotions was stirring up other problems—like a migraine great enough to shatter her skull. She closed her eyes and staggered to her feet, no plan beyond 'escape' foremost in her mind.

She succeeded in navigating her way to the kitchen and was almost to the back door and freedom when the phone rang again. Anger coiled in her gut, and she growled, her eyes homing in on the wall phone where its red light blinked out a rapid, annoying pattern. She stalked across the floor and swiped at the phone with one hand, swatting it with enough force to disconnect it from the wall.

Lillian was rewarded by lovely, blessed silence. She curled her lip at the phone and spun back around to the door. The freedom of nature and the dark, endless forest called to her. Her focus was all on that goal, or she might have acknowledged the sound of footsteps and the door between the living room and kitchen swinging open.

"Hey, Lillian, wait," her brother called from behind. "Did you ever hear back from the...whoa! What happened to the phone?"

"It annoyed me," she hissed over her shoulder.

"You could have simply said you were taking a break, rather than giving the phone a makeover."

Lillian whirled on her brother, not in the mood for his brand of humor.

"Its ring hurt my ears." Her voice came out rich and low, almost a raspy growl, nothing like her own. She fought past the pounding in her head to try to make sense of it, but the need to be outside was more pressing.

Her brother blanched and stepped back, forcing Gran—who was a step behind him—back as well. His move, which was clearly protective, sparked a touch of lucid reason in Lillian's mind. Her brother was afraid. Of her? Why?

Lillian blinked and shook her head, but it did nothing for the pounding in her head or the ringing in her ears. Was she going to pass out? No, her body itched and burned, and it wasn't the tingle of encroaching faintness.

Gran pushed at Lillian's brother, finally forcing him out of the way. She eased past him and stopped a short distance from Lillian. "Darling, you need to listen to me. You're not in danger, and I won't keep you long, but you need to answer a couple of quick questions."

Lillian jerked her head once in acknowledgment of Gran's words. It was all she was able to do as instincts reared up within her and clamored for her attention, to run free, to slide from shadow to shadow as she hunted for prey in the forest. Hunger burned in her belly, making thought harder.

"How long has it been since you and Gregory have had time to spend together?"

"Days," Lillian growled out, not sure if it was entirely true, but it felt like longer.

"I know Gregory has been sleeping in stone to recover faster. Did you see him yet today?"

"Yes," she bit out and turned from Gran, taking a long stride to the back door.

"Lillian?"

She shook her head and gathered her thoughts. Gran wanted to know something else. It was important. She sighed. "Gregory was stone."

"Then he hasn't actually seen you today?"

"No," she snapped. "Isn't that what I just said?"

Gran placed a gentle hand on her shoulder. The slight pressure was uncomfortable, her skin overly sensitive. Lillian was tempted to swat at it but remembered what she'd done to the phone and held back. Something was wrong.

"Lillian, you need to go seek out Gregory now. It's imperative."

"Why?"

"If I had a mirror, you wouldn't need to ask," Gran muttered. "You're going gargoyle on us. Go to Gregory. He'll know what to do."

"He's sleeping."

"He'll wake for you. He'll feel your need."

She did miss him. They could hunt together. Or perhaps he would hunt for her. The wildness in her blood changed focus. Gregory sounded more appealing than a few trees. She had the strangest urge to purr.

She navigated the familiar labyrinth with ease, its cedar scent wrapping around her senses, soothing some of the wildness in her blood. Not much. But enough to reach the maze's center with a relatively clear mind.

With a groan, she dropped to her knees in front of Gregory and bowed her head, pressing her forehead against cold stone as she fought for control. She wrapped the fingers of one hand around the tip of his tail. The stone was cool to the touch, but already growing warmer.

"Gregory," she whispered.

"My Sorceress?" His tail twitched under her fingers as stone gave way to flesh.

"Something is wrong."

CHAPTER FIFTEEN

*A*larm hummed through him even before he was fully awake. It was not danger that awoke him, but Lillian's distress. He inhaled a deep breath and snorted with understanding when her mixed dryad and gargoyle scent hit him full force. It was a lovely scent. One his brain was happy to bask in for a moment more than he knew he should. It also explained her distress.

He opened his eyes and gazed down. She knelt with her head bowed and pressed against his pedestal. No wings. No tail. Still mostly dryad. She hadn't been caught in a painful mid-shift. Not yet, at least.

"Lillian." He touched her shoulder, closing his claws with a gentle pressure to get her attention. "Beloved, look at me now. You have to fight the shift for a little while longer."

She jerked as if his tender urging was the harshest command. But she did as he asked. She looked up at him, and he was relieved to see she was only mildly changed. They still had time to get to the safety of the forest. Though not much, judging by the way her dark irises had expanded until no whites showed in her pain-filled eyes. Her ears had already elongated into points only partially hidden in her hair. She hissed in pain, and her black talon-tipped fingers dug into his calf muscle. As he watched, small black horns erupted from her forehead.

Gregory loosened her hold on his leg and transferred it to his hand, then jumped down to stand beside her. His wings mantled over her protectively. "My beloved Sorceress, I must get you to the forest where we can hide while you learn control. Can you stand?"

She didn't respond verbally but gave a quick, jerking nod. Moaning in pain, Lillian forced herself to her feet.

"This way." He urged her in the direction he wanted her to go, and she didn't fight him. However, she only made it a dozen steps before she grasped her head and sank back to her knees.

"It hurts. Why does it hurt so much?"

"Because you're fighting the change." He gathered her up in his arms and then called his magic to hide them both.

"You told me to fight the shift." Her words came out with a bite of accusation.

"I did. Hold on just a little while longer. I'll get you to the forest, then you can shift where no one will see or hear."

"Can't you just hide me from view? You're doing it now. I can feel it."

Gregory broke into a run. "Your hamadryad is feeding you magic. You may lose control when you shift. I'd prefer we not be near any humans if that should happen."

"I thought you said I couldn't touch my magic."

"You're not taking, she's giving."

"Wonderful," Lillian growled. "What about the demon seed? Are we in danger from that little monster again?"

"No."

"Thank goodness for small mercies. And I think the pain is fading. Actually, I feel drunk." Lillian laughed suddenly. "Now, if fate will continue with this rare streak of kindness, we might avoid any military patrols, too."

The forest was still too far away for Gregory's peace, but at least she was lucid again. As for the human warriors, if they had the misfortune to interfere when Lillian needed him...

A low rumble of threat escaped him.

"Mmm, you have the sexiest growl." Lillian purred the words as she leaned into him. With her cradled in his arms, her head naturally rested against his shoulder, and she rubbed her cheek against his bare skin. Her lips started nibbling on him. He stumbled when her tongue followed the track her lips had just been over. "You taste as good as you smell."

"Lillian!" he rumbled in mild complaint. He didn't need the distraction at the moment. Though he realized almost in the same instant that physical closeness must help Lillian in some way, for she couldn't have been in as much pain, not if she could be distracted by other instincts.

"Sorry. I told you I feel drunk. Or maybe high on endorphins with the pain receding." She let her head lull to the side and her eyes closed as she drew another deep breath. A small smile played at the corner of her lips. His eyes narrowed in thought. Perhaps he could use her attraction to him in some way to aid her through the painful first few shifts.

She made a soft humming sound. "You really are so beautifully male. You can't blame a girl for wanting to touch such muscular perfection."

Gregory scanned his surroundings as he ran. The forest was within a few dozen paces. Safety for Lillian only a few strides distant. When he was under the shade of the first trees, he continued deeper without slowing. There was no time to find an ideal spot for Lillian to shapeshift and then rest afterward. He'd just have to settle for moderately safe at best.

"Hold on, Lillian. We're almost there. Just a few moments more."

He went a little deeper into the forest until they came upon an area of dense undergrowth. A thick carpet of ferns blanketed the ground. It wasn't an ideal 'nest,' but it would have to do.

Guilt twisted in his gut. He should have monitored Lillian more closely for the signs her gargoyle nature was rising again. *Who am I trying to fool? I should have taught her how to master her gargoyle side when it first became apparent she still retained it.*

"Hey, I can practically taste your guilt, it's so strong."

Gregory jerked at the sound of Lillian's voice and found she was intently studying him.

"It's not your fault, you know. Don't feel guilty over something out of your control." She sighed and wiggled in his arms. "You can put me down now. My body isn't trying to tear itself apart at the moment."

Gregory did as she asked, though left a supporting arm around her shoulders, likely more for his own comfort than anything she needed, he suspected. "It is my fault."

Lillian turned to face him. "How so?"

"I should have made time to train you, to show you how to shapeshift, control your gargoyle magic, and to use your wings. But I didn't. I was afraid." Her eyes widened at his admission, but he continued before she could interrupt. "I feared—still do fear—that I lack the willpower to resist you."

Lillian chuckled. "Thanks for the vote of confidence and for making me sound like some kind of super-tramp." She waved him to silence. "I know after the first and only time I became a gargoyle, the title might have been fitting," she cleared her throat with nervous embarrassment, "but it was one hundred percent the demon's influence. I wasn't really 'home' then."

"I know, but it's not—"

"I refuse to believe I'll become some raging hormone-filled beast, unable to control myself, just because I'm the first female gargoyle."

"It's not—"

"I won't become some mindless beast. At least I hope I—"

"Lillian!" he shouted her name.

She froze mid-sentence, and he continued in a quieter tone. "It's me I don't trust."

Rocking back on her heels, she looked up at him, her expression morphing from shock to understanding before finally settling on sympathy.

In a hasty, awkward move, she launched herself at him and wrapped her arms around as much of his waist as she could manage. She mumbled words into his shoulder. They went on for a time. He didn't understand one word, but he didn't have to. Just having her hug him was a comfort.

Finally, she added, "You don't have a clue what I just said, do you?"

"No," Gregory admitted, "but you're very good at non-verbal communication. I think I have an idea."

"Just so we're clear. We're partners. From here on out, we

back each other up. Remember the 'no lies, no secrets' conversation?' Yah, you know the one. Partners help each other during difficult times. I might not have the powers of an Avatar, but I'm pretty sure I can dredge up enough will power to remind you of your 'duty.' Besides, I've got a good memory. I still remember the getting pregnant equals a bounty on our heads, equals the Lord of the Underworld sniffing on our trail, equals death thing. And he sounds like one scary dude. 'Nuff said."

He held his silence throughout Lillian's impassioned speech.

"You can trust me to not fail in this one task. Have I failed in anything I've set out to do since you met me?" Lillian drew in a quick breath, not giving him a chance to respond. "Okay, so some of my plans have been a touch unorthodox, but I haven't failed. I won't fail or betray your trust."

Gregory returned her solemn gaze as he weighed her words, giving them the attention they deserved, but then felt his ears betray him and twitch to half-mast in doubt of her ability.

Her endearing, hopeful expression fell, transforming into one of displeasure. "As if you're perfect!"

"No, as I believe is the root of the conversation. I don't trust myself."

"I... Oh! For pity's sake." Lillian huffed, fisted her hands, and then stormed over to the nearest tree and planted her back against it. "Well, my great and wise Gargoyle Protector, I'm going to shift into a female of the species very shortly, so if you think I can do better on my own or under the guidance of one of the other fae, by all means, let me know and I'll just go seek them out."

Gregory covered the distance in two strides and towered over her. He stepped closer until they were chest-to-chest. "I didn't say I distrusted you. I said I didn't trust myself. Are you so sure you could turn away my advances? Do you want to put it to a test?"

Lillian just shook her head. Though he wasn't sure if it was in answer to his question or denial of it.

"Why the hell are we fighting?" she said at last. "I'm going to shift into a female gargoyle whether I want to or not. Thanks to the Battle Goddess's manipulation, there's no stopping it. Secondly, you're the best candidate to teach me how to be a gargoyle. And thirdly—I can't believe I just used 'thirdly' in a sentence—you're the noblest male I know. You'd never hurt me. I trust you."

Gregory pressed their foreheads together.

She spoke the truth. He would never knowingly harm his beloved sorceress.

She patted him on the shoulder as if to reassure him. "No more stalling or arguing. Let's just get this over with."

CHAPTER SIXTEEN

"Will this spot do?" Lillian asked as she studied her large, winged guardian. "Or should we go deeper into the forest to avoid detection?"

He eyed the area once more and gave a little shrug. "This is not where, when, or how I would have liked to have shown you the finer points of being a gargoyle, yet this is what we have. It will do. I sense no others near—human or fae.

"Good. I don't want an audience the first time. I have a feeling learning to use four legs will be more difficult than two. And wings, those I don't even want to contemplate." She tried humor to lighten the mood, though she wasn't sure if she did it for Gregory's benefit or her own. The thought of the actual physical shift scared her more than the end result. How much would it hurt? And what if she fainted? Would she get stuck halfway?

Strong arms closed around her and pulled her into his warmth. "Do not fear your other nature, it will come naturally to you," Gregory said in a soothing voice. "Only your fear, and perhaps mine as well, have halted the change this long. We are now someplace safe from discovery—it is only your uncertainty holding back your gargoyle side."

After another nervous swallow, she gave him a small nod of acknowledgment.

His hand came up to caress her hair. "Relax, breathe deeply, and put everything out of your mind except my voice."

She found the combination of his voice and the rhythmic stroking of her hair relaxing. Tension slowly eased from between her shoulder blades. She buried her nose against Gregory's neck and inhaled his scent. He smelled like home.

"Don't fear the power within you. It is as much a part of you as your dryad side."

With a snort of humor, Lillian realized she hadn't really accepted her dryad side, which may be why she also feared the gargoyle half. She just wanted to be plain old Lillian. Nothing more and nothing less.

"You are an Avatar," Gregory whispered into her hair. "You will never be 'less' in the way you wish."

"I just want to be me."

"You will always be you, whether you wear the hide of a dryad or a gargoyle, both are as much a part of you as I am."

Strangely, the way he worded it made it more palatable to her. She'd always known Gregory was a part of her. She accepted it without thought or complaint. Shouldn't she be able to accept her gargoyle bloodline just as readily?

Perhaps.

As if her weakening resolve was a signal, magic filled her in a tingling rush, flowing out from her heart, down both arms and legs, and to the very tips of her fingers and toes.

She gasped at the pressure of the building power.

"Easy, it is only your hamadryad sharing magic with you to make this first shift easier," Gregory said in his deep, soothing voice. "Once you learn how, you will be able to shift without needing the extra surge of magic to push you over the precipice."

Her skin became super sensitized, her clothing felt two sizes too small. Heat intensified between her shoulder blades and all along her spine. An enormous pressure built, not pain, but not pleasant either.

"Slowly," Gregory crooned. "You're in too much of a hurry again."

"Maybe you should go mention that to my hamadryad?"

He chuckled, then his fingers left her hair and started to work the buttons of her blouse. When all the buttons were undone, he pushed it off her shoulders and tossed it behind her with little regard. Soon her belt joined her blouse on the forest floor.

He paused, and by his expression, she knew he wanted to say something but didn't know how to word it.

"Just spit it out before my hamadryad sends the next wave of magic."

He flicked an ear in her direction, uncertain. "Once you shift, you may find yourself as attracted to my scent as I am to yours. You needn't be embarrassed by how you may react."

"Ah, thanks for the warning." Lillian toed off her shoes and kicked them in the general direction of her other clothing. She hesitated at her bra, but after a moment, reached back and unhooked it and let it slide down her shoulders. She dropped it on top of her blouse and then folded her arms over her chest. He popped the button on her jeans, pushed them down her hips, and quickly disrobed her of the rest of her clothing. Naked, the night felt much colder than it had earlier. She shivered and tucked herself against his side. One wing curled around her, covering her from head to toe in a living cloak.

"Now what?" she asked, but she knew.

"Surrender."

His hypnotic voice made it sound easy. She acknowledged the command in his tone. Then she breathed in his scent, tasted his ancient magic, and her essence resonated to his silent call. Power flared within her. Gregory placed a hand on her back, between her shoulders and pushed, forcing her to bend at the waist. Instincts flared, and she understood what he was telling her. She dropped to all fours as the power crested within. A burning magic flowed just below her skin, rippling and flaring with a mind of its own.

Lillian gasped and bowed her back, her fingers clawing at the loamy earth. A hot, wet sensation made its slow way over her back and down her sides as something heavy burst from her back. She groaned in pain but was distracted by a new ache radiating from two burning points high on her forehead.

Her body shifted and changed. She grew light-headed, her arms shook, and she would have collapsed onto her side had it not been for Gregory's strong arm around her waist. Another wave of power crashed over her body. Her vision sparked white at the edges before going grey.

Panting and disorientated, with her muzzle pressed into the leaf mold covering the forest floor, she lay quietly for a moment. It came to her slowly. She must have blacked out. She didn't remember completing the change; however, a glance down her body confirmed there was no denying she was now fully gargoyle.

She fixated on her tail, studying it in equal parts humor and uncertainty. Just lying there, she could feel the weight of it against her legs, rather like a giant boa constrictor sleeping coiled against her. She flinched at the mental image, and her tail gave a reflexive twitch.

"You're awake?" Gregory's voice rumbled in her ear, and she realized she was resting against another warm, living body.

She turned her head and found it difficult to lift as if the balance had changed.

"What?" she started to ask and then cracked her horns against Gregory's as she turned to look at him. "Oh!"

Gregory laughed and nuzzled her, purposefully rubbing against her, so their horns clicked together. It didn't hurt, but she rolled her eyes skyward to try to gauge their span. When she thought she knew their impressive size, she was careful to disentangle hers with a muttered apology.

"You have nothing to be sorry for. You did well." His voice sounded husky, or maybe it was her new ears.

"I fainted." Her own voice sounded strange, too. "Hell, I thought I had more backbone."

"Hmm...backbone?" Gregory's arm came around her waist, dragging her a few inches closer. His warm breath wafted against her shoulder and then his muzzle was shifting her hair away from the back of her neck. A gentle lapping made her jerk in his hold, partly in surprise and partly because it felt too good to hold still.

"What are you doing? Shouldn't I be..." Her voice trailed off as he continued to lap at her sensitive neck. A soft prickle of teeth against her skin froze the breath in her lungs and made all her muscles want to melt. It felt nice...too nice.

"Gregory?" She twisted in his arms to try to see his expression. "I don't think this is a good idea."

"No," he rumbled with humor, "but I like it."

He surprised her again when he suddenly rolled away and came to his feet. Crouching next to her, he looked her over with what could only be called interest. She eased up onto her forearms. Her wings came with her, which shouldn't have surprised her, they were attached after all.

"Goodness," she gasped. "How do you move with these massive things dragging after you?"

He glanced over his shoulder. "To be honest, I notice them no more than my arms, legs, or tail. Yours will become natural to you too. Can you stand? Start with all fours. You might find it easier."

Baby steps. Nice and slow, she told herself as she rolled to her knees. Almost of their own accord, her wings righted themselves and fell into place along her back. Her tail shifted, and she gave it an experimental wave as she gathered her hind legs under her.

Gregory coughed into his bent arm, but she could see the tears rolling down his cheeks. His entire chest shook.

"Are you laughing at me?" Lillian aimed a pointed glare in his direction, and he only laughed harder.

"No, yes...sorry." He cleared his throat and wiped at his eyes.

"Well, it's not very nice." Then she realized she was resting on her forearms and the position put her... "Dammit! It's not funny at all."

She pushed up and came to all fours, curling her tail around her hips. It did nothing for her nudity, and Gregory still watched her with avid interest.

"I know it wasn't intended as an invitation," he cleared his throat, "but...in the future, you perhaps should be aware..."

"It certainly wasn't an invitation! I'm still trying to walk! I wasn't thinking of sex!"

She dragged in a deep breath, and Gregory's scent hit her squarely in the chest. She leaned closer to him. He smelled good enough to eat. She very much wanted to lick him. "Argh! Stop that!"

"Stop what? I do nothing." He spread his hands, showing them empty and then gave her a slow, toothy gargoyle grin, and winked at her.

With a show of her newly discovered motor skills, she flipped him the bird.

He laughed and then came over and helped her up. "I did warn you about the likelihood of our attraction. You've always smelled good to me. I suppose it only makes sense I would smell equally good to you."

She wobbled around until she found her new center of gravity. Feeling like she might be able to stay upright, she glanced at Gregory and was surprised to see they were eye level. For the first time since she'd met him, she didn't have to crane her neck.

"Okay, points for being a gargoyle."

He tilted his head in question, but she ignored him in favor of getting a good look at her new body. While she had his height, she was of a slighter build than him, less heavily muscled, less bulky overall. But what she lacked in physical strength, she'd bet she made up for in speed.

"I'm fast, aren't I?"

"Yes."

"Why is my coloring so different from yours? Do gargoyles have variations in skin pigment like humans?"

Gregory cocked an ear. "You're a female gargoyle, there's nothing normal about any of this. But as for your coloring, no, it's different than any gargoyle I've seen. The Lady of Battles likes black and crimson. I can only assume she designed your gargoyle body with that in mind."

Lillian flinched. "Killjoy. I didn't need the reminder about her just now."

"I detect nothing evil within you. The changes are physical only. The Dark Goddess couldn't touch your soul, not even with the demon seed's influence." Gregory dipped his muzzle to nudge her gently. "Soon we will be free of her taint altogether and can face her in battle unhindered by her manipulations."

Gregory seemed a little over-confident on that score, Lillian mused, but he had faced the dark one in the past so she would bow to his wisdom.

Dropping to all fours, Gregory bounded around her in circles. "Come," he called, slapping her flank with his tail as he dashed by. "Run with me."

Gregory's enthusiasm was infectious, and she took a cautious step forward and then another. She remained upright, more trusting of two legs than four. Her wings and tail shifted naturally to aid her balance, requiring almost no thought on her part.

"Lillian, the night grows long." Gregory darted out around her, and she could hear him coming up directly behind.

Not knowing what he planned, she squealed in mock anger and started to run. Her new body responded like she'd owned it all along, her stride stretching into a relaxed, ground-devouring lope. He came alongside and kept pace with her for several strides and then bounded over a fallen tree.

"Be patient." She cast him a dark look. "Haven't you heard the saying you need to learn how to walk before you run?"

"A human saying," Gregory countered. "You're a gargoyle now. React."

With only the one word as warning, Gregory charged, his wings spread to block escape to either side. She backpedaled, lost her balance, and landed on her butt in an undignified sprawl. Gregory landed on top and gave her a sloppy gargoyle kiss before bounding away again. She growled at his retreating backside, wishing she had a well-weighted rock. Rolling to all fours, she scrubbed his residual kiss off with one foreleg and then stretched, loosening and limbering up muscles.

When he doubled back for her, she was ready and pounced on him. Her strike was more luck than skill, but she landed square on his back and was rewarded by his grunt of surprise as she knocked his hind legs out from under him, using only her tail.

Gregory collapsed and rolled at the same time. Lillian suddenly found herself falling sideways with him somehow on top. They were chest to chest, and when Gregory gave a happy little wiggle, she was reminded she was naked.

"Chauvinistic pervert." Lillian issued a light-hearted challenge. "Why do you get a loincloth and I get nothing?"

With another of his slow, toothy grins, Gregory tugged at one of the loincloth's ties. "I would never wish to make you feel you weren't my equal."

"Ha! Nice try, but no getting naked. One buck-ass naked gargoyle running through the woods is enough. And speaking about running. If you want me to run and hunt with you, you better magic up something to bind these with," she pointed at her breasts, "because running with them loose is not going to be any kind of fun."

Gregory sighed longingly. "Perhaps not for you…"

"P is for perverted. G is for gargoyle…"

"I like to think P is for patience."

"That's for me. You definitely get the former." Lillian turned from him and started scanning the ground. When she found a particularly nice patch of moss and ferns, she pointed at it with one long, clawed finger. "Magic me up some clothing like you did once before. Only this time, something like your loincloth and a sports bra instead of a pretty but functionally useless gown."

"As my Lady commands." Gregory turned to the area she indicated.

Dressed in her strange but comfortable mixed plant-fiber clothing, Lillian loped along behind Gregory as he stalked his prey through the forest. At a later date, he'd promised to make her magically warded clothing like his loincloth so the items would shapeshift with her. Which, Lillian had to admit, would be handy.

As promised, she found it natural to run on all fours, and they covered ground quickly. Following downwind of Gregory had the added benefit of being bathed in a wash of his warm, male scent. It mingled in an altogether pleasant way with the night breeze.

Following him for kilometers at a time was far from a

chore. It soothed the wildness she'd experienced earlier in the afternoon when she'd felt trapped in the house, missing Gregory and needing something so primal, she hadn't known what it was. Now she knew.

She needed this—a wild run through her home forest. Hunting with Gregory at her side. Putting on a burst of speed, she came alongside him. He glanced over at her, and she prodded him affectionately with her muzzle, working her way up his side, to his shoulder, and then finally managed to plant a wet kiss along his cheek as they ran.

"*I love you,*" she sent in a burst of emotion.

"And I you, guardian of my heart and soul." Gregory's tail slid along her body, a caress of friendship and reassurance. "But there are still many things I must teach you this night, and you will need nutrition to maintain your strength."

She was feeling mildly hungry, had been for some time, but she'd seen so many wonderful things she'd put it out of her mind. Though now that he'd mentioned it, hunger planted itself forefront in her thoughts.

"*I could use a snack,*" she sent.

"*Follow me. I know a place.*"

CHAPTER SEVENTEEN

Tethys swam deeper, her powerful tail cutting through the water quickly as her eyes scanned the reef below for signs of Surefin. There, near a yawning ravine in the coral, a silver-grey shadow darted around an outcropping of coral and sank into a fissure. She followed the young dolphin, humming and clicking softly. She used no enchantments, wanting him to come to her willingly. Swimming over the crest of coral, she almost collided with the young dolphin. He turned to bolt deeper into the reef.

"Wait. I will not harm you. You are safe with me. Look within my mind, and you will see the truth."

His uncertainty still clear in every flick of his tail and fins, he rose a bit higher.

Taking it as permission, she turned her magic upon herself. Her enchantment allowed the young male a way into her thoughts and emotions if he was brave enough to try.

"Go ahead. No harm will come to you. And you are free to go now

or after." Tethys sent warmth and peace across the mental link. "*I never have and never will enslave one of the ocean's creatures.*"

Surefin cautiously bumped his muzzle against her outstretched hand, then forward a bit more until he positioned himself for a scratch. After a bit of tactile reassurance, his thoughts touched hers. He was more thorough than she would have thought, given his boisterousness and reactive personality. She waited patiently for him to finish picking his way through her thoughts. When he slid back and away, she did not hinder his escape. He picked up speed and vanished around another part of the coral reef.

Her heart surprisingly heavy, Tethys made her way back to the boat.

All was as she had left it. The human male still waited where she had ordered him to sit. Focusing her magic, she sent another mental command. "*Ready the boat. We will be leaving soon.*"

After waiting a moment to assure herself the human did as she said, she frowned down at the dead female. She'd waited a touch longer than was best, but the body wasn't so old as to be useless. With a mighty heave, Tethys dragged herself up and over the side of the boat and flopped down next to the body.

She leaned over and placed her hands on either side of the female's head. Again, the ocean's magic filled her, eager to her command, and with the slightest push, it invaded the dead woman's body. Even with her magic bolstering it, the residual consciousness lacked the sharp clarity of a living mind, the memories accumulated over a lifetime already fading, disintegrating into the grey afterlife. But Tethys found the scraps of what she needed. With a touch of desperation, she hurried to gather those fragile leavings. It wasn't enough to allow her to function in this new modern world, but it was enough to give her the bare bones of a language.

Besides, she still had the male to act as her guide. She trailed her fingers along the woman's cooling cheek, over the line of the jaw, and down the pale column of her throat where the skin was already taking on a grey tinge. With the flick of one sharp nail, the delicate skin parted to reveal the red meat below. With a bit of pressure, Tethys forced a little blood to ooze from the cut. More followed those first sluggish drops, but it wasn't enough for the siren's purpose. With a soft hiss, Tethys turned the body onto its side and pressed her cupped hand underneath the wound. Long moments crept by. When her palm finally contained a few sips, she brought it to her lips and drank.

She grimaced in distaste but drank it all, even licking the residue from her webbed fingers. She was just cleaning the last of it away when a splash at the side of the boat caught her attention. A familiar grey muzzle, with a fish grasped in its teeth, poked up out of the water. Surefin bobbed up and down as if uncertain of his welcome.

With a smile and click of encouragement, she heaved her bulk over to the edge of the boat and gave Surefin a rub of welcome.

"You returned."

"Yes. I come, too."

"You belong with your pod." The siren rubbed under his jaw and along the undersides of his fins to take the sting out of her words. *"Where I go, there is danger. Too much for one so young."*

"I go until there is danger. Then I return to pod. Dolphin family wait."

Tethys sighed, knowing she would have to use magic upon the dolphin to keep him from following. Perhaps he could follow for a short while. At least until they were farther north. She had planned for her human guide to stay close to the shore as they headed north. It would be easy enough to command him to keep their craft's speed down enough so the dolphin could follow them. And to be honest, she expected the journey would prove long and lonely.

"Very well. You may come. But only until we are farther north. Once I go inland, you will have to remain behind."

She winced as an explosion of excited clicks nearly deafened her.

"Calm, Surefin. You may come. But you must tell your family pod first."

Without further ceremony, Surefin deposited the fish in her lap. Then with another series of excited clicks and whistles, he sank back below the waves. His speech too fast for even another dolphin to understand, Tethys could only assume the slur of sound meant Surefin would be back once he had informed his family pod.

She returned to the boat and pulled herself aboard. Turning her attention to the pale, sad corpse, she studied it from head to toe in one long sweep and determined it was of no further use. She grabbed one chilled shoulder and fought with the dead weight until she had it positioned, ready to heave over the side of the boat. One more powerful shove and the body teetered at the edge for a moment before it slid over the side and into the ocean. The dark water rippled as the body disappeared in a flurry of bubbles.

After washing the blood from her hands, Tethys frowned

at her own long tail knowing what she had to do next. Her body had had enough time to process the human's blood.

She closed her eyes and took one deep breath and then another, willing her magic to the surface while at the same time pushing away the dislike of what she must do. Power flooded out from her center, down the length of her arms to the tips of her fingers. She stiffened her spine and grasped the side of the boat in a punishing grip. The webbing between her fingers parted down the middle and was absorbed back into her hand. Her silver-grey skin tinted with a soft rose hue as the magic continued to burn through her body. Scales receded, smoothing into the soft, drab skin of a human. The conversion continued to race down her body, leaving the frail appearance of a human in its wake. More of her magic rose at her command, concentrating in the region of her tail.

A pained gasp, almost a sob, escaped her. She clenched her jaw, refusing to admit any weakness. The pain intensified. Her tail receded. Bones, muscles, and veins all rearranged themselves as her magic continued its work. With a wet sound of shredding, her tail split in two, which made her cry out in a guttural scream. Her vision greyed out, and she slumped to her side.

She drifted for a time on the edge of consciousness, no longer really feeling the pain. But her magic continued the transformation. She could still feel her body shifting as it settled into a new form. For a time, the only thing she was aware of was the gentle rocking of the boat and the soft splash of surf, the calming sound of her home. And there was a louder splash and a heavy, wet thump next to her head. She blinked blurry eyes to clear them. The world came into focus slowly, too slowly, and the edges were still grey. She blinked at the still-flopping fish as it twisted and jumped on the boat deck.

"I bring you fish."

Tethys flinched at the sharp whistle but only sighed at the young one's exuberance. Her ocean born companion would continually remind her of the purpose for her quest, the reason for her leaving the ocean, for the sacrifice of becoming human.

CHAPTER EIGHTEEN

True to his word, Gregory knew of a good hunting spot. It wasn't too distant, perhaps only about five kilometers. The exact distance was hard to judge as her gargoyle body allowed her to cover greater distances relatively quickly. Lillian was rapidly coming to like her new form.

They'd only just reached the place he'd promised when a small, furry creature broke cover and darted off ahead of them.

Gregory snorted and shot off after the creature in the time it took her to realize it was a rabbit she'd seen. Moments later, a minor scuffle ensued, punctuated by a short squeal of terror.

Appearing out of the deep shadows, Gregory padded to her side, the carcass of a rabbit clasped in his jaws. With great ceremony, he deposited the furry creature at her feet. He sat down beside her and curled his tail around his flanks. Daintily, he cleaned a few specks of blood from his muzzle and claws.

When he was finished, he pointedly looked at her and then glanced at the rabbit, his perked ears dropping slightly.

With a mild churning in her stomach, she glanced down at the rabbit, and then back to Gregory. He still watched her expectantly.

Did he expect her to eat the rabbit? Raw, fur and all?

Her brother had taught her the basics of bow hunting, and she'd taken down numerous rabbits and even a few deer over the years, but that game had been gutted and skinned. Not to mention cooked before it came anywhere near her mouth.

"Mmm, thank you." Not wanting to hurt Gregory's feelings, she crouched down lower on her forelimbs and nudged the small carcass with her muzzle.

Warm and furry, the mildly musky animal scent coiled in her nose, but overlaying it was the copper scent of blood. Her mouth suddenly filled with saliva and her stomach cramped. It wasn't nausea; no, it was much worse.

Hunger.

She suddenly found the small carcass far from repulsive.

Jerking back so she wouldn't bite into the rabbit like her instincts demanded, she leaned into Gregory and whined instead.

"Would you like me to gut and skin it for you?"

Burrowing her muzzle between his shoulder and wing, she nodded. She took a deep breath, hoping his scent would drive away the all-consuming hunger. The soft, wet sounds of shredding flesh reached her ears and the coppery smell intensified.

Gregory shifted, his wings folding back and away from her, forcing her to face what he held in his jaws. Dryad Lillian was still repulsed, but Gargoyle Lillian was hungry, and he offered it so sweetly. He presented it to her again, still held tightly in his jaws.

She inched forward, nudging his muzzle with her own. Whining, she licked him in submission. With a grunt of pleasure, Gregory dropped his gift and stood over her. She snatched it up, giving the still-warm flesh a couple bites before gulping it down. Snatching up another piece, she chewed and swallowed it in seconds and bent for another.

When the last of Gregory's small 'kill' was gone, she cleaned her muzzle as she'd seen him do, and then looked over her shoulder at him. He stretched out on the ground less than a body-length from her. Not bothering with words, he merely patted the ground next to him and then rested his head on his folded forearms.

She circled a couple of times before she flopped down next to him. As she curled into his side, she decided a nap sounded like a lovely idea.

When she awoke from her short nap, Gregory greeted her with another wet gargoyle kiss and then stood and stretched.

"Do you feel up to a real hunt now?"

"What? Rabbits don't count as hunting?" She arched her back and stretched, even giving her wings an experimental flap before folding them tight again. Flying was still far outside her comfort level, but hunting didn't sound too advanced.

"No. They are emergency snacks. Come, I'll show you how to track and stalk a deer."

"A deer? Shouldn't I start smaller?"

Gregory sidled up next to her. He landed another one of his surprise swats along her flank and bounded off before she could react. With a mock snarl, she gave chase, playfully trying to snag the tip of his tail each time she managed to get close to him.

They continued their playful run. Gregory sometimes allowed her to catch him and other times she put on a burst of speed, startling him enough to overtake him all on her own. Their wild run continued for an hour in much the same fashion until he picked up the scent trail of a small group of deer.

Gregory ran at a slower gait, dipping his nose to the ground every few strides as he tracked the deer. Lillian matched his pace, her gaze locked on the terrain ahead, scanning for the telltale silhouettes of deer.

Her ears warned her of an incoming beast running toward them. The sounds of snapping twigs and the swish of foliage grew louder by the second. A deer suddenly broke cover on the path ahead of them. It spotted them and veered hard to the left, sailing over a tangled thicket of underbrush. Another deer, running two body-lengths behind the first, followed the same path. Lillian spun and lunged to give chase, but Gregory pounced first, landing directly in her path, blocking the way with the bulk of his body.

"No, stay still and quiet." Gregory turned to study the way the deer had come.

She hunched down next to him and remained silent.

He raised his head and flared his nostrils. Lillian mimicked him and caught a very faint scent. Warm mammal mixed with something metallic and oily.

"Human warriors headed this way," Gregory said barely above a whisper. "Stay close. Don't move unless I do." He curled a wing over her and shifted until they were just off to one side of the game trail, situated in the deepest shadows the immediate area had to offer. "I want to study them while they are unaware anyone else is near."

A tingling, chilled magic flowed over her. She'd experienced his protective spell of invisibility a time or two before, but her new gargoyle senses were able to feel it much more acutely. "Is your spell sufficient to shield us both?"

"Yes. As long as you move with me and stay in contact the entire time." His warm breath washed over her ears and stirred her mane.

It tickled, and she bumped him gently on his shoulder.

He inched back very slightly, still keeping contact between them. A moment later his tail coiled around hers.

"If I had more time, I could have created a spell specific to you, to shield you even if I wasn't near." He absently nuzzled her shoulder while they awaited the human soldiers. "Remind me to create one for you later. It can be part of tonight's spell work with the fae metalsmiths."

"It would come in handy," Lillian rumbled against Gregory's throat.

After a huff of agreement, he turned his attention back to the humans easing their way through the trees.

A voice drifted to her.

"I heard something come this way," one soldier said in a low whisper.

Another soldier, this one a few paces ahead of the man who had spoken, replied in the same quiet tones. "Probably just a deer. We've seen enough of them in the last few days."

"And if it was something other than a deer," a third soldier said as she emerged from around a tree almost beside Lillian, "you two would have frightened it off with all your talk."

Lillian recognized the female. It took a moment to recall her name. Right, Corporal Mackenzie.

"Personally, I'd rather not run into whatever created that crater, or those malformed bodies," the first soldier said dryly. "If noise is likely to scare them off, the more noise, the better."

"If noise is the key, we're not going to find anything anytime soon," the second soldier commented. "Town's too much of a shitstorm."

"What, the reporters getting to you?" Corporal Mackenzie asked with a laugh.

"Them and all the medieval society members running around. It's like the circus arrived. A masquerade ball. Dumb fucking idea."

"Oh, it's far from stupid—tactical, more like. But meant to look like a money grab." Lillian recognized Major Resnick's voice as he spoke for the first time. "There's something strange with the whole family, the ones running the spa. The grandmother is too nice, and the rest of the family is too helpful and perfect."

"How can you not like Gran?" Corporal Mackenzie asked, a big grin spreading across her face.

"Her real name is Vivian. Who actually goes by the name Gran and bakes cookies for complete strangers? I keep expecting to find the Big, Bad Wolf and Goldilocks lurking in these woods."

"You're getting your fairy tales mixed up," the first soldier to speak injected. "It's Little Red Riding Hood."

Corporal Mackenzie's grin grew bigger. "You know a lot about fairy tales."

"Welcome to fatherhood; the truest test of manhood. Come to think of it, my kid would love a picture of Bigfoot."

"Joke all you want," Major Resnick barked. "But there's something strange about the whole family. My money's on cult. And if I'm right, they know something about what has been going on in these woods. I plan to find out what."

"And now you're bullshitting again," muttered another soldier out of Lillian's line of sight.

The leader's laugh grew fainter, but Lillian swiveled her ears and heard a, "Maybe I am."

Gregory held his position until the last soldier had moved on down the game trail. When he deemed it safe, he folded his wings, allowing Lillian to stand. She turned her attention from where she'd last seen the humans. "It's much like Gran feared. The authorities are suspicious of our family. It's only a matter of time before we slip up and get our asses tossed in a cage."

"You could let me handle the humans," Gregory added dryly.

"No...no massive memory wipes, or missing persons. It would only raise more questions." Lillian flicked her tail in agitation. "We'll proceed as planned. Keep working on enchanting the weapons for the Clan. I'll keep working with the Coven to find ways to confuse and confound the humans."

Gregory nodded. "As you wish. However, I think we must continue your hunting lesson tomorrow. Our duty will not wait for us tonight."

"I think you forget one little detail." Lillian waved a hand down her body. "I don't know how to return to my dryad form."

"I'll show you once we're closer to home. Come." Gregory dropped back down onto all fours and started off in a direction that would lead back home without bringing them too close to the human patrol. Lillian followed in his wake.

CHAPTER NINETEEN

The day of the masquerade arrived sunny and bright, with the promise of an equally temperate night, which was good. The better the weather, the better the turnout there would be. She wondered if the Coven had something to do with the perfect day but hadn't asked. She'd add the question to the list of things she planned to ask Gran one day if things would ever quiet down enough in her life to have something as mundane as idle time.

She stifled a yawn and took another sip of tea, and then shifted to find a more comfortable position on Gregory's stony thigh. Her guardian was presently resting on his stone pedestal like he'd taken to doing each dawn. Lillian hadn't seen a reason why she should change her long-standing habit of having breakfast in the center of her maze, in the shadow of her tree while sitting on Gregory's knee. She smiled ruefully. He made a solid bench, but maybe she should start bringing a pillow.

Finishing her bagel, she drew her legs up to brace her feet against his opposite thigh. Sitting crosswise on his lap, with her back braced against his slightly mantled wing, was the most comfortable position. She took another sip of tea and let her mind wander.

In the five nights since she'd first learned to shapeshift, Lillian had met Gregory each evening at sunset, and he would run with her in gargoyle form, teaching her to shapeshift swiftly as well as how to hunt for herself. Last night, he'd started her training in gargoyle magic.

Some things came easily. She could cloak herself from detection without too much trouble, but only if she held perfectly still. As soon as she moved, her shadow spell would break apart like so much fog. Gregory assured her she was a quick learner, but she couldn't help feeling impatient with herself.

Tonight was the Wild Hunt, and she and Gregory would both take part. A small, prideful part of her spirit wanted to be able to match him stride for stride, spell for spell. That, of course, was impossible since she no longer had her Avatar magic to call on, but that prideful part couldn't be reasoned with, it simply wanted.

Mostly to impress Gregory.

Her cell phone beeped again, almost a plaintive sound as if it was saying, "stop wool-gathering and get something useful done." She sighed and picked up the phone from where she'd left it on Gregory's knee.

She was just thumbing through the assorted calls and text messages she'd been ignoring when she caught movement out of the corner of her eye. A stranger already dressed for the masquerade in a long, red cloak emerged from the surrounding maze. Lillian tapped her phone off and then slowly straightened.

Alarm hummed through her veins at the way the stranger homed in on her with a predatory intensity. Sweat instantly broke out in a fine sheen across Lillian's skin. The woman had hair so blonde it was almost white, and her complexion was equally pale. Unmarked by blemish or age, she was strikingly beautiful. So much so, Lillian suspected she wasn't human at all, but a fae. Perhaps one of the Clan she'd yet to meet.

More arrived every day. There were so many strangers coming and going from her life, she shouldn't have been concerned by the arrival of one more. But she was.

"Hello," Lillian called and gave an accompanying wave. The stranger acknowledged her with a bob of the head. "You must be new here."

The stranger brushed at her hair in a half-conscious manner, and she walked closer to Lillian.

"I *am* new to the land. Perchance you could be of service?"

Perchance? What the actual fuck? "Always glad to help."

The woman continued forward and then reached out to stroke Gregory's stony flank. A flood of instant dislike rolled down Lillian's body. How dare the other woman take liberties with her gargoyle?

"I'm sorry, I didn't catch your name..."

"I did not give it. But to alleviate your curiosity, I am of the sea, one of the merfolk. A siren. I see the gargoyle sleeps. Is he unwell? This Realm can sap the strength from even the greatest of us."

Lillian snapped her teeth together. Lying would only anger

the fae, so she told the truth. "Gregory spends the nights weaving metal and magic together. It is exhausting work. But he is well otherwise, he merely rests."

"I am glad." The merwoman nodded. "As I journeyed to this landlocked place, I encountered many whisperings among the fae, the most frequent and interesting of how a gargoyle once again walked this Realm. My inquiries unearthed that this was not just any gargoyle, but the first and greatest of his race—the Sorceress's Shadow. And the Shadow is never far from his Sorceress."

Lillian knew the fae had a number of titles for Gregory and herself, but she'd never heard him called the Sorceress's Shadow, as if he was somehow of lesser value, not worthy of a unique title in his own right. Lillian took an instant dislike to the underlying meaning.

The siren smiled suddenly. It brightened her eyes, making her seem less daunting. "Can I assume you will be participating in tonight's Wild Hunt?"

"That's the plan," Lillian said and then decided to hedge for a bit. "If we can avoid drawing notice from the human authorities."

"You worry over the humans," the siren said absently as she smoothed a wrinkle in her deep scarlet cloak. "Odd. I would have thought humans beyond your notice."

The alarm bells in Lillian's mind revved up another notch. "Other fae may echo your opinion, but I can't say mine aligns with theirs. The humans, while lacking in magic, more than make up for any weakness in numbers. And they have weapons that can kill Clan and Coven. It would be foolhardy to strike out at the humans without provocation."

"You're correct. One should never underestimate one's enemy."

The siren touched the edge of Gregory's stone wing, gliding her fingers up and over the ridges of stone as she made her slow and methodical way around the pedestal. The hair at the nape of Lillian's neck raised to attention when the other woman was hidden from view by Gregory's wings. She didn't release the breath she'd been holding until the siren was again in her sights.

Lillian racked her brain for something to say, finally settling on, "Will I see you at the Wild Hunt tonight?"

"Oh, yes. I wouldn't miss it for all the power in the world." The siren ducked her head in Lillian's direction and bowed in what she could only liken to a deep, courtly bow. The fae turned her attention back to Gregory and gave him an equally deep bow. "Until later, Lillian of the dryads and Gregory of the Livingstone. And if you require me before then, call me, and I will offer what aid I can. Long ago I was called Tethys." Then in an unhurried manner, she backtracked her way through the maze.

Tethys? Lillian might not be up on her ancient mythology, but she'd be willing to bet the name harkened back to ancient times. She made a mental note to Google the name later. She followed Tethys' progress with her newly heightened gargoyle senses. When she was certain the newcomer was gone, she turned back to Gregory and patted his stone knee. "I don't care if the ward stone circle doesn't consider her a threat, something about her sets my teeth on edge. I'm going to go find Gran and see if she knows anything about this Tethys. Rest well, my love."

Her plan lasted a whole ten seconds after she'd exited her

maze, at which point both the caterer and the florist descended upon her like the proverbial pack of hungry wolves. It was close to sunset by the time Lillian escaped the bustle of tonight's masquerade and was able to finally seek out Gran.

CHAPTER TWENTY

The forest was still, only the faintest of breezes stirred high up in the canopy. Nearby, a cardinal sang his location to his mate. Faintly, she heard an answering call in the distance. Lillian wished she still could reach out and touch Gregory over any distance as easily as the bird called to its mate, but that power—like the other magic she'd commanded so briefly—was nothing more than a fading memory.

"Well, suck it up, buttercup," Lillian muttered under her breath. She'd just have to swallow her nagging worry a little longer. She looked down at her watch. For once, luck was with her—she'd made excellent time, and was almost to Gran's rendezvous point, and where Gregory would later join them. From there the Hunt would gather in ones and twos to remain unnoticed, and then ride out once they had great enough numbers. There would be no circle dance in the old sawmill this time, but the Wild Hunt would ride nonetheless.

Who said stress wasn't good for anything? It certainly made her legs move faster.

A dash of white glinted through the trees just ahead. Lillian battled the urge to call out but held back on the off chance a military patrol was out this far. From the reports of the other fae, this sector hadn't had any activity in two days. But it didn't mean it would remain free of mortal soldiers.

Lillian winced at the term—now Gregory had her referring to others as mortal. Just when had that happened?

The blur of white came closer and resolved itself into the unicorn. He galloped to her and then slowed to trot a half-circle around her before coming to a stop at her shoulder. With his usual tact and subtlety, he bumped her in the stomach for a pat and nearly knocked her nose off with his horn. "Watch it!"

Eyes streaming in pain, Lillian rubbed at her nose with another muffled curse. With his head hanging low, his ears forward, and his lower lip quivering slightly, at least the unicorn had the grace to look somewhat sheepish.

"You're forgiven. Is Gregory here yet?"

The unicorn shook his head. *"No, but Gran arrived a short while ago. Come."* The unicorn trotted off, and Lillian followed him to where her grandmother waited.

"Good, you're here." Gran's usually boisterous voice was subdued, barely above a whisper.

Lillian glanced over at her grandmother in time to see her straighten from where she'd been sitting on a fallen log. She brushed at her clothing, switching her staff from one hand to the other, then she motioned Lillian ahead and they started down a game trail. The unicorn took up the rear of their silent procession. Even he seemed subdued, perhaps aware of the need for quiet and stealth.

After another fifteen minutes and unable to hold her peace any longer, Lillian glanced over at Gran, gesturing at her own lips and cupped her ear with one hand.

Gran's one eyebrow crept upward in question. "Dear, I know you were never very good at charades, and I take it the miming is not a mini-stroke, so if you were asking if it was safe to talk, I'd say yes. There are no military patrols close."

"Thanks." Lillian rolled her eyes heavenward and prayed for patience.

"The unicorn said Gregory didn't overtake you along the way. I'm surprised." Gran glanced around at the thickening shadows as twilight descended upon the forest.

The darkness didn't concern Lillian. She had excellent night vision. "Last I talked to Gregory, he said he'd join me later, and he'd make sure we didn't have any spies on our back trail. That was last night. He was already stone by the time I got to the glade this morning."

Gregory's absence was logical, perfectly acceptable, and expected.

And Lillian's stomach was still a knot of tension.

The past week had her on edge and meeting with the newcomer only made everything seem just a touch more sinister.

"Gran, I was sitting with Gregory earlier this morning when a fae I'd never met before came up to us." She paused, noting Gran's narrowed eyes, the beginnings of concern. "She called herself one of the merfolk—a siren."

"A siren?" Gran asked, her face remaining impassive, but Lillian still heard what she left unsaid, a very clear 'why didn't you say something sooner?' "And she was in human form?"

"Yes."

"That is not something a siren will do unless it is absolutely imperative. I don't like this. Did she tell you a name?"

Lillian paused to dredge it up.

"Tethys."

Gran's quizzical smile vanished, replaced by thin-lipped tension. "You're certain of the name?"

"Yes." There was no way she had conjured it out of the air.

"Warn Gregory. Warn him now. Tell him a powerful siren is a threat to all we've worked for." Gran swung her staff up into a defensive position and gazed around at the surrounding trees as if she expected an attack at any moment.

Gran's fear fueled Lillian's own. In a stroke of pure gut instinct, she reached toward Gregory's sleeping mind and then remembered.

"Dammit," she said. "I can't reach Gregory, not over this distance. To be honest, I haven't been able to since I emerged from my hamadryad. I'm as good as useless."

Gran frowned at Lillian, her expression saying they would have a long talk about Lillian's lack of self-worth later. "If you can't warn Gregory over a distance, we'll just have to get closer. Besides, I want to see for myself why Tethys has come. She was never overly fond of land, disdains humans, and dislikes the land-bound fae for their complacency. However, she has her own sense of honor, or so my ancestors wrote in their grimoires."

Forgotten until then, the unicorn drew their attention with a tremendous rolling snort Lillian had come to associate with equine fear of the highest order.

Gran turned her gaze upon him. "Will you help me, old friend?"

The unicorn made another of those sounds of fear but bobbed his head in assent. *"I will aid you as I can, but I will not draw the siren's attention. I will not become a two-legged slave again, not even for the sake of our friendship."*

"I ask no more than you are willing to give," Gran murmured and gave the unicorn a pat on his neck.

When they started back toward civilization, Lillian cleared her throat, for she still had questions. "Tethys is a siren. In mythology, they are known for singing sailors to their deaths. But what of a real siren? Just what can she do?"

"She can sing enchantments."

Enchantments? That didn't sound too terrible, but judging by Gran's white-knuckled grip on her staff and the tight lines around her mouth, 'enchantments' could be far worse than the word conveyed.

Perhaps seeing Lillian's doubt, the unicorn took up where Gran left off. *"Her voice can strip away one's will, enslave one so completely the victim is unaware they are even trapped. If it is her wish, the slave is all too happy to die for her or kill for her."*

Lillian's breath hissed between her lips, more a strangled wheeze than a gasp of disbelief.

Disbelief was far from her mind. It sounded all too terrible not to be true.

"Who is in danger? How many can she enslave at once? And is Gregory immune?"

"Everyone is in danger. At least anyone within hearing distance.

As for your gargoyle, I don't know, but Gregory is male and not at full strength. She may be able to roll him under her spell."

A cold sweat broke out on her body. "We have to do something."

"We will." Gran's barked answer came out sounding drill-sergeant hard.

Together they would assess this new threat, and then they would formulate a plan. And if Gregory were compromised, she'd just figure out a way to disentangle him from the siren's clutches. She owed him for all the times he'd saved her.

Everything will be okay, she reassured herself.

Right. And water runs uphill.

Biting back her own mental sarcasm, Lillian cleared the lump in her throat and asked, "How can I help?"

"Piercing your own eardrums is the best place to start." Gran's tone came across with a deadly serious edge. "I'll create spells for the three of us. If the situation is as bad as I fear, the spell will trigger at the first note of Tethys' song. Then we run like hell and worry about everything else later." Gran paused, her expression thoughtful. "Don't take on your gargoyle form. You heal too quickly. To be safe, you may need to outdistance the reach of her song before you shift."

As far as plans went, Lillian decided it sounded as well thought-out as one of her own.

"To coin a human term," the unicorn injected, *"we're so screwed."*

Gran sighed. "Perhaps the siren has merely come to join with the rest of us to battle the Riven."

Oh, Gran, Lillian whispered in the privacy of her own mind, *you lie worse than I do.*

CHAPTER TWENTY-ONE

The last of the light had fled some time ago, and Lillian navigated the forest pathways as best she could. It was slow going without flashlights or even the glow of Gran's staff. Her grandmother didn't want to risk exposing themselves to military patrols or any of the fae who might now be under Tethys' control.

But they were not in total darkness. The unicorn gave off a very slight glow. The pale light allowed Lillian to see the shapes of low-hanging branches and the occasional gnarled root along the path without summoning her gargoyle senses.

When she had first raised an eyebrow in question, Vivian had claimed no one else would be able to spot the glow. Unicorn magic allowed them to hide from almost anything. Even a hunter like Gregory would have trouble finding the unicorn by sight alone.

Lillian was thankful for the pale glow. However, she would have much preferred her gargoyle form and the ability to see in the dark.

By Gran's intermittent mumbled curses, she concluded her grandmother's night vision wasn't up to the task, even with the unicorn's illumination.

The return journey to the spa felt twice as long, so much so Lillian began to wonder if they were lost.

Casting a speculative glance at the trail ahead and the surrounding forest, she spotted a familiar bear-clawed tree, and then around a bend, another familiar moss and fern-covered boulder.

No, they were not lost. Just crawling along at a snail's pace, with a good two kilometers to still walk before they would reach the spa and her maze, where she'd left Gregory sleeping.

How could she have been so stupid? Her instincts had tried to warn her, but she'd rationalized it as paranoia.

The unicorn came to a halt, his ears twitching forward in question. His skin shivered, but he made no other comment or explanation.

Over the buzz of insects, the chirps of frogs, and the cries of the night birds, she detected a soft crackle of static to the left of her position.

Without comment, the three of them silently moved toward the sound. The unicorn led the way, with Gran a step behind. Lillian followed several steps farther back to better scan the night.

Her nails burned and itched with the need to lengthen and sharpen as the unknown threat weighed on her mind. She fought the urge to shift. Partially because Gran had warned her she'd heal too quickly, and partly because she'd only tried to shapeshift in Gregory's presence.

When they came upon the source of the static, the five shadowy shapes slumped on the ground at random intervals were easy to recognize. It was less easy to determine at a glance what had taken down an entire patrol without a shot being fired. She calmed her own harsh breathing and was able to hear their steady, slow breaths. They were merely sleeping. Well, perhaps there was nothing 'merely' about their sleep, but they were alive.

"Tethys' work," Gran said, answering Lillian's unasked question. "If she were here for a peaceful purpose, she wouldn't randomly leave bodies just strewn about, which tells us she isn't worried about fallout from the humans, likely because she intends to make sure they aren't a problem."

A radio crackled again, drawing all their attention toward it.

Gran cursed. "Let's go. They're bound to be missed soon." She directed a frown out into the surrounding forest. "There might already be others out looking for them."

Lillian glanced back the way they had come. "Then they are bound to see our tracks."

Gran shrugged. "Something to look forward to later, should we survive." On that comforting note, she started off through the forest at a faster pace. Lillian and the unicorn followed after a quick glance at each other.

They found more human patrols and some fae sleeping peacefully under the trees. All attempts to wake the fae proved pointless. Their efforts didn't even elicit a sleepy grumble. And Lillian realized Tethys' enchantment put her victims in a state closer to a coma than natural sleep. "How can we undo this?"

Gran gave Lillian a sharp look. "A siren's enchantments die with her."

Lillian took it to mean it was up to them to find a way to defeat Tethys by any means necessary.

But can I kill?

When she'd been attacked by the Riven, she'd defended herself, killing many of her enemies, but it had been the work of the demon seed protecting its host as much as Lillian's own fortitude. And the Riven were more dead than alive by her judgment. If those Riven hosts had been still alive and aware —she'd probably done them a favor by destroying them.

Images of the helpless, inert forms of humans and fae flashed against the back of her eyelids. They would be such easy pickings if the Riven should happen upon them. And then there was an image of Gregory, how she'd left him sleeping on his stone pedestal, weakened from all the spells he'd been casting these last few days. Tethys had reached out, daring to touch Gregory as he slept.

Could I take the siren's life?

'Yes,' she thought, *'for Gregory and everyone else I love.'*

With that acknowledgment like a promise burning in her heart, she followed Gran out of the forest and into the gardens surrounding the spa.

As they walked the garden pathways, the gravel underfoot the only noise betraying their passage, they came upon more sleeping victims, these a mix of fae, military, and a good couple hundred human civilians.

Ah. The masquerade. What a disaster her clever idea had

become. Now magic had spilled across into the mundane world. Lillian eyed the sleeping people. The siren must be stopped tonight, for dawn would come and reveal far too much to human eyes.

Lillian came around a sharp turn in the path and nearly ran into the pooka. To her surprise, he was still on his feet.

He stood with his head bowed low, hooves planted firmly and tail hanging limp. He didn't so much as flick an ear at their approach, but when she laid a hand on his side, he rolled a dull, yellow eye in her direction.

Gregory had told her both unicorns and pookas possessed a natural ability to see past deceptions. Perhaps it gave the pooka a slight immunity to the siren's magic.

After patting his shoulder, she allowed her hand to rest on his withers, hoping her small gesture would give him some comfort. "No one enslaves my family or friends. I'll get you free and make her pay."

Her words might be a common turn of phrase, but the emotions and fortitude behind them were genuine.

Gran tapped her on the shoulder. "Come, we have a siren to discipline, a gargoyle to extract, and the night isn't getting any younger." Gran sighed out a humorless laugh. "And neither am I, but villains seem not to care about those kinds of details."

"And all before dawn," added the unicorn in a tone Lillian interpreted as ominous.

"Yes," Gran whispered. "Because if we haven't freed Gregory by then, he might be too deeply ensnared for us to release him without help.

"Who the hell is left to help?" Lillian asked, more sharply than she'd intended.

Gran gave her a pinched look and pulled an amulet on a chain from around her neck. She hesitated before handing it over to Lillian. It was surprisingly heavy and still warm from Gran's skin. Actually, it felt too warm, as if it gave off its own heat.

When Gran motioned to put it on, Lillian did, looping it over her head and then smoothed her hair back in place, all the while giving her grandmother a questioning look.

"No matter what else happens, neither you nor Gregory can remain under the siren's control. She must never possess such power. It will start a war with the humans; it might even tip the scales in the Battle Goddess's favor if the fae are forced to battle the humans. War and chaos make her stronger. And I don't even care to speculate what the Riven might try while our attention is drawn elsewhere. Smear three drops of your blood upon the amulet, and it will summon your last allies, and no, I can't tell you more. The less you know, the less you can tell Tethys if you should be captured."

Lillian scowled, seeing a problem with her logic. "Why give me the amulet then?"

"Because I doubt I'll escape the siren's attention either. The best we can hope for is to confuse her if we all attack at once. We'll need to sneak into the cottage and secure some of those weapons Gregory and the sidhe metalsmiths have been working on. We might get lucky and land a good shot. Then, if luck is still with us, you might be able to wake Gregory and finish off the siren. Or if all goes south, escape with him."

We're so screwed, Lillian whispered in the recesses of her own mind, echoing the unicorn's earlier comment. To Gran, she said, "Now there's a scary number of 'ifs' to overcome."

"Unfortunately. It's also the best plan I've got. Tethys is

one of the oldest of her kind. She'll be a difficult adversary to fight, because how does one fight one's own deepest desires? And mark my words, she'll use your heart's wish against you."

"Great," Lillian mumbled as she followed Gran deeper into the gardens in the direction of the cottage.

CHAPTER TWENTY-TWO

Sneaking into the cottage proved surprisingly easy. But then again, stealth wasn't a problem when no other soul was awake to see you, Lillian supposed. Her second greatest fear—that the siren might be holed up somewhere inside the cottage proved false as well. The house was silent, deserted in a way it hadn't been in days. For the first time in her life, the old stone cottage offered no homey reassurance.

"We've been storing the spell-warded weapons below in the wine cellar," Gran explained. She crossed the kitchen and unlocked a side door, which opened onto a narrow set of stairs leading down to the cellar.

Lillian followed close on Gran's heels. They continued along the rows of wooden shelves with their cargo of quality wines, which stocked the family spa in normal times. They filed past the wood shelves, and Lillian found herself in a far back corner of the cellar. The dingy little alcove was devoid of anything of interest, so she'd never had reason to venture over to this part of the cellar.

Gran grabbed the edge of the dumpy little table leaning against one wall and started to move it. The legs dragged on the stone floor and made a painful sound.

Lillian winced at the appalling noise, then looked up at the rafters and cocked her head to listen. Nothing responded to the sound, and she released the breath she'd been holding. While she'd been worrying about something coming up their back trail, Gran had gone ahead and pushed against what had looked like just another section of wall.

But this wall made a grating sound as it swung open into a black abyss. Gran shoved her shoulder against the door a second time and opened it a bit more. With a muttered curse, she groped around in the darkness. After half a minute, there was a hum and a flickering of harsh light as rows of fluorescent bulbs sputtered to life.

Under the cold light of the fluorescents, a large room Lillian hadn't even known existed was revealed. She drew another sharp breath, but only had a moment to marvel at all Gregory's hard work. Knowing he'd been enchanting weapons for days on end was one thing, seeing the hundreds of them was something else altogether. Her eyes swiftly picked out the shapes of swords, shields, daggers, spears, crossbows, and yes, those were longbows resting against one wall. Their beautiful, elegantly carved wood shafts so much more striking than her practical compound bow or the crossbow Gran had given Lillian on her sixteenth birthday.

"Here," Gran said as she shoved first a crossbow and then a wooden longbow into her hands. "Hold these for me."

Lillian did and followed Gran around the room until they were both laden with knives and enough arrows and bolts to do some severe damage.

"One more thing before we go," Gran said as she made her way over to a long, low table. There she pulled a couple of lengths of fabric from a basket and brought them over to Lillian. "Gregory was working on these for you. I think he planned them as a gift. The beading isn't finished yet, but they are functional."

There was a soft rustle of fabric and the gentle clank of beads as Gran handed the bundle to her. Lillian unfolded it to discover one item was a beaded loincloth like what Gregory wore, and the other was a long, scarf-like construction. With a bit of wrapping, it could be secured into a top of sorts, one which looped up over her neck, crisscrossed over her breasts and tied behind her waist. It wouldn't interfere with her wings when she was in gargoyle form.

She ran a thumb over the soft fabric and tiny beadwork. Sudden moisture gathered in the corners of her eyes, and she had to swallow past a lump in her throat. Gregory had been working himself to exhaustion each day, but he still took the time to make this gift for her because she'd asked.

"Here," Gran said, "I'll take the longbow."

It was probably for the best, since Lillian doubted she possessed enough skill to effectively aim one of those deadly weapons with any accuracy. The crossbow suited her better.

She donned the clothing Gregory had been making for her with quick efficiency. And then, as silently as they had come, they left the secret room and made their way back up to the outside world where the unicorn waited in the gardens behind the house.

CHAPTER TWENTY-THREE

*L*illian tightened her hold on the heavy crossbow as she stepped under the shadow of the maze. It was darker inside, the newly risen moon's light not reaching the ground within. She made her way using memory and touch, and still, it seemed an age until she reached the maze's center. Worry for Gran and the unicorn didn't help.

When the maze had first become visible in the distance, Gran had ordered them to split up and breach the maze using a three-pronged tactic. They were each to make their way to the center, searching for traps along the way. Once there, they would await Gran's signal and all attack together, or if the situation inside made it too dangerous, Gran and the unicorn would draw the siren's attention to give Lillian a chance to escape with Gregory.

Not liking the part where Gran and the unicorn might sacrifice their own freedom, Lillian had bridled at Gran's plan but realized there might not be another choice if any of them were to escape.

No one said she had to like the plan. She just had to pull off her part and not fail Gran.

She scanned the central glade while still hidden by the shadows of the maze. The clearing was more than wide enough to allow moonlight to bathe the small glade in its soft radiance. Lillian took an immediate dislike to what she saw.

Arranged in a semi-circle in front of Gregory, with their backs to Lillian, a mixed group of fae stood unmoving. They might as well have been as stone-like as Gregory. Some she recognized: Greenborrow and Whitethorn were two, but the others were strangers or triggered only a vague recollection in her.

She really wished she knew what powers those unknown fae might command.

Her blood drummed in her ears and tingles rushed across her skin, raising gooseflesh in its wake. It wasn't until her claws prickled against her own palms that she drew a calming breath. Gran had explicitly said not to take gargoyle form until absolutely necessary because if they needed to use the deafening spells, Lillian's ears would heal too quickly in gargoyle form. Her grandmother had yet to steer her wrong.

With a mental shake, the last of the wildness bled from her body, and her thick, black claws returned to the soft, pink, useless nails of a human.

Now another worry inched up her spine—where the hell was Gran and the unicorn? Had they been captured? She hadn't heard even the slightest noise to hint at a skirmish. Maybe the other route was blocked or guarded in some way, and Gran and the unicorn were both forced to double-back to Lillian's position?

Well, Lillian mused, she might as well see what she could learn while she waited for any sign of her companions.

From the sheltering dark of her cedar maze, she scanned the small assembly again. Her eyes briefly settled on Gregory, then behind him to her redwood, and finally the large expanse of pure darkness at its base. Moonlight couldn't penetrate its dense foliage, and there might be twenty more fae hiding in those shadows.

Seeing no other choice, Lillian reached for the otherness she associated with her gargoyle bloodlines, calling up that same wildness she'd just pushed away, needing it now.

Closing her eyes, she listened. The night noises sharpened. Crickets, frogs, the hoot of a great horned owl, and even the splash of water as the stream cascaded down the small series of flagstones functioning as a tiny waterfall in the north end of the clearing—all these things reached her ears, making her straining senses tingle.

She filtered all the natural noise out like Gregory had shown her. Now the deep throb of the statue like faes' heartbeats reached her ears and the soft hiss of their breath. Otherwise, the clearing seemed empty of threats, but she doubted it was as innocent as it looked.

Lillian crept forward, muscles tense and senses on high alert as she made her way across the clearing toward Gregory. There was no point in attempting stealth, it would do her little good if she were walking into a trap. She was halfway to Gregory when water surged against stone, disturbing the peaceful night. Frogs and crickets grew silent even as Lillian sought the source of the disturbance.

Her gaze slid to the north end of the clearing, where the largest of the otherwise-tiny waterfalls dropped down into a pool stocked with water lilies and goldfish. The surface moved in an unnatural way for several more seconds, then a head and shoulders emerged through the covering of water lily leaves.

The woman—for it was unmistakably a woman rising partway out of the pool, her bare breasts easy to make out in the moonlight—brushed back strands of damp hair from her face.

Lillian spotted several lines running down her neck, the last ending at the curve of her shoulder. They fluttered and expelled water. If the gills hadn't been enough to tell her this was indeed the siren, the great fan-shaped tail jutting from the surface of the water about five feet from her shoulders was a dead giveaway.

The fae pulled herself up onto the rocks at the edge of the pool. She made no other move. Merely watching Lillian.

The being in the pool looked nothing like the woman who called herself Tethys, but she felt the same, especially that strong current of power flowing against Lillian's skin. After a moment, she identified what it reminded her of. An undertow, the ocean's power far inland from where it would naturally exist, but still recognizable all the same.

The siren's gaze was a physical weight, all stern willpower and focused magic crashing against Lillian's mind, raising gooseflesh along with defensive instincts.

At any moment, she expected to feel a sharp pain as Gran's spell triggered and shredded her eardrums. One moment passed, and then another and another, and still the siren didn't sing.

"Welcome," Tethys said, her voice clear and buoyant, free of anything that could be called musical enchantment.

Lillian only gave the siren a slight nod in answer, but she eased forward away from the green maze walls. She didn't relax, more than ready to launch into a full, heart-pounding, adrenaline-filled sprint for safety but managed what she hoped was an outwardly calm exterior as she said, "Why did you attack my people? What do you want?"

"An attack implies harm. And I have harmed none here tonight. As for why I'm here?" Tethys made an elegant gesture with one hand in the general direction of Gregory. "Why, I want the same thing as him, ultimately."

Lillian was taken aback by the siren's easy answer. However, she highly doubted Tethys and Gregory's endgames were even remotely in the same ballpark—they probably weren't even on the same planet for comparison purposes.

"Nice try." Inwardly, Lillian winced at her flippant tone. It always helped to aggravate older beings of immense power, after all.

The siren tilted her head in thought and fanned her tail to splash water over herself. When her upper body was again thoroughly wet, she pointed at Gregory with one long finger. "Deep down, and it might not even be very deep, he wants the same as me—to help this world find its balance so it can heal."

"You might say heal, and yet your tone implies the opposite." Lillian paced a wide circle around the group of statue-like fae as she made her way toward Gregory. It didn't matter if it was a trap, she had to know her gargoyle's condition.

Tethys aligned herself to Lillian, but she made no threatening moves. "You must not know the other half of your soul as well as you once did. No matter, I still wish for us to be allies against the seductive darkness, the taint which touches all in this land, even you."

Lillian pointed to the statue-like fae. "Not the way to gain allies."

"Perhaps not, but the situation demands immediate action if this world is to survive." Tethys splashed herself with water and then used her powerful tail to drive herself higher up the grass-covered bank until she was three-quarters of the way out of the water. "Humans have a weakness at their core, a rot they've never been able to outpace, a greed which demands more and more. They are never satisfied with what they have. They think only of themselves, never about the planet as a living entity." The siren made a vague, yet all-encompassing gesture with one arm. "They think the planet is theirs. Such ignorance. They are such a young species, and unlikely to become an old one."

Lillian had come here with the plan to save her gargoyle, having to save the whole damned planet hadn't factored into her plans. But she had to do something. "Many of the humans are aware of the crisis and are working to change things."

The siren laughed. "A handful of humans trying to undo the damages created by the rest of the human horde will not save this world or the billions of innocent, non-human victims."

"Then why not help them save the planet? The humans have so much drive, so much potential and creative power, so much passion to offer. They deserve a chance to fulfill that potential and find their place in the universe. You said it yourself. They are a young species. They can still learn. Surely the fae can help heal the damage already done." Even while Lillian's brain spat out the words, she knew they were said in desperation. How could she hope to convince Tethys when she hadn't even been able to sway Gregory, not really?

"You think the humans will just welcome the fae and their guidance? Humans hate anything different. They commit murder over religious differences and even something as trivial as skin of a different tone. How do you think they will treat the fae? Look to the past. They burned their own kind. No, I have wasted too much time waiting for humans to overcome their inherently flawed natures. If one cancerous branch of the evolutionary tree must be pruned out for the survival of the rest, so be it. And if I must lead by example, I shall. But I cannot take on all the billions of humans by myself. I will need allies. First among them will be you and your gargoyle."

"I don't think so." Lillian wished she had more of a plan. But more importantly, what had become of Gran and the unicorn? Aloud she said, "Besides, I have a problem with doing what I'm told. Just ask Gregory. I'm always going behind his back and getting into trouble. Oh hell. Maybe trouble just likes me. But for whatever reason, I've been forced to get myself out of a tight spot a time or two on my own. There's no way I'm going to just roll over and allow you to use us in your genocide."

Tethys gave what could only be called a long-suffering sigh. "I had hoped to reason with you and the gargoyle," she said and then tilted her head and frowned at Lillian. "Did you know you once saved my life, long ago before I mistakenly came to this Realm? I was much younger then, and arrogant in my youth. I'd thought myself strong enough to take on a Void Demon, a true demon from the age of darkness before there was light in the universe—not one of those weak half-breeds that call themselves the Riven. I misjudged the strength of the beast laired in a volcanic vent near my home territory. It was tainting everything near it with its evil. I hunted it to its lair and attempted to slay it. I managed to hurt it, but it did me greater injury, a mortal wound."

Lillian inclined her head when the siren hesitated.

"I thought I was going to die there at the mouth of the vent, surrounded by its evil, my soul forfeit, never to know peace. As a last act, I sent out a call to warn all my fellow sirens of the danger. A siren's power spikes just before death, and my call went out far beyond my ocean realm, out across the realm of magic in all directions. I never expected help to come. But you answered."

Tethys looked Lillian up and down. "The Sorceress, as you are supposed to be, not as you are now. You came, your power a vast light around you, chasing away the shadows, exposing the ocean floor and leaving the demon in the light. So blinded by the brightness, the creature didn't even see your Gargoyle Protector until he'd already cleaved the demon in two. While your gargoyle dispatched the taint and healed the living crea-tures around the vent, you cocooned me in your power and healed me. You made me far stronger than I was to begin with." The siren chuckled. "And you ordered me to ask for aid the next time I planned to battle a demon from the ancient times."

Lillian winced. *I made her stronger? That there was a dumbass thing to do.*

"What unfortunate judgment on the part of my older self," Lillian muttered and then realized the filter on her mouth had failed utterly. To be honest, she had been taken aback by Tethys' words. The siren had known the Sorceress, had actually shared something freely, which would have taken months to drag out of Gregory.

Lillian trusted him with her life; however, he had kept secrets from her in the past, and he rarely talked of what she was like as the Sorceress, or at least he never shared stories about their past lives.

But now wasn't the time to worry over their personal lives, not when there was an age-old siren talking of the extinction of the human race like she was chatting about wiping out a nest of termites.

The siren's gaze grew distant as if in thought for a moment before sharpening upon Lillian again. "I was surprised to find your hamadryad is the Sorceress at the moment. Did you know I tried reasoning with your tree before I attempted to put your gargoyle under my spell? But a dryad's tree, while intelligent after a fashion, doesn't think like either of us, and I couldn't make her understand the threat the humans represent. She knows good and evil, but she doesn't understand why complacency empowers evil. I suppose the nature of a hamadryad is not one of action."

"Never really thought about it."

"Your gargoyle, he and I had an interesting conversation while he slept. He loves the humans no more than I, but he loves you, and you somehow extorted a promise from him to allow the humans to continue as they are without intervention. With such a promise, you made him go against his very nature. He is a protector, a balancer, a destroyer of evil."

"I figured he had enough on his plate at the moment."

Tethys flexed her arms and lifted herself into a sitting position. "Beware, dryad, there is a greater danger than the Riven: you are changing your Gargoyle Protector, infecting him with your mortal weakness and your human-centric moral compass. You have also taught your gargoyle how to lie. He is an Avatar to the father of us all, and yet he has come close to breaking some of those vows for you. He yearns to love you as a mate."

Lillian narrowed her eyes, annoyance overriding fear for the first time in hours. "And what concern is it of yours?"

Tethys' laugh had a tone both beautiful and chilling at the same time. "It will be every sentient being's concern if you do not do something to curb your dire influence over your gargoyle. You say you won't allow me to use either of you, that I and my plans for humanity are evil. But it is you, and your weakness, which taints your gargoyle. If you continue as you are, you will give the Lady of Battles exactly what she wants."

Lillian's stomach cramped like she'd swallowed rocks. The siren's words were dreadful because they struck with note after note of truth.

Had she really forced Gregory to be other than he was supposed to be? And would he be punished for those changes she had inflicted on him? Gregory would never tell her.

Focus. Think of something else, she chanted in her mind. "I can't just stand by and allow you to murder all the humans the world over."

The siren laughed, a bright, clear sound. "They're doing a fine job themselves. I merely propose to help them along. And it need not be all of them, half would be enough to collapse their civilization. Their technology would fail, and they would be back to living off the land and sea within a generation."

"It's still mass murder."

The siren stared Lillian down like she was talking to a

child. "You're living in one of the planet's great death cycles. Only this time humans are the driving force behind it. Humans murder out of greed, desperation, and madness. Do humans not put down rabid animals? I'll merely be doing the same thing on a larger scale."

"What about the people trying to change? What about the innocent children who have no control over what their elders do?"

"Ah, you truly are young. Is this what remains of the Sorceress when all her knowledge and wisdom is stripped away? An innocent. I see why the Gargoyle Protector can't protect himself from you. You work great damage with your wholesome innocence." Tethys snorted. "A deadly temptation to a gargoyle. I'm surprised he hasn't given in and just had you. You wouldn't be able to resist him, even if you wanted to." The siren's lips turned up in a smile. "But you wouldn't really put up a fight."

Lillian's fingers tightened on her crossbow as she fought the urge to just take a shot and hope for the best.

Tethys sighed and made a soothing noise. "Don't get all confrontational, dryad. We both know I speak the truth."

"Your version," Lillian snapped.

"I don't lie. I never have. Sirens are always forthright with our words. Think about what I've said. We are not enemies. I can help free you and your gargoyle from the trap the Lady of Battles devised for you."

"We don't need the kind of help you're offering."

"Yes, your hamadryad is doing a fine job of killing the demon seed trapped within—it was very ingenious of the tree to remove it from you while she healed you. And I would judge the tree to be finished her work in another three or four months. But I doubt you and Gregory have the time. Either the Lady of Battles will send her minions, or you and Gregory will give in to the desire growing between you."

"I won't allow it to…"

Tethys cut her off with a slashing motion of one arm. "I can offer you another option. I am powerful enough to sing the demon seed to death. Then I can help you rejoin your hamadryad, and you can take back your soul and become the Sorceress as she was meant to be. Once you are whole, the Lady of Battles will be unable to withstand the two halves of the Avatar. You can take the battle to her and teach her it is unwise to pit oneself against the Avatars of the Divine Ones."

Oh, it sounded so tempting, Lillian thought, *but for one little detail.* "Is this the same deal you offered Gregory while he slept in stone? Since you're now pandering it to me, I take it your plan didn't go so well."

"No, it didn't have the outcome I'd hoped," the siren answered and laughed openly. "He said he might have said yes but for one detail."

Lillian arched an eyebrow and moved into range. "A rather large detail, I imagine. Well, more like 3.5 billion smaller details. I think that is about how many souls your help would send to the afterlife. I won't barter one soul to save myself; I certainly won't trade a few billion innocent human lives just so I can become the Sorceress again. No bloody deal."

She snapped the crossbow into position and loosed the bolt. It flew true, its trajectory level with the siren's upper body. With an impossible gesture too fast to follow, Tethys swatted the bolt, knocking it to the side where it embedded itself in the muddy bank. Lillian was already reloading it when the crossbow took up a subtle vibration in her hands. It lasted for all of three seconds, and then she was suddenly clenching empty air, gaping with sickening astonishment at where it had been.

"Ah," Tethys said, sounding as calm as a lazy summer morning, as if Lillian hadn't even attempted a shot, "That's what your gargoyle said you would say. Apparently he knows you better than you know him. But that doesn't change my goal. You've forced my hand. I had so hoped you would make this easy. I truly don't want to enslave your gargoyle. He is such a noble beast. So much better had it come from you."

Her heart pounding in her throat, Lillian glared at the siren. "If you could have enchanted Gregory, you already would have, and you wouldn't need me to give him any orders."

"True and false," Tethys said with a mysterious smile.

"And what does that mean?"

"Even though Gregory is male, I'd still have no chance at winning him over under normal circumstances, but we find ourselves in an unusual situation this day. He's still weakened from expelling large quantities of magic to produce weapons for the land-bound fae. It would be the perfect time to enchant him. Unfortunately, while he remains in stone, my power cannot touch him. So now he can heal and grow stronger, all while being impervious to my song. Once he is at full strength, he will awaken. At which point, it won't go well for me. If he lets me live, I imagine it will be locked away behind a powerful spell."

The siren pointed to the maze's northern exit, and then pushed herself backward until her lower half was below the water line. "Lucky for me, Fate has opened another path for me to choose."

Lillian jerked around as she caught an unpleasant odor. Something unwholesome was coming. She could sense it deep down in the soles of her feet. The forest around her gave warning, the trees aware of an evil passing through their domain. She took a step back, the unconscious move drawing Tethys' attention away from Gregory and back to her.

"Young dryad, stay. There is something I want to show you." There was a commotion at the north entrance of the maze, accompanied by much growling and snarling as a tall, humanoid figure was shoved forward at sword-point. The unidentified person dropped down into a defensive crouch. Three fae followed close at his heels, hemming him in and directing his momentum.

Lillian snarled in recognition, and two-inch black claws emerged from the tips of her fingers.

The Riven answered her in kind, its snarl harsh on her ears.

CHAPTER TWENTY-FOUR

While she was less than happy to see one of them here in her grove, she held her position—not truly afraid of one lone Riven. If she had to, she could fight it in her gargoyle form. That nature simmered just below the surface, demanding she answer the challenge, eager to dispatch the Riven sullying her grove. Instead of forcing the dominant bloodline back, she held it in check, ready if she needed it, but stopped short of a full shift, which might neutralize her grandmother's spell. That spell might be her last chance of escaping the siren.

Lillian narrowed her eyes, every sense homing in on the Riven. Actually, the beast hemorrhaged a black ooze from a dozen wounds. It looked like it might expire in front of her at any moment.

"Why," Lillian pointed at the offending creature occupying her grove, "is that Gods' blighted beast here? One alone is no threat to Gregory or me. If this is what you wanted me to see, I'm sorry to disappoint, but I'm already intimately acquainted with the murdering, soul-stealing little monsters. I doubt you can show me anything new about them."

"No, but I did find this one and many others on the edge of your territory. As a favor to you and the local fae, I killed all but this one."

"How nice of you." Lilian's voice dripped with sarcasm, but she was already inching closer to where Gregory slept.

At some point during the conversation, the Riven had turned his attention squarely upon the siren. If anything, the Riven looked more distraught and sank lower into its fighting crouch, fangs gleaming, and claws extended in extreme threat.

"I left this one alive because I thought to use it as evidence in case you didn't believe me about the secondary threat, but then I decided on a better use for the creature." Tethys gestured for the three fae to herd the Riven closer.

Lillian focused on keeping her breath and heart rate slow and even, but she allowed her claws to grow another half-inch. Darting her eyes between the Riven and the enchanted ward stones ringing Gregory in a protective circle, she briefly debated ending the Riven before he reached the stone circle or allowing him to fry himself on the protective wards.

In the end, she decided to leave him to be incinerated on the wards, less tainted blood to contaminate her grove that way.

One of the sword-carrying sidhe made a jab at the Riven. With a desperate contortion of his body, the Riven avoided being impaled and leaped back another dozen steps to land two feet inside the ward stone circle. A second later, Lillian realized the wards hadn't activated, not so much as a spark of magic flickered along their lengths.

Tethys had nullified the protection on the stones.

Her heart starting to pound with the sudden rise of adrenaline, Lillian glanced at Gregory.

What other protective spells had the siren neutralized?

The Riven seemed to think along the same lines, for with one last, disbelieving look at the stone circle, he turned his hate-filled eyes toward the sleeping gargoyle.

No! Tethys planned to use the Riven to force Gregory to defend himself.

Lillian snarled her own challenge and bolted toward the Riven, every logical thought forced aside, only the need to protect her soulmate remained.

She shifted while still in the air, her wings stretching out, carrying her across the distance. She snatched at the Riven, but the creature twisted away from her claws.

With a flash of silver in the shadows, he summoned a demon blade and came at her.

Lillian arched away from the blade. Remembering what one had done to Gregory gave her a healthy respect for the thrice-cursed things. Using her powerful tail as a weapon, she swiped at the Riven's legs, forcing it to jump into the air. She nearly speared him on her talons while he was distracted.

He twisted impossibly fast a second time and darted under a low-hanging branch behind the tree. Growling in rage, Lillian gave chase. A sudden, burning pain sliced across her back, just below where her wings attached. Yowling in fury, she spun, slashing out defensively at an enemy who wasn't there.

A second slice seared across her side, blood welling from a shallow wound that hadn't been there seconds ago.

She smelled the strong odor of sap mixing with the coppery stink of her blood and knew in a moment of lucidity, the Riven was attacking her tree, stabbing and slashing at her hamadryad in a vain attempt to kill her.

Lillian howled out her wrath again. A second, much deeper roar answered her call. It came from behind, and suddenly Gregory was racing past her to circle the tree.

The Riven burst out from behind the trunk, Gregory on its tail and closing fast. The Riven put on a burst of speed, leaping straight toward Lillian with its demon blade extended before it.

Gregory lashed out with a blast of bone-chilling power, catching the Riven in the back. The demon's momentum continued to carry it toward Lillian even as Gregory's magic burned along the length of its body.

Lillian sidestepped and lashed out at the beast. Her talons severed its head from its shoulders as it careened past. For good measure, Gregory leaped onto the corpse and blasted it with a second wave of magic.

With a hiss and final crackle, the Riven's body burned to ash, and then ash swirled into a fog-like smoke until even it was gone.

Gregory raked the ground with his talons, then drew a deep breath and coughed it back out in an enraged snort. He took two steps toward Lillian, his muzzle pointed slightly upward, and his lips pulled back to inhale another deep breath. She dropped to all fours and padded over to him, both to allow him to inspect her wounds and so she could check for any he might have gathered.

They were mere feet apart when a beautiful and eerie song filled the glade. Gregory twitched an ear in the direction of the song. Then he turned his entire head and neck, taking a half-step away from her.

Her own ears swung forward, seeking the source of the sound. Her body was just starting to mimic Gregory's actions when a high-pitched snap echoed in her ears, piercing deep with a sudden agony, and then all the world went silent.

Bereft without the beautiful song, she whined and pawed at her ears, hoping to unblock them, but her hands came back covered in a few traces of blood. She snarled again, thinking this was more of the Riven's work.

But there was something she wasn't remembering.

Something about that beautiful song.

Something dangerous.

Gran had told her about a spell and a song.

Then the web of an enchantment fell away, and everything came rushing back.

She shook herself then stretched, surprised to find herself resting on the ground.

In a sudden panic, Lillian bolted to her feet and searched for Gregory. She found him halfway between her and the siren.

He was crouched, his tail flicking in what she first took as annoyance. She changed her mind after she noticed his long ears flicking toward the siren, and then back in Lillian's direction. Every so often, Gregory would glance at her, his expression vague and uncertain as if he was undecided what he was supposed to do.

At the bank of the stream, Tethys waited, still half out of the water, her tail lazily splashing water over her body as she sang. For the moment, Lillian couldn't hear the song. She'd been lucky her shift to gargoyle form hadn't neutralized Gran's spell, but she didn't know how much longer her luck would last. If she had any hope of helping Gregory, she had to do something now, before her gargoyle blood healed her ruptured eardrums.

A quick glance down at one of her Riven-inflicted injuries confirmed it had already stopped bleeding. Her hamadryad was much stronger from the periodic feedings of Gregory's blood. What she'd normally consider a benefit was, in this instance, an unfortunate side effect. She couldn't assume the healing powers would wait to heal her ears until all the other wounds were healed. For all she knew, her injuries might all be healing at the same rate.

She glanced between Gregory and Tethys.

There was no way she could remove Gregory from the siren's influence—he weighed too much, and he seemed disinclined to move from the spot anyway. She turned her attention back to the siren. Was it possible to eliminate her?

By their very natures, gargoyles were immune to many forms of magical attack. Perhaps her gargoyle body could overcome the siren's defensive magic where her magic-enhanced crossbow had failed.

Lillian leaped into motion, sending a silent prayer that what she did ranked as bravery, not stupidity.

The distance between Lillian and her prey halved. Her talons extended to their full length and her jaws parted in preparation to savage the siren's throat. *Let's see if the bitch can sing without vocal cords.*

Shadows shifted, and suddenly Gregory was piling side-long into her, his greater bulk and massive wingspan carrying them sideways several feet until they both slammed into the base of his stone pedestal.

She took two swipes of his tongue to her face before it occurred that it wasn't an attack on his part. Lillian tried to extract herself from their tangle of arms, wings, legs, and tails. But no matter how hard she tried, it was like pushing against a mountain.

Gregory continued to growl happily as he gave her gentle nips and licks on her exposed skin.

Lillian fought against Gregory's overly happy greeting as it dawned on her that no song the siren sang could ever make him harm her. In fact, Tethys might not actually be able to force a person to do something outside of their innate character. Rather like a hypnotist, maybe her power only allowed her to influence what was already part of a person's makeup.

When Tethys dialed up Gregory's affectionate nature, he became as boisterous as a six-month-old puppy—if ever a puppy weighed in at half a ton.

She forced her head to the side so she could study the siren. Her adversary was still half out of the water, seemingly in no hurry for Gregory to bring her his prize. But then, maybe Tethys couldn't force anyone as powerful as Gregory to do anything he didn't want to do.

That's how the siren will use him, Lillian thought with growing panic. *All Tethys need do is command him to protect his 'Sorceress' against the threat the humans represent. And he would.*

Hell!

She needed to escape, buy herself some time to think and strategize. There had to be a way to shatter the siren's influence on Gregory.

Lillian glanced at the surrounding forest.

Maybe she could escape and lead Gregory deeper into the woods? If she got him away from the siren's immediate vicinity, then he might shake off Tethys' influence.

Lillian forced herself to relax, realizing fighting with

Gregory was getting her nowhere. She lay still while he cleaned her Riven-inflicted wounds, but her mind was far from idle, and she formed the basis of a plan.

He'd loosened his hold marginally as he worked his way lower. When she shifted her weight enough to free one arm, he tensed. Lillian followed through with the motion anyway, pretending his mane had been her destination all along. Once her fingers were buried in his thick mane, she started to groom the few tangles loose.

Gregory's death grip eased enough to allow her to shift positions so she could better reach his mane. As she reciprocated his grooming, her tongue lapped at his skin. After a moment she scraped her teeth over where her tongue had been.

Gregory rumbled in appreciation, shifting his body enough to reach the soft, delicate skin of her throat.

Leaning forward, she nuzzled him in a heartfelt apology and then brought to bear a palm-sized river stone from where it lined the border between the manicured grass and the stream's edge.

The impact against the side of Gregory's head made a dull thud, which turned her stomach. He keeled over sideways with a little push from her, but he caught himself on his arms and braced himself as he shook his head.

Lillian lunged away.

Her leap landed her a good ten feet from where she'd started. She didn't slow or look behind like instinct clamored for her to do. The knowledge that Gregory would follow was equally instinctive.

He had always been her Hunting Shadow. It didn't matter

what spells or enchantments might have been cast, he would always follow.

She might not know what had befallen Gran and the unicorn, but once she freed Gregory from the siren's influence, they would return together to face Tethys and learn the fate of their friends.

Her earlier despair easing, she raced into the depths of her maze with a lighter heart.

CHAPTER TWENTY-FIVE

Lillian made it clear of her maze and quickly left the gardens far behind as she made her way deeper into the forest. The darkness under the trees didn't hinder her gargoyle eyesight. She barely slackened her pace. The only times she slowed was to maneuver around patches of underbrush too thick to go straight through. Occasionally, she was forced to leap over a group of sleeping fae or human soldiers.

She didn't have a destination in mind, as her plan didn't go much beyond running for her life and hoping Gregory followed. Once they were far enough away, she held a small, admittedly naïve, hope he might shake off the siren's spell if he wasn't within range of her song.

Part one of her plan had worked far better than she'd ever dared hope. Her hearing was mostly recovered, and she had only to twitch an ear to her back trail to easily hear Gregory following even over the whistle of the wind in her ears. He wasn't bothering to be subtle, which also told her he was still firmly under the siren's sway. Had Gregory been in sole command of his wits, he'd never have made so much noise.

Refusing to be disappointed, she continued doggedly northward, her gargoyle body not even winded after running for the better part of an hour.

It had to be after midnight now. Four hours of running had worn away her earlier exuberance, but still, she ran. Her muscles burned, and her strides grew shorter even as she ordered her body to run faster. As if sensing victory, Gregory put on a burst of speed until his nose was even with the tip of her tail. She could feel the heat of his breath.

One lunge would spell disaster. She had no doubt if he caught her this time, he would take her back to the siren, and she wouldn't get a second chance at escape. Jumping over a fallen tree, she used the momentary cover it provided to veer sharply to the left.

Gregory leaped over the trunk and changed course in the air, flapping his wings and shooting ahead of her to drop down almost directly in her path.

She dropped to the ground, kicking up a wave of loam and leaf litter in front of her and then kept rolling, right under Gregory's outstretched arms. She felt his fingers graze her hip as she slid by. But then she was off and running again.

Blood surging in her veins, she wanted to shout that she was still free.

For the moment.

But she didn't fool herself into thinking there would be many more moments of freedom. Her body was tiring, it was only a matter of time before it failed her. She was fast running out of options.

Gregory showed no signs of returning to himself, and she had no other tricks up her sleeve.

There was only the medallion bumping against her breast as she ran. Gran had given it to her, and Lillian had never doubted her grandmother's wisdom before, but as she ran and mulled over who else there was to offer aid, her mind kept going to one logical conclusion no matter how her heart shied away from the answer.

Gran had given her the medallion, knowing what could happen. But did she dare to use it?

Was Tethys worse than what aid the medallion might bring?

Lillian feared she was, but also feared Gregory would not agree.

But presently, he was a mindless tool of the siren's making, and Lillian wasn't feeling too confident in allowing the siren to continue unchecked.

Oh please, let this work and not backfire in my face.

With a prayer, she skidded to a halt and brought one talon to her palm and sliced a small line in the fleshy base of her thumb. Three beads of blood welled up as she hastily smeared it across the medallion's surface.

She half-expected the medallion to absorb the blood, or for the metal to flare up with bright fire in her hand. Even a slight glow? Something to show the magic worked.

A whole lot of bloody nothing was what she got for her trouble.

Useless medallion and overrated magic.

Was she doing something wrong?

A full body-bruising weight slammed into Lillian's back. It drove her to her knees and then flat to the ground with her muzzle half-buried in the forest loam. Breath rushed out of her lungs in a pained whoosh. She grunted and dragged in a new breath of air; it hurt worse going in than it had coming out.

Jolly.

Her mane covered her eyes so she couldn't see a thing, but she did feel an earthworm wiggling between two front teeth.

She snarled and spat, trying and failing to get her limbs back under her so she could leverage the dead weight from her back.

A rumbling purr was the only response to her struggles.

"Gregory, get off me."

A warm, wet tongue stroked a path between the joints of her wings. She debated boxing his ears with them but decided he might take it as an invitation to play. Another happy rumble emanated from just behind her head. She supposed she should be glad it wasn't one of the darker sides of his personality dominating him at the moment.

A half-ton of happy, wiggly Gregory seemed a whole lot less dangerous than an eight-foot-tall, winged killing machine.

"Mmm, Gregory, I love you, but get your big ass off me before you break some part of me I'm really fond of, like my spine."

With one last lick, Gregory shifted his weight.

Well, well, he actually listened, she noted with growing interest. *What other commands might he obey?*

With an over-exaggerated slowness, she got up and brushed off the specks of loam and leaf mold covering her body. Her stalling tactic gave her a moment to think. A quick glance down confirmed the medallion still hadn't reacted to her blood in any discernible way.

She was out of options, but at least she'd managed to lure Gregory away from the siren. Frowning, she rolled her eyes in his direction where he quivered at attention like a dog at point, his barely contained exuberance palpable in the air around him.

Lillian amended her earlier thought. She'd managed to extract him physically, but in spirit, the Gregory she knew was still missing, buried under layers of enchantment.

It seemed fundamentally wrong that someone as powerful as her protector could be compromised so quickly and thoroughly by a song.

"Oh Gregory, I know you're still in there somewhere. I hope you can hear me and understand. I'm not sure how I'm going to free you from that over-evolved fish, but I will."

She'd stick with her earlier plan to try and keep him away from the siren as long as possible. Her mad run had bought them a little time. It would take them a good four hours to run back the way they'd come, longer if they walked.

He approached her slowly. Once he reached her, he leaned into her, looking for a scratch.

Then before she knew what he was doing, he scooped her up. Her world tilted until everything was upside-down. One of his steel-like arms clamped across her thighs, preventing her from kicking free. Simultaneously, his mobile tail curled around her shoulders, pinning her wings to her back before she'd thought to use them in some way to leverage herself free.

She was working herself up to deliver a solid bite to

Gregory's vulnerable side when she felt the coldly familiar chill of his magic flowing across her skin.

From her inverted vantage point, she could only peer around Gregory's muscular hip to see him weaving magic. It rose up out of the ground, pale and ethereal, for all the world looking like a thick fog. It spiraled around two tree trunks, climbing them until the silvery haze was above head height and then the two spires shot delicate filaments toward each other, forming a web before Lillian's bewildered eyes.

"Gregory, what is that? What are you doing?"

No answer, though he did pat the back of her leg, which may have been an attempt at reassurance.

"Gregory," Lillian called softly, then changed tactics. "Durnathyne, My Hunting Shadow. You don't have to do this. You don't have to listen to Tethys."

Lillian hoped calling him by his name from his last life would jog some rationality back into his head. He did pause his spell-work and twisted his neck to meet her gaze at the awkward angle, and Lillian's heart jumped with hope, but then he shook his head with a snort and returned to his spell.

Following the direction of his gaze, she saw the spell was now a vaguely door-shaped object. Her fears were confirmed a moment later as the entire construction flashed a blinding white. Still blinking grey spots from her vision, her other senses came to the fore to fill in the details.

The scent of cedar reached her nose. More telling, though, was the distinctive fragrance of tropical water lilies Gran had planted in the small stream that flowed past Lillian's hamadryad.

Her vision cleared, confirming what her nose and ears had already told her.

Gregory's spell was some kind of doorway, and on the other side, the siren waited patiently.

"Don't do this. Tethys is dangerous."

"Yes."

Lillian was surprised Gregory answered her.

"But not to us," he continued as he walked toward the strange, spell-woven door hovering in the air. "She has offered to help us fight our enemies. She will stand with us against the Lady of Battles."

"She lies to gain control over your power."

Gregory sighed and then shifted her off his shoulder and set her down, so she was facing him, her back to the flickering door.

"I have always been able to detect lies. The siren has spoken only the truth to me. She will aid your hamadryad in destroying the demon seed within it, and then you will be free to take up the mantle of Mother's Sorceress once more. All will be as it should."

It was the same promise the siren had given Lillian, and perhaps there wasn't a lie in the offer. And it was the one thing in all the Realms which would tempt Gregory.

He placed his hands on her shoulders and guided her toward the doorway. If it came to a contest of physical or magical strength, Gregory would win.

That only left her with cold, logical reason. "Please listen. I know what she offers is what we ultimately want, but why did you wait to agree until after you awoke from stone? By what she told me, you had already turned down her offer while you still rested in stone. Why was that? What was it about her offer that gave you pause? It's important."

Gregory halted his advance toward the doorway, a frown

line forming between his brows and his ears swung forward in question.

She met his gaze and saw a hint of the old Gregory there. He blinked.

"Gregory, bring your beloved to me where she will be safe from the Riven." The siren's voice floated through the doorway and slid across Lillian's senses like a mother's soothing caress. Her earlier worries seemed unimportant.

Distantly, with only a mild concern, she saw lines of power crawl across Gregory's skin.

He snarled. "I am not yours to command, siren."

His angry words slid past the warmth cocooning Lillian, and she blinked as if waking from sleep.

What? Lillian gave herself a shake.

Gregory. The siren.

It dawned on Lillian the siren had released her to turn her full powers back upon Gregory.

Tethys began to sing, and Lillian felt herself going under a second time even though this enchantment wasn't focused on her. Cold power shimmered along Gregory's skin as he summoned defensive magic. His skin took on the rough seeming of stone.

Tethys sang, and runes blazed to life along his skin, preventing him from resuming his stone form.

Gregory roared in anger and pain, lashing out with magic. The wave of magic was unfocused and shot over the siren's head, though she did hunch lower in the water.

The wave continued past the siren to shear through one wall of the cedar maze. Its momentum carried the magic, and its destructive force, beyond Lillian's field of view.

Having expended so much power in one shot further

weakened Gregory, and he slumped down onto his knees, panting with his head bowed.

Desperately wanting to help, Lillian crouched next to him and flared her wings, mantling them around Gregory in a vain attempt to shield him from the siren's song.

But of course, her action did nothing to prevent Gregory's enslavement.

Helpless to do anything, Lillian could only watch in despair as he fell under Tethys' song a second time.

Her gut tightened. This was a mild version of what the Lady of Battles wanted to do to them. Maybe Tethys would be the kinder mistress. The warm fog was back—soothing, coercing.

"Lillian," a voice called from behind her, the words dark and rich, the tone deep and beautiful. So like Gregory's voice, and yet not.

Swaying, Lillian found herself hovering at the threshold of the magic doorway, Gregory at her side. She didn't even remember standing up, but she was at the doorway, ready to take the last few steps to accept the siren's offer.

Curiosity flared briefly but died as the siren's song swelled to match the dark beauty of the second voice.

"Lillian! I did not sire you so you could become a slave."

CHAPTER TWENTY-SIX

The medallion around Lillian's neck heated to the point of pain, and then a wave of scorching magic raced across her skin. Suddenly, she was herself again, Tethys' voice weaving nothing more than a beautiful song. Shadows to her left shivered, and a gargoyle similar in build to Gregory appeared before her startled eyes.

With a gasp, Lillian stepped away from both the doorway and the newcomer. Her hurried backpedaling nearly had her running over a smaller body behind her.

The delicate female sidestepped in time.

Lillian whirled to face this second newcomer while she tried to determine if there were others with these two, or if they had come alone.

That they were a threat was all too certain.

She'd seen the petite, dark-haired woman and the tall, muscular gargoyle once before. That time it had been at a distance when Gregory had first discovered the demon seed within her and had tried to dig it out with less than favorable results. That day Lillian had only a glimpse of the dryad and gargoyle standing before her now. They had been a part of the first eight years of her life, a time that was nothing more than a blank void except for a few details filled in by others and what she had uncovered. But she knew them on a visceral level, nonetheless.

Her birth parents.

The amulet Gran had given her and the cryptic message now made sense.

It all did—why Gran had been reluctant to give it to her, and the command to use it as a last resort.

Well, this was as last resort as it got. She needed to know one thing first, however, and she modulated her voice to be heard over Tethys' song, which she noted seemed not to affect her at all now that the medallion was hot to the touch. Lillian's parents seemed similarly immune. Handy trick that.

"If you come only on the Battle Goddess's order, then leave me to my fate." Her voice came out strong, almost like she was in command of the situation, though her words were false bravado. She couldn't detect lies as well as Gregory. And even *he* might have trouble judging her parents. If they had been double-crossing the Lady of Battles for the better part of twenty years, they were masters at twisting the truth.

"We knew we could never sit by and allow the Lady of Battles to destroy you." Lillian's mother spoke for both parents.

A loud growl crested above the siren's song.

Gregory and his usual timing. Crap.

She jerked her gaze back toward him in time to see him launch himself at her father. Her mother danced nimbly out of the way and dragged Lillian stumbling along behind as both males rolled past in a biting, snarling ball of winged fury.

"Do you accept our offer of aid, daughter?" her dryad mother asked as she calmly watched the two males continue to inflict damage on each other. "We are running out of time."

Lillian started toward the two, concern driving her forward even when she knew she wasn't ready for a fight in gargoyle form, not like the one she was witnessing. The two fighters would break apart, then, with lightning-fast moves, come together again in a fury of slashing, biting, and lethal kicking. Even their tails and wings were weapons. Both fighters already had an alarming number of bloody welts, bites, and slashes covering their skin.

"Do something. They are going to kill each other."

"Kill each other? Perhaps. But not for days. They're both hard-headed gargoyles and at the moment, fairly well-matched." The dryad made a gesture to the two males. "Normally, your other half could finish your father with ease, but Gregory has had a hard time of it in this cursed Realm, yes?"

The heat from the medallion increased, forcing Lillian to clasp its chain and hold it away from her skin.

"Ah, yes." Her mother nodded at the medallion and then inclined her head in the direction of the siren. "There lays the true danger. The medallions are reaching the limit of their ability to protect us."

At her words, Lillian noticed her mother was also wearing one of the medallions. Had her father been wearing one?

More importantly, could one help Gregory?

"Time to exchange greetings with the siren," her mother said and motioned Lillian forward, back toward the door in the air. When they were almost to the threshold, her mother pulled ahead and gave a formal bow, like something from a long-ago court, or two martial artists facing each other. Her skirts swirled around her, made of some glorious burgundy and black fabric.

Lillian blinked, then a second time to be certain, but yes, her mother had just plucked a bit of black off the skirt.

As she straightened, she spun the bit of glassy, black shadow in her fingers, readjusting her hold on the shard and then flinging it almost faster than Lillian's gargoyle-enhanced vision could track. The bit of black—a tiny little throwing knife made from shadow magic—she realized, flew through the air. Unwaveringly, it hit its mark and buried itself inches deep in Tethys' throat.

Her song cut off mid-note as she gagged on blood and the solid bit of blackness lodged in her vocal cords. Clawing at the knife, the siren bent over and retched blood as she dug it out.

"That will not slow her for long," her mother said as she dragged Lillian away from the doorway. Seconds later, a blast of power streaked through the magic construction, lashing out at the empty space they'd stood in only a moment ago.

"Now!" her mother shouted.

Another gargoyle emerged from the shadows near where Gregory still fought with her father. Instinctively, she drew breath to call a warning to Gregory, but her father sprang away before she could, his momentum carrying him in front of the doorway. Gregory followed close on his tail.

And the third gargoyle struck with a blast of magic. It slammed into Gregory and tossed him right through the doorway and halfway to where the siren still thrashed in the stream. Gregory rolled, his arms, wings, and tail all trying to slow his momentum; however, it was one of the stone rings circling her glade that finally stopped him. Lillian winced at the impact that shattered stone.

Looking beyond Gregory to where Tethys struggled, Lillian saw her lips moving, but only blood came out. Oh, she would have been screaming orders to her other slaves, but without her voice to command them, the other fae stood waiting, blank as sleepwalkers.

Concern for Gregory drew her eyes back to his hunched form. He remained still for several moments, and Lillian's traitorous feet were already moving her toward him.

With a grunt and a shake, he righted himself and then bolted back into motion.

Lillian's mother flicked more of the black shards, but her aim wasn't for Gregory. They collided with the magic doorway, sinking deep into its border. She continued to throw more shards into the weaving until it bristled with them. Then with a high-pitched whine, the magic holding the threshold open collapsed, taking the door and its view of the center of the maze with it.

Gregory vanished still on the other side, trapped there with the siren. Lillian felt hollow inside. She'd allowed her parents to betray him.

She'd betrayed Gregory, her protector, the other half of her soul.

Unaware of Lillian's inner turmoil, her mother brushed her hands clean of residual magic and turned to Lillian. "We must strategize how to capture and hold your gargoyle long enough to free him from the siren's power, but we need to move first before Gregory returns. It will not take him long to build another portal to this place, even weakened as he is. He will be desperate to find you."

"I haven't yet decided whether you're any better than Tethys. It seems everyone wants to use us, or own us, or possess us." Lillian left unsaid the uncharitable thought that that seemed the natural order of things for avatars of the gods. She and Gregory were, in fact, tools owned by the Divine Ones. Gregory might word it slightly differently without a hint of censure, but he'd never tried to hide the fact either. "I'll listen to you, but I make no promises. If you so much as try to force my hand, I'll take my chances with Tethys."

Lillian's father approached, a great dark shadow, but lacking the comfort of Gregory's presence. This gargoyle, father though he might be to her, was a stranger. Thus, a suspect until proven an ally.

Her father's body language was all open curiosity, and she was certain he wanted to come closer for a hug, or maybe a sniff? She hadn't a clue how family relations might work among gargoyles.

The third newcomer, another male gargoyle, sidled up on her right side. Feeling suddenly hemmed in, she shifted her weight, wings spreading for balance and talons coming up.

Her parents both stepped back.

"Lillian, easy, don't hurt him," her mother pleaded softly.

Lillian blinked at her. Don't hurt him?

He was as big as she was, which did put him slightly shorter than either Gregory or her father. And the newcomer was slim, less bulky, his gait somewhat awkward, almost coltish in his movements.

He continued to approach her position, looking for all the world like he was vibrating with excitement.

"Lillian, meet your brother." Her father's tone made it sound like she should already know that detail but uttered it aloud for clarification's sake.

"My brother?" Lillian's mind blanked and kept trying to visualize her older, human brother Jason.

"He's newly emerged from my hamadryad," Lillian's mother said with a touch of pride. "He came early, sensing our distress at your situation. As soon as your grandmother gave you the medallion, we were able to sense the danger to you and your gargoyle. We came as soon as Shadowlight was mobile.

"Brother?" Lillian croaked, still hung up on the fact she had a younger brother. He'd just emerged—by that, her mother meant born. Her little brother had just been born and had already come to help her battle Tethys?

Lillian drew a calming breath. So far, she'd say her family had risked more for her than she'd ever risked for them. The image of Gregory and her father fighting flashed across her closed eyelids. There was no way she wanted Gregory and her little brother to meet, not until her other half was in full possession of himself again. She opened her eyes and speared her mother with her gaze. "I want to hear more, but not here. You're correct. Gregory is going to come storming back any moment."

Lillian's mother nodded and then gestured to where her father was standing next to another portal doorway, one like Gregory had created. Only this one opened onto a night-shadowed meadow, the darker bulk of trees marking the boundaries.

She could well be looking at a very pretty trap. Then again, her parents were presently the only hope she had of freeing Gregory from Tethys's spell. And if they were still serving the Lady of Battles, well then, they had even less reason to want Gregory entrapped by another. Lillian would use them to help her free Gregory, and if they planned to in turn betray her to the Battle Goddess, she would just double cross them first.

A touch of guilt was followed by a strong, protective instinct. It warmed her heart as she looked upon her younger brother. All she saw was innocence and determination in his gaze.

Him she would protect and give Gran another grandchild to mother if Lillian's own parents proved deceitful.

Decision made, she met her little brother's gaze and held her hands out to him. He clasped them eagerly.

"Come," she said with a gentle squeeze of her fingers, "I want to get to know you. My grandmother, the human woman who raised me," Lillian clarified for him when his ears flicked forward in question, "named me Lillian. I heard our mother call you Shadowlight, correct?"

"Yes." His voice was deep and rusty with disuse, or maybe it was more that he was just learning to use his voice for the first time.

They walked through the doorway and into the tall grasses of the meadow. The moon was still climbing the sky, but its nearly full brilliance bathed the field in light bright enough she could make out the fluffy seed heads swaying in the wind.

"Do you know why you're here, Shadowlight?"

"Our parents hope to make this Realm home for a little while. At least until it is safe to return to the Magic Realm."

In other words, until she and Gregory taught the Lady of Battles a lesson not soon to be forgotten, and it was safe for everyone to return.

Ah, the clarity of innocence.

And her little brother, no matter what nasty surprise the Battle Goddess might have planted within him, was innocent of any wrongdoing on his part. It wasn't his fault he'd been born into a situation beyond his control.

And just like that, Shadowlight became one of the things she would protect.

It didn't matter that she hadn't known him this time yesterday. She knew he existed now, and he was a part of her family.

More than happy by his older sister's acceptance, Shadowlight proceeded to sniff every inch of her mane. Then he moved to her face where he started in with big, sloppy gargoyle kisses, which must be a species quirk and not just some inherent Gregory-ism.

After a few moments of mutual washing, Lillian pushed Shadowlight's questing muzzle away. "I need to talk with our parents for a few minutes."

He bobbed his head in that seemingly universal sign of understanding, then wandered off to go chase the fireflies randomly blinking around the meadow.

He looked so terribly young.

But just how young?

From Gregory's and the other dryads' explanations, she knew a gargoyle child was usually gestated in the hamadryad tree until he was ten years of age, at which point the tree would go into labor and birth the fully-grown gargoyle.

Even as ten-year-olds, gargoyles were deadly to evil.

Gregory had come to her rescue when they were both only eight, choosing to be born two years early so he could free her from the Battle Goddess's domain.

Gregory had finished maturing while he'd slept in stone here on earth. She knew Gregory had faced and killed many dangers to extract her from the lady's domain, but he was an Avatar. That powerful magic already his to control, even at the tender age of eight, and he'd had the added benefit of many lifetimes of knowledge to call upon.

And yet her brother had none of that, and still, he'd come to her rescue.

It told her something she'd always suspected about the loyalty and bravery of gargoyles.

It also explained her own well-developed, protective instincts. Those, too, must be a species characteristic.

"Tell me how we can overcome Tethys' enchantment," Lillian paused, her voice shaking slightly, "but first tell me your names because they were stripped from me shortly after I arrived here. And I very much want to know my parents."

Her gargoyle father was the first to step up, and he gave her a huge embrace, lifting her a few inches off the ground.

Lillian held back a sob, only now realizing how much of an emotional void there was from not knowing her parents.

When he put her down, he stepped back and looked her in the eye and said, "I am Stalks the Darkness."

After a moment, she cleared her throat and scrubbed away the tears on her forearm. "Do you mind if I call you Darkness?

"Darkness," her father rumbled, "suits me well enough."

Her mother came forward and placed her hands on Lillian's shoulders and then bowed until their foreheads pressed together briefly. She said something in a language Lillian didn't have a hope of following, but she assumed the alien mouthful was her mother's real name.

Perhaps seeing her daughter's expression, she clarified, "In your human tongue, I would be called Born at the Mountain's Foot Where the River Runs Cold."

Lillian mulled that name over for a moment. "Do you mind if I call you River?"

Her mother smiled softly. "Darkness and Shadowlight call me that. You are welcome to as well."

"Thank you."

Her mother reached one delicate hand out to Lillian's nearest horn in wonder. "I don't care that it was through the Lady's manipulation, but you make a most beautiful gargoyle. Such a strong, brave young woman would make any mother proud, but I am doubly so because I know what you had to overcome."

"Thank you," Lillian whispered. "I would like to know more about my family, but Gregory can track me anywhere."

Her father made a deep huffing sound. "He wouldn't be much of a protector if he couldn't." She thought she detected a hint of reproach as if he thought Gregory hadn't been doing a very good job.

Overprotective gargoyles, she muttered into the sanctity of her own mind before she fully realized she was one of those overly protective gargoyles.

"You said you had a plan to help me free Gregory."

It was her father, Darkness, who answered her. "When Gregory comes to find you, we will already have in place several wards in this meadow to prevent him from building one of the portals that would allow him to return you quickly to the siren. His instincts will tell him to get you away from anything he perceives as dangerous—us being the greatest concern.

"But we will not be here when he comes." Darkness smiled, giving her one of those toothy gargoyle grins that gave anyone who saw one pause. "There will only be you waiting for him. In no distress whatsoever. He'll likely check you over for traps, spells, or injuries. That will be the chance you'll need to follow through with our plan."

River broke in. "You will not like the next part, but it must be done. It's the only way to break the siren's spell while she still lives. And with Gregory and the other fae to protect her, killing her will be far more difficult and risky than freeing your gargoyle our way."

"Your mother speaks the truth." Her father nodded to Lillian, and then gestured to his mate. "Show her."

From around her hips, River removed a great belt—or girdle as they were called long ago—Lillian didn't know what else to call the gem-encrusted band. She wasn't up on her medieval fantasy fashions.

When her mother handed the ornament to her father, and he demonstrated how it would go around a gargoyle's neck, the item went from lavish fashion accessory to slave collar in the blink of an eye.

CHAPTER TWENTY-SEVEN

"*N*o," Lillian uttered the word before her brain had fully registered her intent. "No fucking way."

They watched her, their expressions unreadable.

"Most definitely not. I'll just go serve Tethys, doubtlessly she's the better master."

"You don't mean it, not really," her mother countered, "not when you have the means to free Gregory after you've broken the siren's spell."

"You're saying it's as easy as putting that thing around Gregory's neck, breaking the siren's spell, and then taking it back off again? I'm not that gullible."

"Easy?" Her father chuckled. "I imagine it will be anything but easy to get the ward stone collar on your Gargoyle Protector."

"There is a matching collar which controls this one." Lillian's mother gestured to Shadowlight, and he came galloping over. She held her hand out to him. There was a shifting of shadows around his neck as River unclasped something, and then the matching collar became visible in her hand. "Thank you for carrying this for me, love." Shadowlight kissed her and then darted off to return to his firefly hunting. "Stalks the Darkness is forbidden to carry such a thing from the Lady's realm; however Shadowlight was not there long enough to have such restrictions placed on him yet. And I could only hide the one on my person without the proximity causing them to become reactive." Her mother held out the control collar.

Lillian shook her head and stepped back. River continued to hold it out. Eventually, with a deep sigh of displeasure, Lillian took it because she wanted to see how much a person's freedom weighed.

It was surprisingly light and so very delicate for something so evil.

"I can't betray Gregory like this—I'm sorry, but what are my reassurances that this thing won't just turn Gregory over to the Lady of Battles?"

"You have our word, which likely means little to you, but we are telling the truth." The dryad sighed, her expression closing once again. "But you must know there is no guarantee the siren will not turn you both over to the Lady. We are aware Tethys is bitter about what humans have done to this world. Gregory is already taxing her power, and if the two of you prove too difficult to break to her plans, there is a chance, small I would wager, that she might turn you both over to the Lady of Battles in exchange for aid from that quarter."

Her father made a thoughtful grunt and added, "Or she may fulfill her promise to Gregory and make you whole. Or if that fails, return you both to the master of all gargoyles—the

Lord of the Underworld. There is a chance, a goodly one, Death may offer her a great boon for the return of his dear friend."

"Dear friend?" She really wanted to stop the parroting, but she had to ask. Later, she promised to make Gregory 'magic-up' a concise history of the Avatars. And she would read the damn thing from cover to cover without complaint even if it was ten thousand pages long.

"As relationships go, it is an interesting one. You might think it a father-son relationship as the Divine Ones used you and Gregory to birth the twins, but over the centuries, Gregory and the Lord of the Underworld became more like brothers."

That explained one thing. "Then it's not just the power of the Avatars the Lady of Battles wants? She wants to specifically break Gregory so she can use him against her twin. Nice." Then Lillian saw another option. "I don't have to choose between either a device made by the Battle Goddess's hand or the siren's song. There is a third party. If I run to the Lord of the Underworld, Gregory would follow, and once there, surely Lord Death would set Gregory free."

A long, silent hesitation was punctuated by uneasy looks between her parents. Her father was the one to answer. "Yes, the Lord of the Underworld would restore Gregory."

Lillian took a deep breath. "You're a gargoyle. You must know how to get there. Can you teach me what I need to know to seek him out?"

"As you say, all gargoyles can find the way. Though it is much easier to travel from the Magic Realm to the Mortal Realm than the other way, the trip is possible from here. However, it would take much power, and even more will."

Lillian cocked her head. "What aren't you telling me?"

"Before Gregory started expending large amounts of power to prepare the fae of this world for the coming battle, he had power enough to bring you to the Lord of the Underworld. Yet he chose not to. Why do you think he made that decision?"

Her tail twitched in sudden, fearful understanding. She forced it to still. "To protect me."

"As I said earlier, the Lord of the Underworld would restore Gregory." Her father's look took in her form, from the tips of her horns to the sharp talons on her toes. "He would not stop there. He would free you from what his twin has worked upon you."

"I wouldn't be a gargoyle anymore, you mean." She had feared this side of her nature. It was so primal, and yet it had fast become a part of her. Would she miss it if it were stripped from her?

She flexed her talons in the loam underfoot, gave her wings a little shake, and feared the answer to that question would be a 'yes.'

"Your gargoyle side isn't something the Lord of the Underworld can just unmake," her mother told her bluntly. "You were born this way. And I'm afraid once he was finished with you, you wouldn't still be among the living."

"But surely..."

Her mother made a sweeping motion with one delicate hand. "He would grant you and your hamadryad a swift death and then watch over your soul to prevent his twin from working her mischief a second time. That is the swiftest way to restore you. Once you were yourself again, you would thank him for his aid."

"But what about the Riven? The Battle Goddess's scheme? The siren?"

"If he freed your spirit, you could then be reborn as you were intended. Gregory, too, since your other half would seek a quick end by Death's hand. Once that happened, the plans set in motion by the Lady of Battles would unravel, and she'd no longer be a threat to this or any Realm."

"But surely the Riven..."

Her father interrupted her again. "Once you and Gregory were reborn, you both would make short work of cleansing this Realm of the Riven."

"But it would take at least another ten years before Gregory or I could return."

"Likely longer," her mother added. "Gregory, always choosing to return as a gargoyle, would be battle ready long before you fully matured."

"But by then, the Riven would have claimed hundreds of thousands of lives, if not more."

"The Lord of the Underworld deals in death. He would see it as an unpleasant set of circumstances that might take longer than he'd like to fix, but all would be set right in the end, with the Riven destroyed and the trapped souls freed."

"And this is the being Gregory reveres as noble?"

Her father sighed. "Your thinking is that of a human. The Lord of the Underworld is immortal. Ten or twenty years is nothing to him—a blink in time, a tiny drop. It is as nothing compared to the long years of his existence."

Lillian shivered. To seek the Lord of the Underworld's aid, was that her only option? Was she brave enough to act upon it if it was? She liked to think she would be brave enough to do what was right if that became the only path open to her.

She could never allow either herself or Gregory to fall under the Battle Goddess's power. But the road to the Lord of the Underworld was one she wouldn't be taking either, not until she had exhausted all other options, for she knew that twenty-year delay would doom both the Clan and the Coven. They would be among the first the Riven hunted down. Gran, Jason, Whitethorn, Greenborrow, the unicorn, and the pooka would all die—or worse, become hosts.

"I won't serve the Lady of Battles, and the Lord of the Underworld is only a very last resort. I won't doom this Realm or those who raised and sheltered me simply to make my own life easier. There must be another way to win Gregory back from the siren."

Both her parents relaxed.

"I am glad you agree," Darkness's voice sounded strained, "for no parent should have to help their child find death."

Lillian didn't delude herself into thinking she was as good at reading people as Gregory, but she was certain that was honest concern in their eyes.

Pacing away from her parents' searching gazes helped her think. Out of the corner of her eye, she watched as her little brother hunted something in the tall grasses, honing his newly discovered gargoyle reflexes. He leaped forward and nabbed a bit of brown fur in his jaws. A quick snap stopped its struggles. A rabbit, Lillian idly noted, her thoughts galvanizing around her newly made decision.

She came back to the center of the meadow where her parents waited. "Tell me more about the slave collar." There was no point calling the magical device anything other than what it was.

"Once the final spells are in place, the ward stones

prevent tampering and once activated, none but you will be able to command Gregory. You both must wear a piece for it to work." River held out the chunk of metal and jewels. Reluctantly, Lillian accepted the command collar—it was almost as large as the slave collar. From a dream a few months ago that was not, in fact, a dream at all, but the Battle Goddess's attempt to communicate with her, she remembered how immense the demigoddess was, like the mythological Titans of old, towering taller than a lofty tree. Lillian eyed the collar again. "A little small for a certain goddess, isn't it?"

Her father nodded. "The spells weren't yet finalized, and I was able to shape it into something more to our needs."

It hummed with power. She thought she detected a slight vibration, almost like the device possessed its own electrical power source.

Well, it did have a power source, after a fashion—layers upon layers of spells were woven into the metal and jewels. She could feel them, sense them with that wildness in her blood, her gargoyle heritage. But none of that told her what they were designed to do.

"They protect the wearer from outside magic?" Lillian wasn't completely able to keep her skepticism out of her voice.

"Yes," her mother said, then elaborated. "The Lady wanted them designed so her brother couldn't override their magic—not quickly at least. Of course, the two sets were designed to be worn together. Used separately as we plan, some of their inherent strength might be compromised, but they should still prove enough to overcome Tethys' enchantment. Neither set was finished, but we were only able to steal this pair as Commander Gryton was presently working on the other."

"Why a second set? A backup in case the first set wasn't able to hold us?"

"No. Commander Gryton was confident of his spell's ability to trap the Avatars. You and Gregory were to have worn the slave collars while the Battle Goddess wore the controlling bracelets."

Well. That answered her question, but still didn't change her mind. "I'm sorry, but I can't do this to Gregory. Even if I trusted you implicitly, nothing you've said guarantees these things won't just hand us over into the Battle Goddess's keeping. You can't know that for certain even if I was to trust you."

'Which I don't.'

Her father sniffed at the bracelet with distaste. "Then don't trust us alone. When Gregory arrives, if he is lucid enough, have him examine the collars. He can verify I did not miss anything or have sinister intentions. He will not tolerate them near you if he senses they are dangerous. The siren's enchantments cannot change his nature."

Lillian's ears perked up. She hadn't thought of that possibility. And just before Gregory had tried to drag her back to Tethys, he'd been talking. If not himself, at least somewhat lucid.

"I do not like this plan," her father admitted, "but there is nothing else that will free Gregory from the siren now that her song has had time to dig deep into his spirit. Commander Gryton didn't get his position by being slow of wit. He'll know almost instantly what has happened. Once he alerts the Lady of Battles that she has been betrayed, nowhere within the Magic Realm will be safe for any of us. We'll be forced to remain in this realm for now."

Frowning down at her feet, her tail twitching in agitation, Lillian turned the massive collar in her hands. It reminded her of one of those ancient Egyptian pieces the pharaohs wore.

"What is the chance Commander Gryton might be able to control me through this?"

"You forget, this was made for the Lady. You can imagine what she would do to Commander Gryton if she suspected he attempted something to undermine her authority."

"She's not much for independent thinking among her underlings, I take it?"

"No," came her father's dry reply.

She hadn't really thought about what her parents were risking to help her. She glanced over at her younger brother where he was finishing his meal. "If she catches you, she'd kill you both, and my little brother, too. Probably him first, just to watch you suffer."

It wasn't a question, and her parents didn't need to answer. It was cold, hard fact.

"I'm going to bring that temple of hers down around her ears and make it her tomb or die trying." Lillian hissed more to herself than anyone in particular.

She pinned her father with a fierce look. "So how is this going to work?"

Her father tilted his head suddenly, taking in the surrounding meadow and scenting the breeze. He snorted with distaste.

Then Lillian caught the scent as well. The undeniable stench of Riven, an unholy mix of death and dark magic.

A stronger waft of Riven reached her nose a moment later. Just what she didn't need. But fate was doing its usual thing.

Lillian flexed her claws. "If I have to kill a few Riven before dealing with Gregory, so be it."

The exercise might help her work out some of the fear and frustration currently churning in her blood.

"No," her father ordered, "you will stay here and await Gregory. By now, he will have escaped the traps we placed to slow him down."

Her ears flattened against her mane, and her lips started to peel back in a snarl, protective instincts rising again.

"Peace. They weren't designed to harm, only to slow him. However, if we don't put some distance between us, Gregory will do *us* harm."

Shadowlight came bounding up to her. Surprisingly strong, he scooped her up and spun her around.

"I'll help our parents hunt down the Riven. I'll make you proud." His happy rumble was rather loud in her ear.

"Mmm. Thank you," Lillian answered and patted his arm, not wanting to hurt the young gargoyle's feelings, but also a touch confused.

River stepped up and gave her a hug as well, though a much more sedate one. "Dryads and gargoyles pass on instinct, memories, and life experiences to our offspring. Shadowlight knows you through our memories, and gargoyles are naturally very clannish and loyal. He already loves his older sister."

Her mother moved off then, allowing Darkness to embrace her.

Before he broke away, she asked the one question that had been bothering her. "Even if Gregory looks at the collar and doesn't blast it into next Tuesday, how am I supposed to get it on him then?" She pointed at the slave collar where her mother had left it. "Its appearance doesn't inspire confidence."

Her father laughed, surprising her. She'd thought him much too dour and standoffish for humor. "Then offer him a reward as an incentive. You're the first full-blooded female born to our race. It shouldn't be too difficult to get him to remain in one spot long enough to put it on him."

CHAPTER TWENTY-EIGHT

Alone in the meadow, Lillian paced around the bejeweled enslavement tools, still heartily uncertain of her plan, but not knowing what other choices she had. She already despised their jeweled beauty, the overdone gaudiness that failed to hide their sinister purpose.

And Gregory, when he came back to himself, would he understand and forgive her?

She feared he might not. But still she'd see her decision through—a few billion lives were in the balance. She wouldn't sit by and do nothing, not if there was even the slimmest chance she could use the collars to shape a more favorable outcome.

God, she hated gambling.

A sudden shift in the air currents and a tingling of magic against her skin caught her attention. She pushed away all her unhappy thoughts and prepared for what was likely inbound.

Unlike the first two times she'd seen the magical portals earlier today, there was no slow gathering of power or swirling mists. From this side, the threshold just appeared fully formed in the air. A second later, Gregory hurtled through it.

His gaze locked on hers, and then it swept away a moment later to scan their surroundings. He sniffed the air, circling around the meadow's perimeter as he searched for signs of danger or other traps.

Gregory continued to circle, drawing closer with each pass until he was only ten feet away. He continued to sniff, emitting small huffs of anxiety or anger. The scents of other gargoyles and the much more distant scent of Riven would be as easy for him to read as it was for her.

Lillian held her position next to the ward stone collars for a couple of seconds longer, then decided it would look more natural if she went to him. With a gruff rumble as a greeting, she dropped to all fours and made her way over to him, her wings and tail held in a natural, relaxed position.

With a slight flaring of his wings, Gregory studied her with a determined look in his eye. Gone was the loving and playful—if overly happy—gargoyle from earlier. In his place was one of Gregory's darker aspects—The Gargoyle Protector. Her Hunting Shadow.

His eyes narrowed and the powerful muscles in his thighs bunched.

Ah. It seemed she was today's prey.

Lillian leaped clear as Gregory landed in the place she'd been mere seconds ago. She circled him, her head tilted to the side, ears canted forward, tail flicking in a challenge, her entire body saying, 'come play if you can keep up.'

Another mad dash and a leap, and she was crashing into his side, her momentum managing to shift him off his balance enough, he had to sidestep. While he was collecting himself, or more likely just stunned by her behavior, she darted away, using her gargoyle speed to bolt out of range of any retaliation.

A glance over her shoulder showed she need not have worried. Gregory was sitting on his haunches, his wings tucked loosely against his back and his tail flicking slowly, his expression bemused. While he was still dumbfounded by her actions, she inched closer to where she'd left the collars in the grass.

"Gregory, I need you to look at these for me and determine if they are safe."

He still hadn't said one word to her, but Lillian saw a spark of intelligence in his gaze, buried underneath the many layers of the siren's enchantment. Now if she could only reach that one, small part.

Gregory tilted his head, sniffed, and closed the distance between them until only a couple of feet separated them. His gaze strayed to the collars for a moment and then slid back to land solidly on Lillian.

Sidling up next to him, she gave his shoulder a playful nip. Gregory's lightning-fast response caught her by surprise, and she found herself on her back, her wings trapped under her and the heavier bulk of a male in his prime, pinning her to the ground.

Gregory watched her with something other than the earlier vacant look. No, the heat there was far from vacant. However, a heated look and returning intelligence were not the same thing. But a little heat might make him more biddable and willing to listen to her. She really did need him to study the collars.

He sniffed at her, and then ran the underside of his jaw

along her shoulder, up her neck, and over her muzzle. He did the same strange routine on the other side. Poking around a bit with his muzzle, he found another spot, the inside of her lower forearm, and shimmied his muzzle along there as well.

He was scent-marking.

"You smell the other gargoyles. They were my father and brother, nothing for you to get jealous over. They mean me no harm. At the moment, they are dealing with the Riven to give me the time I need to free you from Tethys."

A non-conversational grunt was his answer. He worked his way lower, rubbing all along her side, hitting each and every rib, and then over her flat belly before moving back up the other side, the same path in reverse.

She waited until he was back up by her collarbone again, then started placing gentle nips and kisses along his shoulders and throat. Gregory froze in place. Only his tail continued to sway, the movement somewhat jerking. Then he began to purr.

Scent-marking was one thing. What she was embarking on now was altogether something else, and far more dangerous. But Lillian saw no other way forward.

"The siren is trying to steal you from me."

Gregory stopped his rumbling purr and narrowed his eyes at her.

"It's true. She wants your power, to use you like everyone else wants to use you. I won't let either Tethys or the Lady of Battles have you." She brought her hands up and clamped them around his forearms, her fingers digging into his biceps. "You're mine, and no one else's."

His rumbling purr started up again, and he dipped his muzzle down to kiss her shoulder, then the hollow of her throat. She nearly started purring herself. Who would have thought that little dip between neck and shoulders could be such an erogenous zone? She lowered her muzzle to her chest, forcing Gregory to move from his designated target long enough so she could regain the ability to think.

His scent had intensified, swamping her senses with his pheromones. Somehow his tail had found hers where it was trapped under her body, and he'd planted one knee between her thighs. Her jaws parted, hoping for more air without the drugging influence of his pheromones, but it only made it worse. She could taste his essence. Each lungful of air drew it deeper into her body. She did purr then, surprising herself.

Another species characteristic and not just a Gregory quirk.

That little bit of information seemed to stimulate her brain enough to get it functioning. Her plan had somehow derailed—rather more quickly than she wanted to admit—and it was her failing, not Gregory's.

Touching him, she could feel what he was feeling. His deep love for her was still there, but what he was feeling at this exact moment was more physical than emotional. And that fact was an icy bucket of water on her own lust. Suddenly, what she was doing felt very, very wrong.

The last tendril of lust wilted, and Lillian dug her heels in and tried to push out from underneath Gregory's greater weight. His arms tightened around her, and his purring changed into a growl. Her heart tripped into a pounding rhythm at the sound.

Yet because he was also pressed against her, she could touch his mind, and it opened to hers, his thoughts completely unguarded for the first time.

And so many things became clear, she wanted to cry. Not in fear. Even when he growled, she knew he wouldn't hurt her. It was the siren's command to capture Lillian and bring her back, getting mixed up with Gregory's more physical instincts. When she stopped struggling, he immediately relaxed and returned to grooming her. The scent-marking, licking, and gentle nips were all part of gargoyle courtship.

Needing to know more about Gregory, she pushed her own body's reactions to the back of her mind, ignoring them as much as possible to better focus on what her other half needed. There was something, just at the very edge of his thoughts, something buried that he didn't want to face himself, a dark secret he wanted to remain hidden.

She knew Gregory was packing a lot of blame and guilt about everything that had gone wrong in this lifetime, but the magnitude of that guilt became clear when his thoughts flowed over hers. He felt responsible. He was the protector, and it was his duty to protect his Sorceress from all dangers. But he'd failed so many times recently. And now even his body betrayed him, craving an unwholesome relationship. He was unworthy of her.

"Oh, Gregory." She kissed his jaw, then rubbed her muzzle against his. "You are worthy. You are the bravest, noblest, and kindest person I know. No matter what you crave, I am your other half, and I exist to fill that need."

She opened her heart and mind, offering up all she was to him.

And he took what she offered, absorbing her love and acceptance into his soul. Slowly, his emotional turmoil subsided, and his purring increased in volume. The delicious vibrations traveled over her skin—even her breastbone reverberated gently to the rhythm of his deep croon.

Now was the moment. It had to be now, or she'd lose her nerve.

"Beloved," she called softly, pushing away her doubts and reservations for what she was about to do, "I want you to belong only to me."

"I have ever been yours," he growled softly against her ear, his voice raw with emotion. "No one else's, not even those few times when I gave my seed to another to beget a child so we might have the raising of it."

Hating herself a little bit more she said, "That was once true, but it's not entirely accurate anymore, is it?"

Gregory whined softly, his ears flicking and then flattening to his mane as if they wanted to vanish, to hide. He buried his muzzle in her hair and pressed harder against her.

"The siren holds some influence over you." She ran her fingers through his mane, soothing, caressing and then tugging gently when he wouldn't face her or her words. "You can't hide the truth from me."

"Her magic infiltrated my defenses while I was weak. She said she'd make you whole, make us one. Once she had you, she promised that she'd convince you to possess me, hold me so close to your heart and soul that it would be like we were one again. I would be complete." Gregory shuddered in her arms. "I so very much wanted it to be true, even as another part knew it to be wrong. I tried to fight it in the beginning. But she didn't want to harm you, she wanted to make you whole."

"I know." Lillian caressed him, whispering soothing words. "She promised me the same thing."

As he poured his heart out to her, she held out hope he was returning to himself, that he might be able to break the siren's hold without the collars.

"Tethys' spell grows stronger by the hour as she takes strength from the other fae. I can feel her tendrils tightening around my mind."

Now that didn't sound good.

"If she had only tried to order me to do something to harm you, my magic would have tagged her as a threat and destroyed her while she was still weak enough. But she knows what we are, what we mean to each other, and had the wisdom to order me to protect you."

Lillian tightened her hold on Gregory. "It's okay. I have a plan to free you from her influence. I have two magical artifacts I want you to examine. I'm told they will protect the wearers from outside magic—I just don't know if I can trust the source. I'm rather hoping you might know better by looking at them. Because if they are safe to use, we will be immune to Tethys' magic and able to neutralize the threat she represents. Gran told me a siren's enchantments die with her."

"That is true."

"While my plan will free you from the siren, there is something I will be asking for in turn. And I fear it will be a heavy price."

He braced himself on one arm, so his upper body lifted away. His gaze sought hers, and twin pools of shining dark anguish looked down upon her. "Anything. I would pay anything to solely belong to you again."

"I must own you body, heart, and soul...though I hope it will only need to be for a little while."

Gregory shuddered above her. "All those things have been yours for a hundred millennia, all you ever had to do was claim them. Take them now, I offer them freely."

Her heart pounding with dread and shame, she took up a collar from where it rested in the grass. It was the one intended for her own neck, she saw, its workmanship of a more delicate nature. Fear sparked through her mind, but she forced her hands to snap the collar around her own neck. It was heavier than she'd expected, and cold, so cold. Only slowly did it begin to warm to her body.

The second collar remained on the ground, untouched.

She ran her fingers over the unmistakable shape of the collar around her own throat. This was wrong. She knew it was, and yet what choice did she have?

If Tethys remained in control of Gregory, it would only be a matter of time before Lillian became a slave as well. And if that were to happen, there would be no one left to save the billions of innocent humans from the siren's vengeance.

She took up the other collar. It was heavy and still her hands shook uncontrollably. With agonizing slowness, she inched the collar closer to Gregory. He merely watched her in silence.

He trusted her, she realized in a moment of absolute self-loathing.

No matter how many ways she tried to justify it, she'd still be betraying Gregory by enslaving him, and it didn't matter if the collar was a better choice than the siren, Lillian still couldn't bring herself to collar Gregory.

"I can't," she choked. "Not even to free you from the siren."

"Yes, you can. For me," Gregory said, almost pleading.

"No," she repeated, her voice growing stronger. "I won't. I will not make you my slave."

With a desperate decision, she attempted to whip the offensive magical device as far from her as she could, but Gregory caught her wrist, preventing her. As she watched, he gently pried the collar from her clutched fingers. He turned it over in his hands, and she felt him call magic as he studied it with a sense more acute than sight. He sniffed it, huffing softly to himself as he continued his study. Then as she watched frozen in horror and denial, he placed it around his own neck.

Golden light, bright enough to force her to blink and shield her eyes, twisted among the jewels embedded in the collar. Her own grew warm around her neck in answer to the magic triggered in his. The heat intensified, warming the metal and her skin. She reached up, intent on prying loose the one around Gregory's neck, but two powerful hands locked around her wrists, preventing her.

Magic boiled up from deep within his spirit. She felt it wash over her body. Then with a snap, it severed the ties that had bound Gregory to the siren. Waves of magic continued to roll out across the meadow, making the grasses sway violently.

She was still gasping in shock at the force of the magic swirling around them when Gregory shifted enough to free himself from his loincloth and then tore hers away as well before she knew what was happening.

"Yours," he rumbled, "I am yours now and forever."

Gods, no. "It's forbidden!"

"My beloved, my soul's mate," he roared. With those words, he pressed between her thighs, jerked forward, and slid home in one thrust. He tossed his head back and groaned, his wings jerking open and flapping once, twice, and then a third time before folding down around them both. Magic continued to flare wildly for a moment, rippling over them both and then the light vanished, taking the weight of the collars with it.

Lillian gasped and tensed at the first, sharp flush of pain from Gregory's sudden invasion, but within moments, her magic welled up and her body began to adapt, welcoming him home. He bowed his head down to bury his muzzle in her hair as he started to move against her with his powerful strokes.

A new heat stirred low in her abdomen and he soon drove any thoughts of the collars and what they'd done out of her mind.

He gentled after a few strokes, murmuring words of love to her in an unending stream, sometimes aloud and other times only in her mind. It was so clear, just there for her to see, that no matter how forbidden it was, he needed her in this way, required this closeness, a moment more vital to him than the next breath.

Belatedly, Lillian wrapped her arms around his shoulders. She told him of her love with everything that she was. "My heart, I'm here. Take what you need. I offer it freely, and I promise we will get through the coming days together." Shifting slightly, she wrapped her legs around his hips, crossing her ankles under his tail for better leverage.

Her actions drove him right to the edge and on over.

"My Lillian," he roared, back arching. After a few short, urgent strokes, a great spasm shook his wings as his entire body quaked with his release. He slumped against her and just panted while he tried to catch his breath.

Gradually, the waves of magic emanating from Gregory's

body grew less until all that remained was a shimmering, knee-high mist swirling around the meadow grasses.

Exhaustion stole over her body, and she allowed her head to slump back onto the ground, but she continued to gently stroke his back and wings in a soothing manner. Her eyelids drooped. Even though she hadn't found her own release, her body felt heavy and sated, rather like she had shared Gregory's, and now she was drifting at the edge of sleep.

She may have indeed slept then, for when her senses sharpened once more, everything came rushing back in horrible detail. In contrast, Gregory was still a warm, heavy weight draped across her body, his wings cocooning them from the chill of night, and his scent soothing to her.

But they'd just done the one thing that they weren't supposed to.

The Big Rule.

Shattered to little tiny bits.

It was all her fault. She should never have let the collars within a thousand kilometers of him. No matter that she'd thought her parents were acting in good faith or that Gregory had looked them over, it was she who had accepted the gift and presented it to her poor befuddled gargoyle.

She'd gambled and lost.

Her mistake was still there, glowing ever so slightly in the moonlight. This mistake didn't look like it could be easily fixed. Encircling his neck, where the collar had been but a short time before, was a gold tattoo-like brand. It twisted in elegant whorls all the way around his throat. When she ran a finger over it, the skin felt slightly raised, but otherwise unharmed. She fingered her neck and felt the same raised pattern circling it. With a heavy heart, she turned her gaze back to Gregory.

As if the focus of her thoughts caught his attention, he stirred from his lethargy.

"Lillian?" he asked and cracked an eye open, his voice sounding a touch confused and groggy with sleep. He didn't bother to lift his head from her shoulder. "Where am I? I feel strange."

"Rest, my love. All is well, and we are safe for the time being." Though that was probably a lie, she thought as she looked at what the collar had wrought.

He huffed out a contented snort and slumped farther to the side. Enough that only a little push was required to get him to roll off her. She disentangled their limbs and slowly sat up, taking a quick inventory as she did.

She ached in a few interesting places, and that wasn't really a surprise. However, the faint streaks of blood on her thighs made her glad Gregory wasn't awake to see. He never handled the sight of her blood very well, and somehow, she was sure he would blame himself for every little drop.

He would never forgive himself for this. She worried this event might kill a small part of him. He held duty and loyalty in such reverence, she knew he'd see what happened as a personal failure on his part. Then an even more troubling thought surfaced. Would he believe he'd just raped his Sorceress?

She replayed what had happened in her mind. Was it rape? Gregory might think so. She knew him well enough to know that he'd blame himself for centuries. This night would certainly haunt her for many nights to come, but did she see it as rape?

It was an ugly word, but accurate. Though she was not traumatized by the act. She hadn't been afraid, not of him, never of him.

But if it was rape, she wasn't the sole victim. Gregory was compromised by the siren's enchantment through no fault of his own.

Sighing, she admitted that if she'd just allowed him to take her back to the siren, none of this would have happened. She'd known the stakes and the risks if things went badly. Oh, and they had. But she might still be able to avert complete disaster if she acted quickly.

"Gregory," she called gently. His one ear swung around to listen, but he didn't open his eyes or otherwise move. She touched the tattoo encircling her own throat and loathed herself. It was quickly becoming a familiar feeling. "It is important that when you wake, you don't remember anything that happened here in this meadow."

Gregory made a worried little growl at her demands. Lillian was quick to stroke his mane to soothe him.

"It won't change the fact that I am your mate, and I love you more than life, but this is to protect you, to keep you strong so that you may better protect me in turn. I need you strong and undivided in your convictions. Do you understand?"

"Yes," he breathed out on a sigh and drifted into what appeared to be a deep, restful sleep.

She and Gregory had promised to tell each other everything, to abstain from telling lies. Would omissions count as lies?

Yes. But just this one time more, she would omit something. Oh, he might figure it out. His heightened senses might scent the truth, or he might read the emotions on her face, but in the end, the risk justified the means. They both needed Gregory strong and his faith intact if they hoped to defeat the Lady of Battles in the coming months.

She rested a hand on her bare stomach. And if something more became of this than another one of her mistakes, well, she'd just deal with the consequences.

Surely, she wouldn't conceive just from this one time? The odds were against it. The only thing that kept complete and total panic at bay was that presently she wasn't the Sorceress. Her hamadryad tree had that honor. She was merely Lillian, not an Avatar capable of birthing a monster with god-like powers. And besides, in the past, Gregory had broken his celibacy on a few rare occasions to beget a child with another. He'd even said that she'd done the same thing at least once.

And those times had never brought down the wrath of the Divine Ones. Surely, this time would be no different if the worst did happen?

Lillian shook herself out of her reverie. What was she doing? There was probably almost no chance of her getting pregnant. She had greater concerns to deal with now. Like what to do about the collar tattoos, Tethys, her parents, and the Riven. Oh, and there was the small problem about what to do with the naked gargoyle asleep next to her.

Somehow she had to keep him from finding out the extent of her mistake.

Well, to start, she'd just have to hide the evidence. She'd already done what she could to keep him from remembering. Though she didn't know if that would be enough. Gregory was good at ferreting out the truth. And there was no hiding the collars.

Then again, he might be so angry over the collars that he'd completely overlook the foggy, dream-like events that led up to the collaring and never think to find out what other events might have occurred afterward.

But he certainly wouldn't mistake it for a dream if she didn't get them cleaned up and the evidence washed away quickly. She untied her scarf-like top and dropped it next to her discarded loincloth. A glance at Gregory showed him still sleeping. She didn't dare go far, or as past situations had shown, he would wake if she strayed too far from his side.

Lifting her muzzle into the air, she scented the surrounding meadow, this time looking for a water source. The only water within the needed radius was a small, brackish little pool, home to a few bog plants and an assortment of amphibians. The boggy smell was enough to make her eyes water, and when she stalked through the muddy edges into deeper water, the muck proved to be worse than the water alone.

She splashed herself with liberal amounts of the pond water. To call it a bath would be a gross injustice as she came out far dirtier than she went in. However, the pond water—and the mud now sticking to her lower extremities—certainly performed the function she wished.

It was doubtful if she'd be able to smell anything other than the little pond for days, no matter how many times she showered. Jaws gapping, she breathed through her mouth in a desperate effort to defuse the wretched stench, only to snap her jaws back together after the first breath. She could taste it on the back of her tongue.

She gave herself a shake, sending drops of water and pond muck flying, and then walked back to Gregory and her discarded clothing. She donned her beaded loincloth; one of the right-side sashes was now shorter than the other, but she rigged it so it would hold together. Then she tied on the scarf-like top.

That done, she couldn't ignore it anymore. "Oh gods, that smell." She almost felt sorry for what she was going to do next. With a delicate shudder, she returned to the pond's edge and scooped up generous handfuls of the muck, then returned to where Gregory still rested. After another half-hearted apology, she proceeded to smear his lower extremities with the mud in such a way it would look like he'd chased her through a bog.

CHAPTER TWENTY-NINE

He awoke by degrees, fighting off sleep as if it was one of his more insidious adversaries. It clung to his mind, almost dragging him back to the land of slumber more than once. With a mental snarl that in the waking world might have been a sleepy mumble at best, he shook off the clinging tendrils of sleep, and his mind finally sharpened enough that his other senses started to relay information to him.

That part of him, buried deep in his brain where his soul resided, the one that always knew where Lillian was and what her condition was, began feeding him details about her. She was close at hand, her mind alert, scanning the world around her for dangers while also keeping an eye on him. There was no panic or fear or pain, no urgent need for him to wake to defend them—his weary body tried to convince him that he could nap for a little while longer.

He snapped fully alert then. No, that wasn't his body's weariness trying to woo him back to sleep. It was most certainly the dregs of an enchantment, a very powerful one, too.

Ah yes, Tethys, a demigoddess of the ocean. The spell had been broken. Only a few fragments remained, but it was no wonder why he'd slept. That spell was no trifling thing.

Another scan of Lillian showed she wasn't under the siren's sway, though there was some residue from where Tethys had tried to enslave her. Shame flared to life in his heart as he remembered how he'd chased Lillian down like a deer. Well, maybe not a deer. She'd put up a fight worthy of any gargoyle, and he was a little proud she'd been able to outrun him for so long. Her speed and stamina would only grow with practice and time.

Hearing was the next sense to sharpen, and he tracked Lillian as she rose from her crouch and paced over to him. He detected another emotion he hadn't noticed earlier. Anxiety. He reached further and found her mind, her thoughts and feelings coming to him.

Her distress and worry were over something she'd done—worry that he'd be angry and never forgive her for a rash mistake.

Gregory bolted upright to discover what was causing her so much stress.

And he choked on his first deep breath.

The second wasn't any better.

Glancing down at himself, he found he was coated in a layer of the vilest-smelling mud he'd ever had the misfortune to encounter in all his lifetimes. Merciful Father, what had he been doing? Rolling in a bog?

His gaze sought Lillian, looking for an answer since he didn't remember how it had come about.

Come to think of it, there were a few other holes in his memory. He remembered the siren, and hunting Lillian, capturing her and then losing her—to another gargoyle! Lillian's parents had come to her aid. Against him.

Had she called them?

He feared she must have.

"How are you feeling?" Lillian asked, her voice holding an edge of uncertainty.

"Like I've been stomped on by the Lord of the Under-world," he answered her truthfully. What had happened? He hardly dared to breathe, for more than the obvious reason. It couldn't be good if Lillian were acting skittish around him.

"Fancy you should mention him. He might be the only one able to save us from my stupidity."

Lillian ducked her head and swallowed hard, he could see the muscles working in her throat and could smell her guilt even over the stench of the bog mud. Why in Light's name was he covered in the sticky crap?

He refocused his attention on Lillian. "Tell me what has happened."

Over and over, throughout their many lifetimes, he'd always bowed to her command in every facet of their lives except when it came to her protection. In that, his word was law. And she'd always bowed to his demands without question.

But not in this lifetime. This time around, she repeatedly tried to protect him when she judged him to be in danger, every time at the expense of her own safety. On the one hand, he secretly admired her, for she valiantly defended those she loved. But on the other hand, she was going to give him a stroke.

By her expression, she'd found her way into another great, steaming pile of trouble.

"You're going to hate me," she said in a weak voice.

He was about to say that was nonsense, but she tilted her chin up and brushed her mane back from her neck and he saw it.

It circled her neck, the golden glow of its spell shimmered ever so slightly in the moonlight.

With equal parts shock, horror, and disbelief, Gregory reached up and touched the twin to Lillian's tattoo where it circled his own neck. At his touch, the ward spells flamed briefly but didn't cause pain or otherwise incapacitate him.

The stirring of power was more of a warning. One Gregory acknowledged by moving his fingers away from the slightly raised skin.

"Lillian..." He pitched his voice low, holding steel in the tone. He needed answers, not evasions, or worse, apologies. "Tell me what happened. Tell me everything. Leave out no details. It might mean our survival."

Lillian swallowed nervously, but she started to speak, haltingly at first, and then with more certainty. "I'll tell you what I remember and what I think I know." She paused and fidgeted with the tattoo around her own neck. "There were times when things became foggy. The siren almost rolled me under with her tidal power more than once. I only escaped because you fought, and she had to turn all her attention back to you or risk losing us both."

What she told him coincided with the few snippets he did

remember when he wasn't fully under Tethys' control. He still didn't relax since nothing she'd said even remotely hinted at an explanation about the powerful weaving circling their necks.

She continued her tale, and Gregory interrupted at key parts for clarification. A hollow pit opened in his middle where his stomach should have resided. He'd never been ill a day in any of his lives, but for the first time, he thought he just might discover what it felt like to heave up one's last meal.

"Why didn't you stay away where you would have been safe? Why must you always act so rashly?" The words flowed out of him. He hadn't meant for it to happen, but more came flying out. "Had you only gone to ground somewhere, I would have remained as stone, out of the siren's reach."

Lillian jerked like he'd slapped her. Then her eyes narrowed, and her nostrils flared. With her tail flicking in agitation, her anger was impossible to miss. "Well forgive me for caring, I was concerned." She snapped her teeth at him, her wings unfurling as if she prepared for a physical fight. "Tethys was enslaving everyone in sight."

"And you, what? Thought it would be a good idea to make it easier to get to me through you?"

"You're an ass," she said and whirled away from him, then spun around and slapped him on the chest. "How dare you judge me? If our positions had been reversed, you would have run to my side without a second thought, even if I'd been standing upon the steps leading up to the Battle Goddess's bloody throne. So, you don't get to judge me for coming to your rescue."

"I protect you. It's my purpose."

"Says who? Did the Father sit you down on his knee when you were a mere speck of power and tell you that was your role?"

"It was implied!"

"Ha. I call bullshit! We're two halves of the same being, equal in power and purpose." She smacked him along one arm for emphasis. "I bet in the beginning we were more similar than we were different. How could we not be? We were one creature. Did our separate personalities develop over time? It makes sense in a way. You always choose to be born as a gargoyle, whereas, from what you've said in the past, I'm more varied in my choice of forms. You're stuck in a rut. Always choosing to be a gargoyle, imbibing more and more of their nature into your own. Gargoyles are protective. It's hardwired into them, and it's becoming hardwired into you. Tell me I'm wrong. Tell me to my face without lying. Go on, tell me."

"Why must you question everything? Can't you just do what you're told?"

"Do what I'm told? Like a child! Is that what you think I am? I'm twenty. By human standards, I am an adult. Start treating me like one."

Gregory slapped his ears flat against his mane. "I'll start treating you as an adult when your actions show rational, mature reasoning behind them. Choosing agents belonging to the Lady of Battles over Tethys is not a mistake my Sorceress would ever have made."

"Well, I'm not your Sorceress, am I? I don't have her memories or her magic. I don't even possess her soul now. My hamadryad stripped me of all that. Even she didn't think I was worthy." Her voice quivered, and she turned from him.

"Lillian, it's not...that's not what I meant."

"But it's still true. An ugly truth, but true all the same."

"No," Gregory said, feeling that sick heaviness again in his middle, but for different reasons this time. His words had harmed her, and he would do anything to take back that pain. "Your spirit is beautiful. You're brave, noble and protect those you love with everything within you. Perhaps you're not, at present, the Mother's Avatar, but you are and always will be *my* Sorceress."

Lillian turned back to him. "But I lack her power and knowledge, and we sorely need it."

She fell silent, and so did he. In good faith, he couldn't contradict her.

"We're supposed to be equals, Gregory. But we're not."

He sighed, feeling cold seep into his body. "I know."

She gripped his chin and lifted it until his gaze was level with her throat. "I may not be the Mother's Sorceress at the moment, but as a mature adult, I accept that this," she touched the tattoo-like brand, "is one hundred percent my fault, and the stupidest thing I've ever done. I just hope it doesn't kill us. I gambled and lost. That's my epic fail to live with. But I had to get you away from Tethys. She was going to use you, use us, to kill millions of humans."

"All the Magic Realm will suffer if the Lady of Battles can now command us."

Lillian flashed fang. "So, save the Magic Realm and screw all the humans in the Mortal Realm?" She sounded more tired than angry, or perhaps defeated was a better word. He could understand that emotion.

He shook his head, his own anger and frustration spent.

"All the Realms will suffer equally under the Battle Goddess's rule."

"Okay, you win this round." Lillian drew in a big breath, her shoulders squaring, and with a little shake, she seemed to rid herself of her weariness. "We'll just have to defeat her, but first we need to free our allies from the siren. As I see it, I tossed a wrench in her plans. I'm free of her influence and, now, so are you." She gestured at him. "You're coherent and capable of logical thought. Which, I might add, you couldn't have claimed two hours ago."

Gregory drew in a deep breath and let it out again. He couldn't really counter her argument this time, either. He had been, without a doubt, firmly under the siren's sway.

Oh, but he knew in his gut Tethys would have been a better choice for the greater good of all. "It shames me I failed you so badly, that you were forced to make such a terrible choice to begin with."

Lillian took three swift steps toward him, and then she was hugging him with all the strength in her arms, even her wings came up to encircle him. "Can we stop raking ourselves and each other over the coals for a while?"

"Yes." He hugged her back, the act giving him much-needed comfort.

"Promise?"

"Yes," he rumbled. "And Lillian, it is you as you are now—sweet and rash dryad and fierce and equally rash gargoyle—who has captured my heart. It is you, not the Sorceress of old, who I fell in love with all over again in this life."

He seemed to have shocked her speechless but then she tightened her fierce grip, as if unwilling to release him. "Would it be naïve of me to hope the villains will take a break for a while, long enough to allow us to figure out an action plan?"

Gregory barely refrained from snorting in humor. Instead, he said, "Tell me more about your family, and everything they said about the collars they gave you."

After questioning Lillian twice, he debated what he'd learned for some minutes. When she talked about her parents, it was with a bitter tone, though it softened when she mentioned the unknown brother.

Clearly, she had come to the conclusion that her parents had, in the end, purposely betrayed her.

Gregory was not so sure now. Not after learning more about the collars. From what he had gathered based on his long experience with magic and his enemy's tactics, the physical collars were merely designed to carry the true enslavement spell. It was an ingenious way to ensure that the victim could not simply cut off or use magic to otherwise remove a physical collar.

What made Gregory think Lillian's parents were innocent was that the collars, at least the physical ones, had disappeared within seconds of attachment. He could only surmise that the solid collars were designed to return the wearer back to the Magic Realm, probably to some dark chamber deep within the Battle Goddess's temple.

That he and Lillian were presently still here in the Mortal Realm, instead of enjoying the dark twin's hospitality, must mean that Lillian's father had tampered with the collars as he'd said, changing the spells woven into them, thereby preventing Lillian and himself from falling victim to the Lady of Battles—at least not this day.

Of course, they still had the secondary spell burned into their skin like a brand. But that didn't prove malicious intent on the part of Lillian's father. In fact, the spell was very similar to the type of magic his adversary had used to graft the demon seed onto Lillian's soul.

And *he* had very nearly missed that spell's existence until it was too late. The other gargoyle could have overlooked a well-hidden secondary spell.

However, he wasn't telling Lillian any of his theories yet. She'd already been hurt enough. He wouldn't intentionally give her false hope, only to cause her more pain later.

In the end, the only way to learn what the newcomers intended was to confront them and use magic to determine if they spoke the truth.

His plan had only one glaring problem.

He couldn't call on his magic. It was walled off, out of reach for now. He had a sneaking suspicion only Lillian's command could now unlock that power.

They hadn't tested that theory yet. Gregory was reluctant to try, fearing any order might open a mind-link between them, which, with his thoughts so focused on her parents, could only give away more about his theories than he wanted to risk.

And that, as Lillian would say, was a Catch-22.

Looking over at Lillian where she sat on a fallen log, he wondered if they dared risk finding out what the ward spell would and wouldn't allow them to get away with.

One of the first things he found was that the spells

wouldn't let them travel more than twenty feet apart, which suited Gregory fine.

Lillian wouldn't be able to get into trouble without him knowing about it, and the forced proximity might allow him to find out just what Lillian was keeping from him.

She was still visibly upset by today's events. Her tale had been reasonably detailed, except for a few parts. Like the times when she'd almost fallen prey to the siren's song and later when the collars activated.

By all accounts, Lillian's distress was justified, but he still couldn't shake the feeling something was off.

What wasn't 'off' about this situation? With a mental shake, he gave a great, huffing cough.

Regrettably, that action graced him with a big whiff of his own scent.

Mercy, that stink certainly didn't mellow with age. Even with the mud now mostly dry, it was still breathtakingly terrible.

The sound of distant hoof-beats reached Gregory's ears, and they swung around to the south, tracking the sound as it grew closer.

"Now what?" Lillian asked, echoing his own silent thought.

Honestly, Gregory didn't know.

Though by the sound, the hoof beats came from two different equines. His pooka and unicorn allies always seemed capable of finding him, even when he didn't particularly want to be found.

This time, he couldn't assume they were coming to his aid.

CHAPTER THIRTY

From his hiding spot in the deepest shadows underneath the boughs of a young fir, where even the light of the full moon couldn't touch, Gregory watched and waited. No more than ten feet from the same tree line, his other half sat in a patch of moonlight, intentionally badly hidden in the waist-high grasses.

It was Lillian's idea to act as bait.

He hated it but agreed only because it was the best way to observe the two equines and judge whether they were presently still his allies in truth.

Besides, he mentally reassured himself, *I'm close enough to protect Lillian.*

Even without using his Avatar magic, which he feared to use until he learned more about the tattoo around his neck, he was still more than capable of taking out both the unicorn and the pooka, should that be required.

He sincerely hoped it didn't come to that.

A glimmer of silver between the trees quickly resolved

itself into the unicorn. He galloped into the meadow and stopped when he spotted Lillian.

He approached her with a nicker and craned his neck to sniff at her. *"You're not actually trying to hide, are you?"*

"Yes," Lillian said. Gregory watched as she slapped playfully at the unicorn's muzzle.

"It's good to see you. I'm surprised you escaped Gregory at all if that's your best attempt at hiding," the unicorn said with an accompanying bob of his head.

"She's not hiding, you twit," said another mind-voice that was familiar with its liberal dose of disdain. *"She's playing decoy to Gregory's hunter."*

A black pony emerged from the shadows. He looked directly at Gregory and said, *"At least that's a better attempt at hiding."*

Lillian stood up, her expression losing its earlier joy. "I'm glad you both escaped the siren, but what became of my grandmother?"

It was the pooka who answered. *"Vivian is safe. She stayed behind so we could reach you faster."*

The tension in Lillian's shoulders and wings visibly eased.

Gregory emerged from the shadows and joined Lillian.

"It's good to see you're both free of the siren. Maybe now we can do something to teach her to be choosier about whose territory she invades."

The pooka froze in place, his eye showing white for a few seconds in surprise, but after a moment he stretched forward to nose at Gregory's neck. *"It seems you have escaped the siren's snare merely to be caught by an even more powerful faction."* The pony tilted an ear forward and back in question. *"How did such a thing come to pass?"*

Gregory remained silent, not in the mood to give answers to the pooka's surly tone.

Lillian stood, brushing off bits of grass. "I was foolish enough to trust my parents."

"Ah. They showed their true colors. How disappointing. I rather liked them."

That caught Gregory's attention enough to draw him in. *"We never did find the time to have that particular conversation as I recall."*

"Yes, I was there when Gran first stumbled upon them in Lillian's grove while you both were still deep in your healing sleep. That time I only witnessed them aiding both of you by sharing their power. They seemed genuinely concerned." The pooka gave a mild shake of his head, his equivalent of a shrug. *"I suppose the concern could be real, and they still might serve the Lady of Battles."*

Gregory hadn't expected the pooka's words to be reassuring, and they weren't. However, he had hoped for something more substantial.

Eyes narrowing, he accepted that he'd just have to hunt down what he needed to know himself.

"We have some hunting to do," Gregory said, including the other three. His instincts cried for him to find some safe place to hide Lillian until he ascertained the siren's condition and the Riven's strength and numbers, but the brand on his neck would not allow that, so she came with him.

He dropped to all fours and raised his nose to the breeze, seeking the trail her parents had taken.

Lillian dropped down next to him and gently bumped his shoulder. "We hunt."

"We hunt," both the unicorn and pooka echoed.

Gregory snorted. It hadn't been what he'd meant, but the

Wild Hunt would ride this night after all. What remained to be seen was if Lillian's parents would join the Hunt or become its prey. Whatever the outcome, Gregory would make certain this Hunt left many victims in its wake.

Tethys, too, would have that same choice, and then the Riven would feel the cold, passionless wrath of the Wild Hunt of old.

Gregory bolted into motion, Lillian at his side, with the pooka and unicorn two strides behind them. This Hunt lacked the starting dance, the howl of the dire wolves, the call of hunting horns, and the baying of the fae hounds. But in its oldest form, the Wild Hunt did not need those things. It only needed blood and sacrifice at its final destination.

CHAPTER THIRTY-ONE

They ran through the night-shadowed forest, twisting, leaping over, or darting around anything in their path. Sometimes the pooka or unicorn would pull ahead. Gregory seemed content to allow them the honor for a short time before he would surge ahead once more.

Lillian stayed with him, determined to be as his shadow. As the night grew longer and the scent of their prey steadily stronger, she noticed something else of interest.

She'd already run far this night and should have been tired, but each step came as easily as the first, some unseen power buoying her up.

And she wasn't alone. Both Gregory and the two equines seemed to feel it as well. Magic swirled around them at the edge of her vision, sparks and whorls like tiny incandescent snowflakes formed in the air, only to break away and drift behind.

Lillian chanced a glance back, curious to see what became of the magic they summoned from the Magic Realm, even without the aid of the great circle dances. It was as she thought. Wherever the tiny sparks landed, they nourished and renewed the land.

Even while in gargoyle form, her dryad nature sensed the land and trees growing stronger. With a smile, she bounded a stride ahead and stole the lead from Gregory for a whole ten seconds.

She was just easing back to run alongside him again when three shadows began to pace them. Turning her head, she studied the massive wolves as they communicated silently with Gregory.

She'd never forgotten the dire wolves she'd seen in her first Hunt, but she hadn't seen any since she'd woken from her hamadryad's healing. Gran had said they were in mourning, and once that was over, they would start the selection of new leaders.

Lillian wondered if their arrival meant the dire wolf packs had a new alpha king and queen. She and Gregory could sorely use the help in the coming fight.

"The dire wolf packs are still far to the north," Gregory explained, crushing that small hope, "but these three and others along the way were sent to howl back the news of what they learned. Apparently, other Clan members sent word of our awakening to the packs, and later a second message about our preparations to fight the Lady of Battles."

A nod to each was the extent of her greeting, for even as those three aligned their magic to the Hunt's, more of the Clan joined them. These were the ones who had no reason to be near enough to the spa to hear Tethys' song and so had avoided capture. Two blazing white elks, a male with a massive rack and a yearling female, galloped at the tips of the dire wolves' tails.

She flashed to another time when a similar white buck had attempted to carry her to safety only to be brought down by the attacking Riven, his beautiful coat awash in crimson blood. Yes, the Riven had much to answer for, and she planned to make them pay it in their own blood.

A family of foxes burst from a thicket and flanked Gregory on his other side. Farther along the path, a bull moose awaited them. Perched upon his back, like she was born there, sat the banshee.

Lillian flicked a questioning ear at the banshee. The last time she'd seen that fae had been earlier in the day while they were finishing details for the masquerade. She'd just assumed the banshee was captured along with the rest of the fae helping at the spa.

The banshee guided her moose closer to Lillian and then smiled down at her from her higher perch. "Be at ease, young gargoyle. A siren, no matter how powerful, can't out-sing a banshee's keening. When I saw how many she was able to enslave, I fled into the forest and joined with the other free-ranging Clan. We will fight at your side. First the Riven, then the siren, and finally even the humans if they leave us no choice."

Lillian nodded her head. There was no time to get into an argument about the humans just now.

Other Clan joined the Hunt, sliding out of the deeper shadows of the forest. Several sidhe joined them, riding either deer, elk, or moose. By a quick count, Lillian estimated that there were close to two dozen hunting hounds running silent at their hooves. Next to them, three massive bear-like creatures loped along, their giant strides easily keeping the pace. There was even a black hunting cat ghosting at the edges of the Hunt.

The Wild Hunt, which started four strong, had grown to over sixty in number by the time they reached the location where close to twenty-five Riven battled two gargoyles and one dryad. As the Hunt swept down upon the rear-most Riven, Lillian realized they had to leap over many already killed.

With a small part of her mind not already engaged in battle, she noted how deadly her family was. Even her baby brother was lethal, she admitted, as she watched him dispatch a Riven with a decapitating stab of his tail. Her father moved with brutal efficiency, but Lillian spotted wounds. None of them were without injury, mostly claw and bite marks.

Gregory surged ahead, making for the left flank of the Riven horde. Lillian followed with the rest of the Hunt howling at her heels.

It wasn't like the movies, no glorious clash of steel on steel. There were only the nauseating sounds of tearing flesh, popping cartilage, and the dull thump of dead meat hitting the ground. The Riven did not use conventional weapons. They were the weapons. Their fangs and claws venomous with evil corruption, their blood a burning poison.

But worst of all was the smell—she'd never forgotten the charnel house smell of a Riven body torn open. The stench threatened to steal the breath from her lungs.

She fought as they did, with tooth and claw and blade-tipped tail. One Riven she tore nearly in two, baring its spine to the moonlight. Her powerful jaws promptly gifted a second Riven with a severed neck.

Spitting tainted blood, she scrubbed at her mouth and briefly worried how harmful it might be to her gargoyle body. The Riven didn't give her long to worry, as two more attacked at once. Gregory, gripping his own opponents in each hand, tail-speared one of hers before she was forced to fight two at a time.

All around was death and the wails of the wounded. The Riven only hissed in rage as they died. She hated the monsters' otherwise stoic silence, for it meant each of the grunts, yelps, and cut-off screams belonged to one of her people.

And there were many sounds of anguish filling the air.

For every cry, she sought to pull down another Riven as payment in kind. She didn't know how long the battle raged. Seconds? Minutes? An hour? But between one ragged breath and the next, the battle was over, the last Riven dying upon Gregory's talons.

With a snarl of disgust, he shoved the corpse away and glanced over at her where his gaze quickly scanned her for injury. An assortment of slashes and bite marks decorated her upper body and lower arms. Blood seeped from them, but she did nothing to stop the minor bleeding, deciding it was the best way to cleanse the wounds for now.

Lillian's mother was examining a nasty wound on Darkness's belly. It looked like he'd almost been eviscerated by one of the Riven.

She would have been more concerned, but her father was still alert, studying his surroundings as if prepared to continue the fight should more enemies appear.

A soft whine drew her gaze to her brother. He struggled to his feet and stumbled toward her location. Her eyes narrowing, she looked him over and didn't see a wound deep enough to cause his distress.

He tugged at something along his side, just under where his last rib ended.

She saw it then, the hilt of a demon blade.

She'd taken a couple of cuts from one of those blades but hadn't allowed the Riven who wielded it to land a stabbing thrust. Her brother hadn't been so lucky.

Taking a step forward and opening her senses once more, she felt it too, the slow, deadly suction that could drain all magic from its unfortunate victim. Intent on offering him aid, she started forward, only to be warned off by a low growl as Gregory put himself in her path.

"Let me by," Lillian said, surprised her voice sounded anywhere near normal.

"No." Gregory didn't turn his attention from her family when he answered her.

Frustrated, but also respecting his reason for distrust, she didn't challenge him about being overprotective this time. He had reason. But she was also sure that her baby brother was innocent. "Gregory, he's got one of those cursed blades buried in his side. You know how much those hurt, and what it will do to him if we don't get it out quickly."

She could already see the ring of stone forming around the blade where his body tried to protect and heal itself.

Lillian's parents looked up, just noticing the youngster's distress. Shadowlight had been doing an excellent job of not broadcasting his pain, but now that he was closer, she could smell it even over the stench of battle.

"Shadowlight?" River called. Then the truth dawned upon her features, and her eyes grew large. "Shadowlight!" She ran, sprinting around bodies and over the gore-slicked ground to reach his side. She sank to her knees and brushed his hands away to better see the damage.

Darkness was at their side a moment later.

"I have no magic left that will touch this," her mother whispered in horror, glancing between her son and her mate. It was easy to see her grief.

Darkness moved one hand from where it was braced against his own wound and raised it to the demon blade. As his fist engulfed the hilt, his muscles went taut, his wings trembled at the strain.

Lillian's stomach dropped in sudden understanding. Her father was too weak to heal both himself and his son.

She glanced at Gregory, silently pleading for his help.

Gregory rumbled something under his breath as he fingered the tattoo around his neck. "If they came to achieve some mischief, they've already done their worst."

He stalked forward, his tail poised over his back in threat.

Lillian trailed him. He glanced over his shoulder long enough to glare at her for not staying where he'd left her, but he didn't reprimand her aloud.

Bodily pushing Darkness out of his way, he did a quick examination of Shadowlight's side, then look back at Lillian.

"The collar won't allow me to access this level of magic without your order," he said without a hint of emotion. "Make it a command that I heal all our allies, all who serve the Light."

Lillian sucked in a breath, surprised to find the Hunt had encircled them while Gregory examined Shadowlight. Many had wounds as grievous as her brother's or father's. "Do you have the strength for all that?" she asked in a low voice, more for a respectful tone than an attempt to hide her questions. The fae around them could clearly hear every word of their exchange.

"No." Gregory gave a little shrug to Lillian's question and then turned to address all the rest of the Hunt. "But it will not be my will that will allow the healing, I shall beseech the Spirit Realm, and all healing will be by the Divine Ones' grace. Stay and be judged by them or go into the darkness."

Gregory turned back to the wounded young gargoyle without further comment.

In that moment, she understood how Gregory was going to judge if her parents were allies or enemies.

There was some uneasy shifting among the other members of the Wild Hunt, but none fled that Lillian spotted.

Her father bowed his head and closed his eyes, preparing.

Lillian didn't know how the Divine Ones would judge her parents, but she wanted the chance to know more about them before...before what might happen next.

Gregory speared her with a look. "This is your choice to make, you must make it soon. There are many more Riven to be hunted this night."

More Riven? Of course, aren't there always? She thought with bitter resentment.

"Heal them," she ordered. "Heal everyone here who serves the Light. Let it be the will of the Divine Ones."

She rested her fingers lightly upon the brand circling her neck. By Gregory's earlier words, it sounded like anyone the Divine Ones judged to be tainted weren't likely to see the dawn. Then she realized the gods might view her and Gregory as tainted.

Was that Gregory's plan all along? To end them both before they could become the Battle Goddess's playthings?

"So ordered, so shall it be." Gregory's somber tone matched the ritual words.

He mantled his wings, and they flared outward like two great sails. His eyes drifted closed as his voice rose in a melodic chant.

Lillian didn't know what the outcome would be, but if she'd just ordered their doom, well, by the God and Goddess, she'd watch it come with her eyes wide and her mind free of fear.

Gregory held his hands out before him, palms facing each other like he held a globe-shaped object between them.

Cold air flowed downward from some unknown spot above her head. A breeze picked up, growing stronger by the second until it was kicking up debris in a circle around them. Cross currents continued to build as silvery, blue fog rose from the ground. Lillian's lungs burned, and she released the breath she'd been holding.

Between Gregory's outstretched hands, a spinning vortex of pure, cold magic formed. Brighter flares of magic twisted up through the opposing currents of air and a small twister began to swirl down from a denser, cloud-like mass of power overhead.

A tornado?

That was to be the mechanism of Divine justice?

Poetic justice too, perhaps, for Gregory had been like a tornado coming into her life: powerful, awe-inspiring, possessing a deadly beauty, and fully willing and capable of disrupting an orderly life.

If this was to be her end, she wanted to say one more thing.

"I'm sorry," she shouted above the noise of the wind. "So sorry I made such a muddle of things. I only ever wanted to be worthy."

Gregory's eyes slid open, and his expression was serene.

"I know," he whispered into her mind. *"And you were always worthy, my beautiful dryad, my fierce, gargoyle huntress."*

He dropped the glowing ball of power he'd been holding. It fell slowly as if gravity's hand had little effect upon it. When it finally hit the ground, it shattered, exploding outward in all directions.

A powerful force knocked her from her feet and rolled her a few times until she collided with a tree. The force flowed onward, feeling more like an ocean wave, one with a powerful, accompanying undertow than it resembled storm-tossed air currents.

Lillian gasped and shuddered before she managed to roll herself back into an upright position. All fours was the best she could manage.

A tingling sensation raced along her nerve endings, similar to the pins and needles of restored circulation. Though this was probably something far less harmless. The magic sank beneath her skin, seeped into her bloodstream, and then deeper yet, through muscle and into bone, until its cold tingle settled deep in the marrow. It paused then, and Lillian took a courage-strengthening breath. Nothing more happened for several heartbeats. She was just glancing up to see how the magic was affecting the others when a wave of pain welled up from within her bones.

The pain stole the strength from her limbs, and she

grunted as she rolled onto her side. Her body twisted and quaked as it began to shapeshift.

The weight of her wings grew too much for her to hold up away from her body. They might as well have been two lumps of dead flesh for all she could move them. Then with another body-spanning shudder, her wings vanished, pulled back into her body in one quick and extremely painful surge.

Shapeshifting hurt. It always had. But this made the first few times seem easy.

Her jaws ached from clenching them, but the alternative was crying out in pain, and that might distract Gregory from the spell. She'd already caused enough trouble, she wouldn't call down more.

Besides, with that mighty power riding him, she wasn't sure if that was really Gregory. He stood, head bowed and wreathed in shimmering, flame-like magic. Even over the distance, she could feel the cold magic of the Spirit Realm flowing outward from where he stood, feeding the spell, which was presently controlling her change.

Her gargoyle features vanished and left her weak and shaking in the smaller body she'd known far longer. Though, at this exact moment, her dryad body seemed no more in her control than her gargoyle one had been.

She continued to shake and quiver for a good minute. Slowly, her limbs regained feeling and strength, and she sighed in relief when they moved at her command.

Blinking, she found herself curled in a fetal position. The earth was soft under her, and its scent was reassuring. She didn't want to move but forced herself back to her hands and knees. Only then did she realize there was still magic sliding through her, examining her. It shifted from the center of her chest upwards until it settled in a circle around her neck. The tingling increased.

Threat or warning?

She didn't know but breathed a hardy sigh of relief when the magic moved on. If the power wanted to kill her, surely it would have done that at the first touch. No, the magic seemed more interested in studying her, which gave her no comfort whatsoever.

The magic continued to coil through her blood, a seemingly random examination.

She was just acclimatizing to the chilled presence when a tendril snaked lower and touched her womb with its insubstantial fingers. There it paused as if it found something of great interest.

Lillian shivered at the power's creeping touch, and fear reawoke, rocketing her to new levels of dismay.

But several heartbeats later, the magic gave one last probing search and then the power disappeared.

In its wake, she was left weak-kneed and very, very cold inside.

Slowly, her pounding heart eased its frantic tempo and warmth returned to her body.

With a half-conscious gesture, she reached to finger the skin of her throat. Disappointment rose within her at the feel of the raised brand. That it was still there came as no real surprise, for if it were that easy to get rid of, Gregory wouldn't have been so angry.

But she was alive. And a quick survey showed all her injuries healed. That was something.

The gods hadn't smote her after all. Gregory looked equally whole. As she watched, he reached for his own brand, then he fisted his fingers and let it fall back to his side. Maybe she wasn't the only one with that small, naïve hope.

Turning away before her gaze caught his, she studied the power as it continued to flow farther out from its magical epicenter. Wherever it encountered one of the fae, the winds would spin and whirl until, with a little burst of magic, the accompanying healing spell would migrate to the next nearest fae. In counterpoint, wherever the power touched upon a Riven's body or a spot of tainted blood, the magic would lick along it with pale, blue flames until all was consumed.

Others were still gaining their feet after the initial surge of magic had tossed them on their asses. Lillian's little brother was one and seeing him moving stiffly and awkwardly, she hurried to his side. A soft, but otherwise happy whine greeted her.

After giving him a once-over and examining the smooth skin where the blade had been, she enfolded him in the best bear hug she could manage now that she was once again a much smaller dryad.

Her eyes turned to her father to find River already there, bending over him, checking for injuries. That they had both survived gave Lillian some hope that she might one day explore those family bonds to see how deep they ran. But unlike with her brother, she had no urge to go and hug either parent.

They were strangers. As was her brother, she supposed. But there was something very engaging about Shadowlight—his friendly openness would melt even the most guarded heart.

A shift in the flow of magic against her skin alerted her that Gregory's spell was winding down. In its wake, all were healed and the bodies of the Riven had vanished. Strange though it was, she could still see the broken underbrush, torn up grass, and smell the scent of crushed vegetation where the individual battles had occurred, but the blood and gore were absent. Slowly, other things seeped into her consciousness. While the Wild Hunt still milled around Lillian and Gregory, awaiting direction, a quick tally showed that their number had decreased.

Killed in battle or killed by Gregory's magic?

"All who ran with us were loyal. Only the dead are gone, free to journey to the Spirit Realm. May they have a long, peaceful rest before starting the journey of life once more."

Lillian looked around, disconcerted for another reason. She didn't know the members of the Wild Hunt, not personally. Though they clearly knew each other.

What if she'd lost friends or family she'd known for years? There one minute and then gone the next. No chance to say goodbye. Nothing of the physical left to shed tears over, no burial for a final farewell. Wiped clean off the earth by divine power in the space between heartbeats.

Gregory had called to that mighty power, and he'd received an answer. He'd told her all along what he was, what she used to be: an Avatar.

And Avatars belonged to their gods. But those same gods somehow belonged to their avatars, and couldn't or wouldn't deny Gregory their power, even when it was clear he had been compromised by the brand of enslavement.

What Gregory was capable of had never been as real to her as it was in that moment of clarity. It was such a beautiful, horrifically fierce power. And she now commanded it. She'd never felt so tiny, or completely inadequate, in her life.

Somehow, she had to release him from the influence of the brand.

That barely contained force must never belong to the Lady of Battles. Lillian's earlier conviction was based on more personal reasons. He was her friend, beloved companion, the other half of her soul. She'd wanted to protect him out of her love for him, their sense of duty to each other.

Those were romantic reasons, but now she'd seen the far more deadly and far-reaching reason why she couldn't let them fall any further into the Battle Goddess's manipulations.

She and Gregory were now the greatest threat the universe had ever encountered—because even with the Battle Goddess's slave collars around their Avatars' necks, the Divine Ones still shared their power.

Gregory's little experiment proved that.

"You finally understand?" he asked as he padded over to her on all fours. "The Divine Ones love all they create. They would not destroy the Lady of Battles, even when her war with her twin threatened to tear apart the Magic Realm. They love us no less—in essence, we were their first-born. It seems they will not or cannot deny us their power. I had expected as much but hoped otherwise." Gregory fell silent as he fingered his tattoo.

"I do understand why you see Tethys as a better choice than trusting my biological parents. And I would not have used these cursed collars knowing what I know now. However, I would have still fought the siren and attempted to free you or died trying."

"I am glad you did not die," Gregory whispered hoarsely.

A soft swish of long grasses in an unfelt breeze and the shifting of shadows announced when her father joined them.

"I am truly sorry for our part in your current predicament, First One." Her father bowed to Gregory. "There must have been a secondary spell hidden in the intricacies of the outer casing. My failure to find it is a stain upon my honor." He tilted his muzzle toward the night sky and waited, his vulnerable throat exposed.

Lillian saw her mother's look shift from concern to terror.

Gregory huffed. "Considering where you spent the last twenty or so years of your life, I can only imagine that this most-recent failure is just one of many stains upon that honor."

Darkness stiffened, but held his position, waiting for the killing blow.

Then Gregory raised a hand and patted the other gargoyle on the shoulder, surprising her father, and everyone watching, into a group flinch. "It is not for me to judge you. Though I can only imagine what choices you had to make to protect those you love. And ultimately, I owe you and your dryad mate for siring my beloved."

Her father sighed softly. "I've made many mistakes, but Lillian and Shadowlight will never be among them."

"We all make mistakes," Gregory agreed. "I have committed more than my share in this lifetime already, and no doubt will make many more." His tone darkened. "But should you attempt to betray my trust, know that I will set both you and your mate before the Lord of the Underworld's throne. As a personal favor to me, he will grind your bones under his hooves until they are dust."

Just then the pooka trotted up to Gregory and rubbed his head against the gargoyle's shoulder in what could only be called a loving manner. Gregory met Lillian's gaze while absently returning the pooka's show of affection with a good scratch along his neck, just under the fall of his mane.

A soft whine pulled Gregory's gaze away from hers as he tracked the sound. Lillian wasn't the only one disturbed by her guardian's fierce ultimatum. Shadowlight paced closer to Gregory on all fours and whined a second time, his tone a clear plead.

Gregory's expression softened, and he reached down and ran his fingers through the smaller gargoyle's mane. "Be at ease, young one. Your parents will not betray me of their own free will. But it had to be said as a promise and a deterrent to anyone here who would betray me."

Shadowlight's ears perked back up, and he licked at the older gargoyle's fingers, happy and reassured once more.

While she was glad Gregory wasn't going to indiscriminately execute members of her family just yet, recent events had ensured that she wasn't quite as trusting as she'd been six months ago, so she wondered what his next move might be. However, the night was chilled and so was she now that she was merely a dryad again. Deciding that was excuse enough, she covered the six feet separating them and bumped her shoulder against Gregory's until he took her under the shelter of one wing.

It had been a hell of a night, and it still wasn't over. They needed to find Gran and then deal with Tethys.

CHAPTER THIRTY-TWO

"There are still other Riven headed toward Tethys' location," said a voice Lillian identified as her father's.

And just like that, Lillian was tossed back into the here and now. With a rumble, Gregory nodded in the general direction of the waiting fae as the Wild Hunt shifted back into its deadly, predatory readiness.

Gregory glanced at her smaller form but didn't say anything about what possible reason the magic might have had for stripping away her gargoyle form.

But Lillian could guess. There were no female gargoyles for reasons not entirely known to her. As such, she was somehow in violation of the natural laws, and apparently, the Divine Ones didn't care for the new look.

While Lillian woolgathered, the rest of the Wild Hunt had moved off a little way, leaving only her parents and little brother in their immediate area.

Her gaze returning to her mother, she found the other

dryad already mounted on Darkness's back. She sat on him like it came naturally to her. Well, she probably had lots of experience.

Her parents did another of their silent exchanges, which she couldn't fault them for since Gregory utilized that gargoyle trait frequently, but it did leave her wondering what they discussed. Apparently, she wouldn't have to wait long for an answer. Darkness approached her location less than a minute later.

When he was a stride distant, River reached out and handed over one of her swords. Lillian looked up from her study of the blade to find her mother holding out a second blade, a twin to the one already in Lillian's hand. From out of the air, River produced an accompanying shoulder harness with scabbards for the two short swords.

Lillian's eyebrow rose at the show of magic. If she wasn't mistaken, River had been drawing on a handy bit of Darkness's gargoyle magic. She hadn't even known that was possible. Later, she would question that in more detail. By the slight tremor in the tip of Gregory's one ear, he planned to do the same thing.

With a bit of instruction from her mother, Lillian was able to wiggle into the harness and secure the blades so they would come free easily but wouldn't bump against her back when Gregory ran. Throughout the whole exchange, Gregory merely looked on with what Lillian couldn't mistake for anything other than approval.

Her sword skills were limited to fencing, and these were slashing weapons, their weight and balance nothing alike, yet it still felt good to have the weapons. They gave her a purpose.

Gregory dropped to all fours and arched his one wing out of her way so she could mount with ease.

She only hesitated a moment before she mounted in silence, but inwardly she mourned the loss of her gargoyle body. After all, she felt so much more secure when it was her own feet doing all the work.

Leaning forward, she wrapped her arms around Gregory's neck. He leaped forward, her father and brother taking up flanking positions, and then Gregory was out in front of the Hunt, leading them back toward civilization, the siren, and most-probably a whole host of Riven rabid for blood and magic.

A tendril of familiar power brushed her mind a moment before Gregory's essence joined their thoughts. *"It's good to have you on my back again. Do not misinterpret my words, you made a lovely gargoyle, but I missed my dryad."* His tone held hints of his old self, which she hadn't heard since before he'd been taken by the siren.

"It's good to have you back, too. I'll figure a way to get us out of this mess."

He twisted enough to brush a quick gargoyle kiss against her shoulder. With her arms around his neck, it was the only part of her he could reach. *"We'll work together to solve this. I think that is where we have failed. We each keep trying to do things apart, to protect the other, but that is what allows harm to find us."* Gregory paused and then glanced back to where the rest of the Hunt ran at their heels. *"The Lady of Battles may have made a mistake with the collars, for in tying us even closer together, neither of us will be able to get into trouble without the other knowing."*

Lillian laughed. "That's one way of putting a positive spin on winning the shitstorm sweepstakes." She pressed a kiss to the back of his one shoulder, then straightened up enough so she could twist her upper body and look behind. She met her mother's gaze.

River gave a slight nod and then whispered something in Darkness's ear. In reply, he lengthened his stride and came alongside Gregory.

Lillian tilted her head in River's direction. "What do you know about the Riven?"

Her mother pressed her lips together in thought. "They seek power. They probably are after the siren, though that won't be their primary goal. They need your hamadryad."

That made horrible sense. "Because she's now the Sorceress and they want that power?"

"No, actually," her mother countered and then clarified a moment later. "They want to use the bridge your hamadryads can form between the Mortal and Magic Realms."

Lillian felt Gregory stiffen under her. She stared at her mother. "Hamadryads. Plural?"

"Naturally." Her mother quirked an eyebrow. "You know there are two, surely? The one in this Realm, and the original in the Magic Realm—the one you took the cutting from in the first place."

Cuttings only came from other plants. Of course there was a second tree.

"And it still lives?"

"Yes. Your tree is very strong and is in fact flourishing. She's almost twice as large as the one growing here. Though that shouldn't surprise you either since she's had an extra eight years to grow and absorb power from the Magic Realm."

"Hmm, I really don't like the idea of a part of me still trapped there," Lillian mumbled more to herself than any particular person. "What's to stop the Lady of Battles from somehow using the hamadryad against me?"

Gregory rumbled at her question, apparently not liking the thought any better than she did, though he'd probably thought of that angle long before her.

"Hamadryads, being a hybrid of tree and faeblood, are not something our enemy can influence. As a tree spirit, a hamadryad lacks thoughts or emotions that the Battle Goddess can grasp, understand, or corrupt."

That might be true, but it didn't mean she liked the idea any better.

"However, there is a way to exploit both your hamadryads, and I think the Riven plan to try." Her mother frowned darkly.

The terrain forced Gregory and her father to veer around the opposite sides of an ancient oak, following two different game trails. To Lillian's dismay, she couldn't continue the conversation for several strides. When Gregory and Darkness finally merged back onto the same path, Lillian sought her mother's gaze. "Tell me what you mean."

"You're aware that travel between the Realms is difficult, yes? Normally, one must fight their way through the Veil. The trip here to the Mortal Realm is less strenuous than the return journey. In fact, besides gargoyles, only dragons, phoenix, and gryphons have enough inherent natural power to return to the Magic Realm. Of those, only the most elite of their kind could make the return journey without damaging themselves. All others would require aid directly from the Magic Realm or some form of powerful talisman that could enhance their natural magic."

Lillian thought she knew where this was going without

needing more details. "And somehow, my hamadryads can circumvent the Veil."

"Yes, the two hamadryads can act like a bridge for those of us who know that secret."

Lillian quirked an eyebrow. "That's how you and father came here."

River nodded in answer.

"And now the Riven have discovered that little detail?"

"I can only assume," River agreed. "I would also guess that they now wish to bring more of their brethren here. The blood witch has been busy building up their numbers. We can't allow them to reach this land. If they do, they will use the humans to multiply faster than we can kill them. All the Riven must die."

Lillian was in complete agreement with her mother on this.

"I don't know how much you know about the Riven," River continued. "But once housed in a suitable host, that seed of evil grows. It multiplies and infects all parts of the host body, tainting and warping it to the Riven's needs. As the speck becomes a flood, it overwhelms the host and the Riven becomes a sentient, thinking, reasoning being."

"Gods above. It's like a virus or cancer." Lillian shivered in horror as another thought occurred. "An intelligent cancer that consumes you, body and soul."

Her father flicked an ear in her direction, and suddenly his voice was in her mind. *"The Riven traps the host's soul and uses it as a link to the body. Being more of the spiritual than the physical, without the soul to act as an anchor, the Riven couldn't remain in the host and would drift away and be torn apart by the cleansing power of the elements."*

It was too horrible for words, so she said nothing, merely tightening her hold on Gregory.

Perhaps sensing her distress, Gregory interjected, *"It's all right, my Sorceress. When we destroy a Riven, we are freeing the soul to return to the Spirit Realm where it can be cleansed and healed of all scars. And we will kill all the Riven, take peace in that."* Gregory twisted to nuzzle her shoulder. It was a small gesture but eased the tension in her spine.

Yes, they would destroy the Riven to the last bloody one. She was immensely sick of them always sneaking around and then striking when one was weak.

"If the hamadryad can be used as a bridge, why haven't the Riven from the Magic Realm just flooded down the bridge and conquered this realm?"

Her father glanced at her. "Because they can't. The hamadryad shields against anything that evil attempting to breach the bridge from that direction. But the magic of this realm is much weaker. If the Riven can bypass the hamadryad's defenses here, they will be able to bring their army through."

Lillian tightened her hold on Gregory as he gathered himself and leaped over a fallen tree. When the way was smooth again, she asked, "But the hamadryad allowed you, River, and Shadowlight to come here."

"The hamadryad read our intentions and judged them to be good."

His words confirmed a theory she'd been bouncing around. Nodding, she said. "Let's go stop the Riven once and for all."

Nodding his agreement, he gave her a wide gargoyle grin, flashing his deadly fangs.

Her father and brother's motives she understood but her mother's remained a mystery. Glancing at River, she frowned. "You I don't understand. Why are you helping us, really? If the Riven conquered this realm, surely that would aid the Battle Goddess."

"Yes, I was loyal to my Lady. All her subjects are, and I would still be serving her if I thought her actions wouldn't bring about the death of my children. But the Riven do not care how many they kill."

A cold lump formed in Lillian's stomach, but River continued with barely a pause.

"We were her subjects long before the loss of her consort and the schism with her twin, which led to a millennium-long war. She was not always as she is now. Long ago, her battles were against evil, her twin fighting at her side. She once was a goddess of justice."

"*The glory of what one once was, no matter how great, doesn't remain untarnished by the misdeeds of our present existence,*" Gregory said with undisguised censure.

Her mother bowed her head ever so slightly. "That truth took me a long time to understand. I held out hope for eons that time or reason would gentle the rage burning within her. A small part still hopes for that one day, but I could not sit by and wait for that day, not when my own flesh and blood would suffer at her hand to sate her need for vengeance."

Lillian would have questioned her mother more, but just then the abusively loud crack of gunfire split the night. And not the type of guns used by hunters. No, these were the kind she'd only heard in the movies, not real life. Instinctively, her back muscles knotted with tension, as if waiting for bullets to rip through her body. None did, though.

"Those are the weapons the human warriors carry, aren't they?" Gregory asked with another brush of his mind against hers.

"Yes."

"Then either Tethys has released everyone under her control so they can fight the Riven, or the enemy has already overrun her position and her enchantments died with her."

Lillian sent up a silent plea to the heavens for the siren's survival. Three hours ago, she wouldn't have believed she'd be praying for Tethys life, but they could sorely use a fae of her strength in the coming battle.

Then again, the phrase 'choosing the lesser evil' had originated somewhere. She wasn't the first person, nor would she be the last, to eat her own words and side with a former enemy to face a greater threat.

CHAPTER THIRTY-THREE

As they drew closer to the savage sounds disrupting the night, Gregory winced at the bruising noise. He skirted wide, not wanting Lillian or any of the Hunt to get caught in the path of the tiny vicious projectiles.

At his mental command, six sidhe archers broke off from the Hunt to aid the human soldiers. The sidhe took to the trees, that relatively high position might offer them some protection from the path of the bullets.

"The poor humans," Lillian whispered. "Their guns can't kill what's already dead."

Having no time to partake in the smaller skirmishes, he continued to run, intent on the main Riven force closing in on the hamadryad.

"The sidhe will do what they can for the humans. We must stop the Riven force before they reach your hamadryad." Gregory allowed compassion to bleed across their mental link. *"I'm sorry, but I fear there will be many deaths this night—Clan, Coven, and human alike."*

Lillian's thoughts brushed his in return, the depth of her understanding strong. "Run swiftly, my Protector, and perhaps we can prevent greater losses."

He lengthened his stride in silent agreement. They passed several other smaller skirmishes along the way. Gregory ran down two Riven with the poor judgment to get in his way. To either side, he saw Lillian's father and brother take down their own share of the enemy.

On the outer edge of the gardens, Gregory ordered Lillian to draw her blades. She did as he asked even as more Riven poured out of the night-shrouded greenery, forcing the Wild Hunt to slow. This particular horde fought and died with a greater ferocity, and he assumed they were there to slow the Hunt no matter the cost.

At first, Lillian's two long blades must have felt awkward compared to the type she was accustomed to, for her moves were cautious to the point of hesitation. Gregory brushed his thoughts with hers. *"Merge your thoughts more fully with mine."*

There was a small hesitation on her part, and then he felt her thoughts brush more firmly against his, then deeper until they were fully merged.

His spirit thrilled with happiness and pleasure, uncaring that it was battle that forced the bond. With her astride, they were of one mind, body, and soul. It fed that all-consuming craving to belong, his greatest weakness, and as close as they were merged, he couldn't hide it from her. The shame at his personal weakness was still there, but mild and muted by the sheer joy of running into battle with his lady upon his back.

Her essence moved deeper, almost touching his soul. The soothing wash of her voice filled his mind. *"There is no shame in what you feel."*

Another six Riven in his path forced him to bury his fierce joy and focus on the battle. More bodies fell before his claws and Lillian's silver blades. Within moments, the pristine gravel path darkened with blood and more unwholesome substances.

He continued down the path with reckless speed, spearheading the mad charge, the rest of the Hunt swift on his heels. He didn't slow until he came upon the hulking shadow of Lillian's maze. A great mass of Riven had already made their way inside the south entrance. Distantly, the sounds of battle reached his ears, and he knew there must be another group of Riven attacking from the north entrance of the maze as well.

The wind carried the snarls, grunts, and screams of battle. More importantly, his keen hearing told him that the fight hadn't yet reached the middle of the maze where Lillian's tree grew.

Within, an unknown number of his people still fought.

A familiar voice rose above the din of battle, shouting orders and encouragement. Vivian's tone confirmed there was still hope, still time to stop the Riven. The gods had been merciful.

Gregory felt Lillian draw in a breath. He pinned his ears just in time as she screamed, "Gran, we're coming! Hold on!"

The three massive bears bolted past, drawing the Hunt into a new charge.

He and the other gargoyles followed close behind the bears, decapitating the carpet of broken Riven bodies they left in their wake.

Decapitation proved the most effective way to neutralize the Riven until their remains could be burned in purifying fire. The bears' lethal claws did an excellent job for the most part, but a few demons had been agile enough to avoid killing blows. One such Riven snarled at Gregory.

It was not so lucky as to avoid *his* claws.

The Hunt pushed onward, breaching the maze. Within, the fighting grew more intense, the confined space forcing the fighters on both sides to use uglier tactics.

He found himself unable to get a good swing without tangling with the warrior next to him, and he resorted to severing the Riven's head from its body using his jaws. Spitting out the tainted blood from his last kill, he took down the next Riven in a similar fashion.

Lillian was left unable to swing her swords without hitting one of their allies. By her inventive curses, she wasn't pleased with being unable to contribute.

The going was slow, but when they turned a corner in the maze, they were able to see Vivian and a dozen other Coven members defending their position against close to thirty Riven. With the enemy stretched out between them, he went about the business of reducing their number. Lillian's father and brother took up flanking positions a few steps behind.

Seeing three gargoyles advancing sent the Riven into a frenzy. Some of their numbers attempted to escape by scaling the maze's cedar walls.

A stirring of magic drew his eyes from the Riven to the cedars themselves.

Ah. He smiled. Now he sensed what Greenborrow had been doing in the maze of late, and why the enemy had opted for the longer route to the center of the maze instead of cutting, climbing, or clawing their way in a direct line through the greenery. But desperation now made them attempt the walls.

One Riven was making a good bit of headway and had climbed a good two-thirds of the way to the top when the dense greenery shifted and pulled the demon's upper body inside.

There were several moments of snarling and screaming before the cries were cut short by a wet, tearing sound. The cedar walls gave themselves a shake and spat out the Riven's lower body first, followed a couple of seconds later by the upper portion. Five other Riven attempting the same climb met with similar resistance and outcome.

Lillian gasped. "I know why Gran wanted me to increase their blood-meal feedings. God, it wasn't to make them grow. It was to keep them fed."

Lillian might have said more, but she had to take out a Riven that got past his claws when four rushed him at once.

She shoved the body off her long blade as he continued forward. They left the still-struggling beast for Shadowlight to finish.

Several more Riven fell before him, and he was suddenly standing before Gran as she battled one of the last enemies. She slammed her staff down on the Riven's skull, then looked up at him and gave him a weary smile.

"Glad to see you finally showed up. And you brought the Hunt. I always knew you were a dependable boy." Gran leaned on her staff for a moment and panted. Sweat dripped down her temples and covered her face. She and the others with her were covered in blood and gore—too much of it their own.

As Lillian slid from his back to give Vivian a hug, Gregory

admitted to suffering similar bites and claw marks. None of them were unscathed, but they were alive.

"I'm sorry," he said with a formal half-bow in a show of respect for Gran. "We came as soon as we could."

"Forgiven, my dear gargoyle," she said as she and Lillian broke apart, and she hefted her staff once more. "But we need to get to the center of the maze. The Riven attacked from both directions and the others don't have the Hunt to aid them, they may already be overrun."

He nodded and shouted orders to the rest of the Hunt for the fastest to come forward. Out of the corner of his eye, he noted when Lillian's brother came alongside Gran and bent a wing.

Gran took the arrival of more gargoyles in stride, and with a nod accepted Shadowlight's invitation. She mounted in one smooth motion despite her numerous injuries. Gregory dropped back to all fours and Lillian silently remounted him as well.

Without needing to speak, the three gargoyles bounded into motion. They ran as swiftly as the twists and turns of the maze allowed. The Wild Hunt kept pace. He was proud of their valiant efforts this night because none of them had had an easy task to complete.

Shadowlight pulled up even with him, and he realized Gran wanted to speak.

"Tethys sensed the Riven coming and released everyone from her enchantments so we could prepare for the coming battle. She stayed behind with Lillian's hamadryad to protect it should we all fall before the Riven onslaught."

"What happened to all the guests?" Lillian asked.

Yes, what had happened to all the humans? He'd not

noticed their lack until Lillian mentioned it, when in fact, he should have been tripping over their Riven-ravaged bodies. He was glad that wasn't the case, but he still wanted to know the answer to that mystery.

"Tethys commanded the civilians to the north end of town, well away from where she sensed the Riven coming. She saved their lives, though I think it was mainly so the Riven couldn't use them as new hosts. Heaven only knows what the townsfolk will do when they return to themselves." Gran gave a little, half-hearted shake of her head. "If we survive this night, I don't know how we're going to spin this to keep the humans in the dark."

Ahead, a sharp bend marked the inside edge of the maze. Their destination was almost in sight.

They took the last corner without slowing and burst out of the maze into the small glade.

A quick glance showed many Riven had already forced their way free of the narrow north entrance and were now shoving back or overrunning the few surviving defenders. As the tide flowed into the glade, it broke into three distinct flows. One group swarmed the defenders, forcing them against one of the inner cedar walls where the sidhe didn't have room to swing their deadly long swords and were forced to use smaller blades to hack and thrust.

Behind him, more of the Wild Hunt emerged from the maze. He motioned half their number to attack the Riven at the opposite entrance. They had to slow the amount of Riven reaching the inner glade, or they'd simply mob the Hunt and trap the defenders with sheer numbers.

Vivian led the first wave of the Hunt to engage the enemy. If they were able to keep the remaining Riven trapped within the close confines of the maze itself, they had a chance to end the conflict relatively quickly, with less of their own blood decorating the ground.

Or so he hoped.

As the second wave of the Hunt gathered behind him, he did a quick tally and found seventeen already at his heels, with more pouring in behind them. Out of time, he led the charge toward the siren's location. The first batch of Riven had started to encircle the tree even before Gregory had covered half the distance.

As he closed in on the hamadryad, he spotted Tethys at last. She rose up from the stream, her power falling from her like water, where it swirled around her in an ever increasing current. Then with a subtle shift in her shoulders and a flick of her great tailfin, she loosed a wave of magic upon the unsuspecting Riven.

Her spell-wave crashed over the first row of them, physically forcing them back even as the defensive magic triggered in bright flashes of light. The powerful spell ripped the moisture from the Riven, leaving dry husks incapable of movement in its wake. Even over the distance, Gregory felt the pressure of that spell dance along his skin. By her sudden, sharply drawn breath, Lillian felt that fearful power, too.

Tethys continued to lash the demons with blast after blast of her magic.

But there had to be close to eighty Riven already within the glade.

Gregory slammed into the nearest one and twisted its head from its shoulders with a mighty heave. Lillian decapitated another with her swords while he was busy with his own enemy.

He speared another with his tail as it tried to slip under his guard. Horns, claws, tail spikes, and teeth—he used all his natural weapons, but he needed more. Lillian's father used magic as well, sending bits of shadows and moonlight to devour his enemies.

Gregory was mildly envious. But this close to Lillian's hamadryad, and its link to the Magic Realm, combined with the new tattoo circling his throat, made him leery of using his magic for fear of somehow falling under the Battle Goddess's sway. Yet he had no choice.

If even one Riven reached Lillian's hamadryad and was able to circumvent the tree's protective shields, the beast would be able to open a bridge and summon the rest of its kin here while the Clan and Coven were weakened. If his allies fell, he and Lillian would become easier prey for the Battle Goddess.

Such an outcome could not be allowed to come to pass.

"Lillian, you must order me to use my magic again."

"The tattoo, you said it was too dangerous."

"We don't have a choice." When there was a momentary break in the fighting, he turned his head to glance back at Lillian. "Give the order."

"Gregory." Lillian paused, her hesitation lasting only as long as it took her to draw back her arm and send a knife flying with practiced accuracy at a demon about to maul his side. Then she turned and met his gaze, giving him a slight nod of understanding and agreement. "My Hunting Shadow, call your magic and eradicate the Riven." She slashed at another beast, removing its head.

"As my mistress commands," he purred happily as his magic rose within him to do her bidding.

All around them, the chilled magic of the Spirit Realm poured from him and flowed across the ground in an ever-increasing circle.

It rose above the ground, floating and whirling slowly like thick fog birthed from cold air and warm ground. He let it build for three more beats of his heart, then he ordered it into a hunting spell, shards of shadow and light that sought out the nearest Riven with vicious accuracy.

The magic stabbed deep into the nearest creature, shattering it from within, reducing it to specks of light and vapor. It died in silence, unable to cry out in pain or warning to any of its fellows. Even as the first blew apart, Gregory's magic sought more, first in ones and twos, then in greater numbers as his spell spread out before him.

He followed the trail his magic had cleared, drawing closer to Lillian's hamadryad. More magic poured from him, becoming shadows and light and in turn hunting more of the Riven.

Another ten Riven fell before his magic, their bodies still disintegrating when an anguished wail drew his eyes back toward the siren. Several of the demons had gotten past her defensive spells and were savaging her with claws and the dark glimmer of what could only be demon blades.

The area between his shoulder blades twitched with phantom pain as he remembered all too well the agony those things inflicted. He sent a current of magic across the distance to the siren's aid. His spell caught four of the attackers, but several managed to jump clear. They retreated to the far side of the stream.

A wave of magic rose from the water and slammed them

into the cedar walls twenty feet away. The cedars swallowed their newest victims in a swift, hungry fashion.

Tethys continued to lash out with power, even as her blood turned the stream red. From what he could see, two demon blades were still embedded in her side. Hissing in frustration, pain, and anger, she blasted more Riven out of existence.

Several Riven continued their attack, venturing into the water only to discover that ancient siren blood was as toxic to evil as gargoyle blood.

They screamed as they died. Gregory nodded to the siren over the distance, and she returned the gesture in kind, then bared her teeth at the next wave of demons descending upon the hamadryad.

Gregory turned his magic upon the ones coming closest to the tree. Shadows and moonlight hunted them while he dealt with the ones near his person in the more mundane manner of tooth and claw.

The battle raged on for many more minutes. Lillian called encouragement the whole time until suddenly there were no more enemies within striking distance.

There were still a few other battles raging on, but even those would shortly be won.

Lillian's mother and father had moved off to aid Gran and Shadowlight. Other Clan and Coven members were finishing off the few Riven still within the glade.

Gregory loped over to inspect Lillian's hamadryad. The tree seemed whole and unharmed, and there was no taint of Riven essence upon her. They'd managed to prevent that at least.

Lillian dismounted for a better look.

A black shadow circled around from behind the tree, and Gregory nodded to the pooka. The unicorn joined him a moment later, and they took up positions on either side of the tree, acting as sentries. He was about to thank them for their loyalty when Lillian whispered his name and then tapped him on the shoulder. He followed where she pointed, and he soon spotted Tethys where she lay in the stream, half up on the bank.

"Guard the tree," he ordered the two equines.

They bobbed their heads in unison.

With Lillian a step behind, he approached with caution, but none of the Riven bodies piled up three deep along the stream banks showed any signs of movement.

Tethys lay almost as unmoving as her conquered enemies, only the slow flutter of her gills and the slight rise and fall of her chest showed she still lived. No part of her body was untouched, and blood still welled sluggishly from a hundred wounds. She might have survived all that, but her own trident had been broken, and both parts speared her body. The lower shaft had been driven through her chest, and it pinned her to the bank. The three-pronged crown was buried in her abdomen.

It looked like it had been plunged in several times before the hand that had wielded it had given out, or more likely, had been killed by Tethys's dying will.

"Tethys, can you hear me?" he asked directly into her mind, hoping a spark of her fierce nature and pride were still there.

"Yes, Avatar." She answered in kind, though her essence was weak and pain filled. *"But even you can't save me. Grant me a boon and give me a merciful ending."*

"It is as you said. I can't save you. But I can thank you for protecting Lillian's hamadryad."

"It was the least I could do after what my actions almost allowed. The Riven would have violated this Realm far more quickly and far more thoroughly than the humans ever could."

"I am glad you saw that before the end." Gregory pulled her broken trident from her abdomen and then wrapped both hands around the broken shaft, just above where it speared through her chest. *"But there is one more thing you can do for me, one last task only you can perform."*

He yanked the shaft free, and Tethys issued a weak, bloody gurgle, but her eyes blinked open as he lifted her into his arms. *"I can send you back to the Magic Realm, in spirit at least. Before you pass on into the next life, I would ask you to carry a message to the Lord of the Underworld for me. Tell him all you know and have seen here. As a reward, he might gift you with more time to seek vengeance for what the Riven have done, but I cannot promise you that."*

"Send me then, and I will tell Death everything before I venture forth into the next life. It matters not if he gives me more time. I do not deserve or crave it, but if it is granted, I promise to spend it well."

Gregory nodded at the words. There was no deception in her, she meant what she said.

He bowed his muzzle to her forehead and placed a kiss there. *"Go, regain your honor."*

He lowered her body to the ground at the base of the hamadryad, but her spirit was already on its way, speeding toward the Magic Realm and Lord Death.

Gregory could not say how the Lord of the Underworld would react to the news of everything that had happened here tonight, but at least Tethys could give him some valuable details, especially about the Riven army amassing in his twin's territory.

And Death would be clever enough to see Gregory had just given him a way to dispatch that army without violating the duality curse that held the Lady of Battles imprisoned.

Gregory smiled harshly as Tethys' body turned to sea foam and seeped into the ground under the hamadryad. Lillian made a surprised exclamation. He merely tucked her against his side to reassure her.

"What was all that about?"

He waited until Lillian's parents, brother, and grandmother joined them under the hamadryad before explaining.

Vivian's expression hinted that she already knew the answer, and her smile grew bigger, turning into what Lillian had always called her grandmother's shit-eating grin—which was a repulsive human adage, but that smile always drew an answering one from him.

"What I wouldn't give to be there to see the outcome of that," Gran said with a chuckle.

Lillian's parents merely watched Gran with puzzled looks.

"Come," Gran said in a tone that was all business once again. "We need to see to the wounded, dispose of the Riven's remains, get cleaned up, and then sit down for proper introductions." She eyed Shadowlight with open interest. "If I'm not mistaken, I believe I just inherited another grandchild. The more the merrier, I always say."

Shadowlight practically vibrated with happiness. He was as bruised, battered, and bitten up as the rest of them, but he galloped over to Gran and bumped his muzzle under her hand. With a chuckle, she obliged. But she multitasked even then, giving Lillian's biological parents a once-over that was civil, though a touch cool. "We'll divide into groups and triage the scene. Lillian, you can take Shadowlight and introduce him to Jason. You'll be aiding him in cleansing the tainted blood." Gran turned her attention to her next set of victims. "Gregory, I would like you and…" She glanced at Lillian's father with a raised brow.

"Stalks the Darkness," he supplied, "though my daughter finds Darkness an easier mouthful."

Gran smiled. "Darkness, I would like you and Gregory to lead another group in disposing of the Riven corpses and dispatching any stragglers. When you find allies, please report them to Whitethorn and Greenborrow. They will oversee bringing the wounded to me. If Lillian's mother is willing to help?"

River nodded. "I have done many healings during my long life."

"Good. We'll need as many able bodies in the healing tent as soon as possible."

Lillian, who had been silent until then, perked up. "You taught me basic first aid. I could help."

"You could indeed. But only after several rounds of full biohazard decontamination protocol. You and Gregory both smell like you've been wallowing in a cesspool for the better part of the night." She made a vague, full-body gesture at Lillian. "At present, you'd kill more souls than you would save."

Lillian blushed but nodded in agreement. "We ran afoul of a bog. It was richer than most."

"To put it mildly," Gregory rumbled, unable to keep quiet on the topic.

"Dawn isn't far off," Gran said and then paused as a

newcomer approached. A tall sidhe warrior, her bow still at the ready and dressed in full battle armor, came up to them and bowed graceful to Gregory and Lillian before she pulled Gran aside for a moment. Gran conversed with the fae for some time, and then met Gregory's eyes. "It seems we have a more pressing deadline than just the rising sun. The human military is gathering itself. Some of their numbers must have made it back to base and notified their superiors."

Lillian muttered an expletive, and for once Gregory was inclined to agree and added a few of his own.

Gran just sighed at their language and took command. "Change of plans. The siren may have provided us our scapegoat when she sent all the townsfolk north. Lillian, you're still on cleanup detail with the gargoyles. You'll just have to do it without your brother. I need him to lead the Coven members that are uninjured and gather any Clan that can pass for human and take everyone to join the townsfolk as quickly as possible. Once there, they can pretend to blat in fear and confusion with the townsfolk, all the while using persuasion magic to swing the blame firmly on some super-secret government experiment gone wrong. The human authorities can spin it any way they want. I don't care, as long as we aren't exposed to the general public."

"While that's the craziest plan I've ever heard, people will be more willing to believe that than the truth about magic and demons." Lillian gave her head a little shake, her expression darkening as another emotion slid across her face. "The average person might believe that tall tale, but the military personnel in the woods tonight know otherwise."

"Exactly." Gran motioned another fae to her side, this one a dire wolf already shifted to human form. "We need to get this done because we know the human authorities will be all over us, since the masquerade was our idea and it coincided with the Riven's attack. We need to make it look no more or less strange here than what's happening in the rest of the town with the townsfolk waking up from the siren's enchantment."

Nodding her head sharply, Lillian added, "So no bodies, body parts, blood, or gore. But lots of leftovers from a big shindig suddenly abandoned when the partygoers wandered off after getting exposed to a—what, a hallucinogenic gas or something along those lines? Got it."

"That's my girl," Gran said. "I'll ask any other fae not helping with the wounded or the cleanup to create a diversion in the forest and give the soldiers something more interesting to chase. A three-pronged diversion should work. Besides, we've flooded enough magic into the land tonight to confound any tech they will have with them. Do what you can and then meet back here in an hour and a half."

Gregory gave himself a shake and stretched muscles stiffening in the cool night air.

"All right, boys," Lillian said with a wave encompassing him and the two other gargoyles. "You heard Gran, let's do this in record time because I want to shower, eat, and then dream about sleeping for a week."

Gregory rumbled his agreement, and they set off, starting at Lillian's hamadryad and working their way out from there. He quickly showed Lillian how Elemental fire summoned from the Magic Realm served their needs much more efficiently than gasoline and a match.

CHAPTER THIRTY-FOUR

The cleanup took less time than Lillian had estimated, but then again, with three gargoyles ridding the land of taint and her own dryad magic repairing the damaged grasses and other landscaping around the spa, maybe it shouldn't have surprised her. In the days to come, there would be more work far out in the forest, such as adding layers of protection to the dwellings of the other fae, where wounded were even now being transported.

When they'd finished their task, they had gone back to meet up with Gran. Once there, she'd assigned Darkness and Shadowlight new jobs. Which, Lillian had noted with amusement, they accepted without as much as a flick of a questioning ear. After that, Gran had looked Lillian over from head to toe. Gregory got the same treatment, and then they were ordered to "go find a shower in all haste before someone expires from the smell alone."

Hence, Lillian now made her way back to the house with little guilt about leaving others to contend with the military threat. Gregory seemed unconcerned as well—but that might just have been exhaustion. He padded along beside her, silent and physically 'drooping' with his ears at half-mast, wings loose at his sides, and tail dragging in the dirt behind him.

"Come on," she said as she ran her fingers through his mane and caressed his silky ears, "I'll get a quick shower first and then make you something to eat while you get yours." By her calculations, of the two of them, he'd done the lion's share of the work during cleanup. It was only fair she hunt up food for them.

Gregory rumbled happily and leaned into her touch, though she didn't know if he agreed with her idea or was simply reacting to the physical contact. They trudged up the back steps and crossed the veranda and into the house in a companionable silence.

It wasn't until they had crossed through the kitchen and into the living room that it occurred to her that they'd done this exact thing after the last Hunt. "You know, in the future, we might want to excuse ourselves the nights the Wild Hunt rides. We never seem to escape it unscathed."

Beside her, Gregory tilted his head to look up at her, and he started to chuckle. "No, I suppose we don't, but imagine how much worse the outcome could have been if we weren't there both times."

"Hmm," Lillian debated as she climbed the stairs to the second story. "There's that silver lining. Guess I'm glad all these aches and pains were gained for a higher purpose."

It was the thought of hot water, shampoo, and copious amounts of body wash that sustained her to the top of the stairs. She shed her clothes as she crossed the threshold into her bedroom and continued into the bathroom with the determined shuffle of the terminally drained.

Gregory plodded into the bathroom behind her. She'd initially wanted to shower alone so she could scrub off any incriminating evidence that she might have missed with her hasty wash in the pond before she'd smeared herself in the bog slime. But Gregory had proven a fantastic mind reader in the past, and if she tried to chase him from the bathroom now, he might get suspicious.

And a suspicious gargoyle was far too much for her to cross wits with in her present state of brain fog.

In the end, Lillian had emptied half a bottle of body wash on the two of them before Gregory had stopped crinkling his nose up every time he took a deep breath. She'd finished up first, and then gone in search of something to eat. To her surprise, she'd opened the door to the hall only to bump a tray with her toes. No harm had come to either her toes or the trays, of which there were two, and both piled high with steaming food. A glance up and down the hall showed no hint as of how they'd gotten there, but she'd bet a night's sleep Gran's invisible hand was involved, even if she'd not stepped foot within the house herself for hours.

Gregory was still in the shower, so she set the trays on the bedside table and pulled the towel off her head and started to work on the snags in her hair. She'd managed about half the job when the door to the bathroom opened. A moment later, the bed shifted behind her and Gregory took the comb out of her hand. With a gentle nuzzle, he continued the work in silence. He was in one of his touchy-feely moods, but she didn't mind, taking comfort in his presence. He slowly teased out the tangles with gentleness and patience far greater than her usual efficient brushing.

In a moment of weakness, a part of her wanted him to catch some betraying thought or scent, to discover that they'd crossed a forbidden line because she was terrified that her worst fears might come to pass, and she'd have to face that truth alone.

One hand strayed to her flat belly. Reason returned, and she quickly tied her robe's sash to make the move look natural. Now was not the time to fall apart or panic, especially when nothing might come of her foolish mistake. Gregory didn't need yet another thing to worry about. She'd just have to dig deeper and find a bigger backbone.

"Lillian?"

Her stomach plummeted. Had he already discovered her shameful secret?

"Yes?" she asked, proud her voice sounded normal.

"What are you afraid of? I can smell the sudden spike of fear." A large, muscular tail curved around her waist and tugged gently until she softened her stance and allowed her head to drop back against his chest. "Me?"

Breath froze in her lungs, and she couldn't answer as her heart did a strange little flip in her chest.

"Is it me you fear?" he asked again.

Hearing uncertainty and dread in his tone, she turned and straddled his lap. Entwining the fingers of one hand with his, she pressed the palm of the other against his chest where she could feel the throb of his heart. Then she raised their joined hands to her own breast and pressed his hand over her heart. "No, never."

"I would never harm you. Not even when I was fully under Tethys' enchantments, could she have made me harm you."

"Shh, I know. It's not you I fear. It's the future." She stroked the tattoo around his throat. "I've made so many mistakes and bad choices. I don't know if I can ever make it right."

He took her hands and cradled them in his larger one, and then in an elegant, old-world way, he pressed a kiss to the back of each. "We will face this new obstacle as we have always faced challenges, together."

I dearly hope so.

She hugged him in a fierce embrace.

Gregory must have caught her thought, for he dipped his muzzle down and nuzzled her damp hair for several moments before one large hand came up and started to caress it in long, soothing strokes.

Even after her inner turmoil finally quieted, she continued to hold Gregory in a fierce grip until her arms grew tired, only then did she release him with a sigh and asked, "Are you hungry? Food magically walked to our door while you were still in the shower."

He gave her a slight nod, and she padded over to where she'd set the two trays.

Gregory was just finishing off his meal when his gaze took on a distant look, which meant he sensed something or someone was communicating with him. "What is it?" she asked, fearing bad news.

"Your hamadryad," he rumbled, sounding happy. So perhaps it wasn't bad news.

"My hamadryad can talk to you?" she prompted when he didn't seem inclined to explain.

"Of course, she is the Sorceress," he said, sounding perplexed at her question. "Though from this distance, the best she can do is send emotions. When you have finished your meal, your hamadryad has something she wants us to see."

Lillian glanced down at the food she'd been 'worrying' instead of eating. "I'm not actually that hungry. We can go now if you'd like."

Gregory glanced at her plate of partly eaten food with a disapproving huff, but didn't say anything, or, thank the gods, try to get her to eat more. Her stomach was twisted in too many nervous knots to know what to do with food just now. Maybe whatever good news her hamadryad had would help distract her from other, less pleasant things that had occurred this night.

She tilted her head toward the door. Still, Gregory hesitated.

"Let's go," she said, sounding as tired as she felt. "I could use a little good news."

Gregory nodded and led her from the cottage. Dawn was a pink hint on the horizon as they made their way back to her grove, where they'd battled the Riven not five hours before.

Lillian trudged along beside Gregory, thinking that whatever news her hamadryad wanted to share, it damn well better be good.

CHAPTER THIRTY-FIVE

Tethys fanned her upper body with water, the gesture more out of routine than necessity, for the air was crisp and moist outside the Lord of the Underworld's cliff-side temple. Absently, she speculated if that was natural, for she could hear the crash of waves and scent the salty-brine of the ocean, or if the pleasantly hospitable climate was his doing.

The pool she presently basked in was likely new as well, or perhaps simply a bit of repurposed architecture. She eyed the great temple where it reared high above, surrounded by terraced gardens and stairs cut into the rock. There were five terraces and hundreds of steps composing the entrance to the megalithic structure. Greenery and the sparkle of waterfalls and pools dotted each level.

Odd though it was, Death's domain held more life than what she'd seen of the Battle Goddess's lands when Tethys arrived in spirit form beside Lillian's original hamadryad.

The hamadryad had shown her many things about the

goings-on within the Magic Realm. Much had changed during the long eras she'd been gone. And yet, much was still the same. She was home at last. And she wouldn't sit idly aside while dark forces planned to abuse its bounty.

With a burst of empathy, and what Tethys would have called well-wishing in a flesh-and-blood being, the hamadryad had sent her spirit to the Lord of the Underworld's temple.

She had no memory of arriving here, but she'd awoken in this pool some time ago to find her spirit housed in her old body—or what was a perfect replica.

Apparently, the Lord of the Underworld had given her spirit a body once more and then just left her here.

To think?

Perhaps.

Was she to become a tool in the war against his twin? A tool he had no plans for at present but would use at a later time? Her present location didn't look like a prison. Behind her, the open cliff-side vista and the great blue ocean called to her spirit. Reaching out with her siren's senses, she learned that the drop from the terrace edge to the ocean below was a goodly distance, but not one that would harm her.

Freedom was only a short distance away; she could even follow the meandering path of the streams and small waterfalls to the edge of the cliff.

Death's actions were not what she'd expected.

Nothing here was.

He hadn't been chained as the hamadryad had shown the Battle Goddess was. At least not by any physical means. His chains were self-imposed, created by the considerable power of his iron control and the Divine Ones' duality curse placed upon the Twins. As long as one was imprisoned, so too was the other.

His was a willing, noble self-sacrifice and she now knew why the gargoyles revered him. She wasn't sure if she'd be able to make such a sacrifice for the good of all else.

Deep in her own thoughts, she missed when he first emerged from his temple.

It wasn't until his massive size dwarfed the small trees and lush greenery lining the rough-hewn stairs cut into the cliff that she became aware she was no longer alone. The immense strides of his horse-like lower body devoured the stairs twenty at a time. Each hoof was as massive as her entire body.

Tethys had seen many strange species, both natural and magically altered, but perhaps none as unique as the form Death wore.

At a glance, she was reminded of the old-world centaurs with their equine bodies and human-like torsos. But that was where the similarities ended. Two massive wings erupted from just behind his equine shoulders. The membrane stretched between the stout bones looked soft and supple, not unlike a gargoyle's wings, and they were not the only gargoyle-like attributes.

Instead of an upper body like a centaur possessed, Death's was far closer to a gargoyle's, complete with a blunt muzzle and a pair of great, glossy black horns that swept back from his forehead as they reached for the sky. A thick mane cascaded down past his shoulders. It fluttered in the strong breeze blowing in from the ocean beyond, and he reached up with two of his four arms to tie it into a knot behind his head.

His other two arms remained in place, his fists loosely clasping the hilts of two of his swords where they were tucked under his wings. She spotted the hilts of the other two poking out from behind his shoulders, where they'd been half-hidden in his mane.

While she studied him in silence, he folded his legs under himself and sat next to her pool. Even then, he still blocked out the sun, and an involuntary shudder ran through her body.

"I thank you for housing my spirit within my body once more," she inclined her head in a show of respect, "for there is much I must tell you."

"Your spirit already told me all that has gone wrong in the Mortal Realm." Death's voice flowed across her senses—dark, full of mystery, and utterly beautiful.

Beguiling. The word was invented to describe his voice.

The power contained in her own voice was nothing in comparison to his. She wondered once again why he'd given her back her body. What use could he possibly have for her?

"Others would say I gave you life on a whim."

Others? Who would be so foolish to mock death?

Instead, she said, "But you don't do anything on a whim, do you?"

"No," he said, voice echoing softly. "The Avatars sent you to me for a purpose. I gave you back your life out of love for them. You have a choice to make, siren."

She inclined her head, knowing what he would ask now, and already knowing her answer.

"You may stay and become one of my subjects or go out into the world, free to do as you choose."

"Thank you, wise one. I am honored by the choice."

He gave her a slight nod in acknowledgment and then with a flick of his wrist, he pulled her trident out of the very air, whole and unblemished, its internal song resonating deep inside her. He released it, and she snatched it before it hit the water.

"Take as long as you like to decide what path your life will take."

The siren bowed. "Once again, I thank you. But it will not be necessary. My path leads out into the world. There is something I must finish, a debt still to be paid."

Death nodded, his solemn expression unwavering, but she felt his thoughts brush hers, felt a tendril of his contentment. He already knew about her new quest and was well-pleased with her choice.

He'd likely known her decision before she had.

"Go with the Light's blessing, Tethys." She felt his power swirl around her. "May your hunt go well, and your debt be paid in full."

With his words fading into a faint echo, his power surged, and she was pulled from the pool. Her mind and senses blurred, and she sensed she'd traveled far, half-way across the Magic Realm until the cliffs at the edge of the Battle Goddess's kingdom became visible in the distance.

The open ocean, and the voices of the other oceanids, called to her and she went.

It didn't take her long to travel the rest of the way to her intended destination. She sang as she swam, summoning all the oceanids to her. And her siren daughters came, welcoming her with joyous song.

Just inland from the shore, a range of black mountains

rose high into the sky. On the leeward side of the tallest mountain sat a temple equal in grandeur and size to Lord Death's, though this one was cold, hard, and devoid of all warmth and beauty. Tethys studied the structure, the place where the Lady of Battles ruled her domain—a strange mix of prison and seat of power.

Tethys looked away, for the temple held no more interest for her. It was not her target, after all. Her gaze followed the path of a glacially fed river; its cold, clear waters cascading down the mountainside until it finally emptied into a wide-mouthed estuary.

She scanned the shoreline, pleased to see how the shoulders of the mountain came right down to the water, its foothills flanking the river so conveniently.

Lining the sandy beach along the bay, just on the outskirts of the Battle Goddess's domain, a mass of bodies congregated at river's mouth—the Riven army.

Tethys smiled and began to sing. Other voices joined her song, but the power for the spell came from her alone. She had innocent blood on her hands, and it might take an age to redeem herself, but she would start with this debt. It was hers alone to pay.

Her daughters merely came to sing and witness as she'd asked.

Power gathered in the ocean water surrounding her, answering her lilting summons. The slowly rolling waves grew in height and frequency as her song stretched out, away from her.

For leagues around, the ocean stirred to her call, and she absorbed the magic into her body. Her song increased in volume, the gentle melody becoming something harder and darker. The ocean reared up, great waves coming toward her. She held up one webbed hand, palm out, facing the massive incoming wave. Its forward momentum froze, but the press of water behind the wave continued forward, forcing the wave to rise, the only direction she allowed.

Magic continued to flow into her body, faster now. Her body began to glow, illuminating the ocean with pure white light. Above, the teal-tinted sky grew darker, the clouds amassing to the east, hurrying to her call as well. Warm, magic-laden air met with the cold low-pressure front and flashes of lightning, and a power that was more than electricity, bled between the clouds.

She sang, her voice rising above the crash of the stormy seas and the equally turbulent storm winds. Her body brimmed with magic, her bones ached with it, and still, she sang and absorbed the bounty of the ocean.

Far away inland, she felt the dark army's attention swing out to the ocean, sensing her and the threat she called down upon them. The Riven began to stir, seeking to toss up defenses or use their demon blades to shift to another location, but the power of her song washed away their dark magic, swirling, shattering, and cleansing.

Pain bombarded her overtaxed body, it had for quite some time. With a sudden, sizzling anguish, her nerves flared and died in a million tiny pinpoints of pain. Her body grew numb, the light brighter, the veins under her skin stood out stark and clear. Blood and magic swirled away from her dying body, but still, she sang. Her spirit took up the song when her voice grew weaker.

She only had moments left, her spirit was already preparing to leave her body. With a fragment of her consciousness not focused on the destruction of the Riven army, she looked back to her daughters with her mind's eye.

"Tell the Avatars that I paid my debt in full, and I thank them for showing me back to the Light."

With a flick of thought toward the stormy skies, she loosed the magic-laced lightning down upon the Riven. Strike after strike pounded the beach, burning the Riven to ash and turning the sands to glass.

"With my power and sacrifice, I send you back to the abyss from which you crawled," Tethys sang from her spirit. "May you become naught, know naught, and forever be naught. Let all others forget even your memory. Go now and perish."

Her spirit surged free of her flesh. From her position above the waves, she saw her own body flash as magic ripped it asunder, becoming nothing more than flecks of light and foam on the sea.

The great wave, which had been held back by her living will broke free and raced toward shore. Contained within, the purifying spells she'd been singing all along flowed with it. She watched with calm assurance as the wave slammed into the bay, rose up over the beach, and continued deep into the mouth of the river valley, cleansing everything it touched.

Her oceanid daughters sang a lament to the sea, singing her onward to her next journey.

"*You did well.*" Death's voice echoed in her mind, as soothing and beautiful as the first time she'd heard it. "*Go now and rest. I would carry you to the Spirit Realm as I did for the heroes of old, were I still able.*"

"*You honor me, my Lord. When you see the Avatars again, tell them I gladly paid my debt to them for saving my life so long ago.*"

"I shall." With those last whispered words, Death was gone from her consciousness. But in his place, there was a gentle tug on her spirit.

With a burst of joy, she turned from the power of the ocean, and the song the other sirens sang in farewell, following that tug as she began her journey home.

CHAPTER THIRTY-SIX

Gregory removed his hand from Lillian's hamadryad and smiled at what the tree had shown them.

"Goodbye, Tethys. I thank you for paying the debt so rarely paid. Until we meet again in the Spirit Realm." With a full body shake and a much lighter heart, he dropped to all fours and watched as Lillian removed her hand from the tree with a thoughtful expression.

The Riven, at least, were destroyed. There would be other enemies and other battles, but Tethys had bought them much-needed time. He promised to use that dearly bought gift wisely.

"You saw clearly what your hamadryad showed us?" he asked.

"Yes, but I hadn't expected that. Tethys sacrificed herself. For us, for our cause. For all the humans of this world." Lillian's tone rang with honest bafflement.

"She was misguided, not evil. In the end, she found her way again." Bumping his muzzle under Lillian's hand, he guided her out of the glade and into the maze beyond. *"Come,"* he sent silently, wanting the intimacy of his thoughts touching hers. *"We will rest and then on the morrow, see to all the problems this night has spawned."*

Lillian tensed, her eyes growing troubled. When he was on the verge of delving into which one of tonight's acts caused that look, she took a deep breath, squared her shoulders, and nodded sharply.

"You're right. We need to rest and regroup. Tomorrow is soon enough to learn what all this night has spawned. Perhaps we will be lucky, and it won't be half as bad as I fear."

Her fingers found their way to the base of his horns and rubbed with blissful pressure. His eyes drifted closed.

"But whatever comes, know I'll always stand by you."

"And I, you," he said with a playful bump of his head to her hip. With that, they exited the maze side-by-side. Gregory hadn't felt this content in days.

It wasn't likely to last, he knew. But for the rest of this night, there would be peace.

THE END

Lillian and Gregory's adventures continue in Sorceress Hunting.

Hey before you go, can I interest you in signing up for my author newsletter?
You get my free starter library as a gift for joining.

http://lisablackwood.com/join-the-newsletter-here/

Did you enjoy Sorceress Rising?

If you have a moment and wouldn't mind leaving a review, that would be greatly appreciated.
Reviews help other readers to decide if a book is something they would like.
It doesn't need to be long. Even a few words is tremendously helpful.

None of this would have been possible without, you, my readers. You're awesome! Thank You!

Bye for now,
Lisa Blackwood

ABOUT THE AUTHOR

Lisa Blackwood is the author of the bestselling Gargoyle and Sorceress urban fantasy series. Her work has also landed on the Wall Street Journal and the USA Today Bestseller lists as part of the Dominion Rising Anthology. When she's not reading and writing, she also enjoys gardening and spending time with her horse and her dogs.

At present, she grudgingly lives in a small town in Southern Ontario, though she would much rather live deep in a dark forest, surrounded by majestic old-growth trees. Since she cannot live her fantasy, she decided to write fantasy instead.

BOOKS BY LISA BLACKWOOD

Gargoyle & Sorceress

Dawn of the Sorceress

Sorceress Awakening

Sorceress Rising

Sorceress Hunting

Sorceress at War

Sorceress Enraged

Legacy of the Sorceress

Sorcery & Firedrakes

Scion of the Sorceress

Sorceress Eternal

In Deception's Shadow Series (Epic Fantasy Romance)

Betrayal's Price

Herd Mistress

Maiden's Wolf

Death's Queen

The Prince's Gryphon (forthcoming)

Ishtar's Legacy Series (Epic Fantasy Romance)

Ishtar's Blade

The Blade's Beginning (short story)

Blade's Honor

Blade's Destiny

The Blade's Shadow

First Queen of the Gryphons

The King of the Anunnaki (forthcoming)

The Anunnaki's Blade (forthcoming)

Huntress vs Huntsman (Epic Fantasy Romance)

Master of the Hunt

Night Huntress

Dragon Archer

Soul Mage (forthcoming)